DAJAHA DIOR HALLIDAY BLAIR

A Black Girl's Trauma Volume One: Rose Colored Lenses

Content Warning

This book contains depictions of sensitive subject matter that may be distressing to some readers, including:

Childhood trauma

Sexual abuse and assault

Domestic violence

Substance abuse

Mental health struggles

Profanity and mature themes

A Black Girl's Trauma: Volume One: Rose Colored Lenses is a deeply personal and raw exploration of pain, identity, survival, and healing. Reader discretion is advised.

Please prioritize your well-being while engaging with this work.

First edition

ISBN: 979-8-9989023-1-4

This book was professionally typeset on Reedsy.
Find out more at reedsy.com

This novel is a tribute to my late mother—
a woman whose strength anchored me,
wisdom guided me, love sustained me, and grace shaped me.
She was my compass through life's fiercest storms.

To my beautiful sisters—
Thank you for teaching me the meaning of loyalty, how to survive in an unkind
world, and for reminding me to laugh even when our hearts ached.
Together, we turned pain into poetry.

To my beautiful daughter, who will read this one day. This is for you.

Contents

Acknowledgments

This book has been a journey—years in the making. The first of many, and a dream realized. But none of it would have been possible without my husband, who never stopped believing in me. Malcolm Alexander, you championed my voice before the world ever heard it.

You sat with me through countless days and sleepless nights, listening patiently as I shaped story after story, idea after idea.

You poured encouragement into me as I poured my soul onto these pages— speaking life into the writer I was becoming.

Thank you for always seeing me.

I

Bitter Beginnings

"An open rebuke is better than secret love."

— *Proverbs 27:5*

1

Born Into Fire

Philadelphia, PA. June 24th, 2004

Someone once told me pain makes you a woman. It seems a little unfair—to be born into a war you didn't enlist for, hear the doctor shout, "It's a girl!" and from that moment, watch Fate roll up his sleeves while Destiny sucks her teeth and turns her back.

I didn't choose this. I was just... here.

Would you believe my Momma thought I was going to be a boy?

The whole time I curled inside her, I sat "Indian style," she said. Her prayers, blocked by my mere existence. All she ever wanted was a son. A strong, handsome boy she could mold into a man—the man she never had but always longed for. But after hours of labor, her body torn open, blood dripping like a warning, all she got was me.

Another Black girl.

I was the only one who ripped my way out. Literally. Split her open like I was trying to escape something, not enter. My arrival was loud, messy, and defiant. Covered in blood, wailing like I already knew the world I was born into wasn't built for softness.

My father frowned when he saw me.

His fourth daughter. Another disappointment, he wouldn't know how to love. He never understood girls, and he didn't try. The older his daughters got, the more he drifted from them, like ships he never learned how to steer.

The first woman he ever loved abandoned him under a summer moon, leaving him barefoot in the street with nothing but heat on his back and hunger in his chest. That wound became permanent, stitched into the essence of his soul. It turned every girl born to him into a bitter reminder of the one who left.

I don't remember what I looked like as a baby, but I've heard the stories—frail, ugly, they said. Compared to the likes of a dog named Cujo. A horror film that would later echo how I felt when I looked in the mirror. I'd stare at my reflection, searching for someone I recognized. A nose too round to be his, cheekbones that hinted at hers, eyes too big for my small, confused face. They said I looked like my grandmother. That's where the eyes came from—big, bright, brown. Framed in a face the color of honeyed caramel. Thick lips, a nose that curled at the tip. Every inch of me screamed Black girl.

And with that came a lifetime of being watched.

My body bloomed before I even knew what it meant to be touched. My hips spread like they were running out of room, breasts swelling in secret while I still played with dolls. I noticed the stares first. Eyes that belonged to uncles, cousins, neighbors. Not strangers—people who should've looked away. People who knew me by name.

I learned quickly: men didn't care who you were, only what you became. And in their eyes, I had become something tempting.

"Change yo shirt," Momma would snap. "You don't see how them men looking at you?"

I thought it was protection. But really, it was projection. She had seen those looks before—on her own flesh. Now it was my turn.

By nine, I was pretty. By thirteen, I was dangerous. Strangers would holler at me like I owed them something.

"Smile, lil mama!"
  "Damn, you thick!"

Their words stuck to my skin like oil. It didn't feel flattering. It felt like being hunted.

No protection. My father chose the streets. My mother chose survival. I was left chasing a reason to exist.

I found myself envious of TV characters—girls with story arcs, happy endings, and scripted purposes. I wanted a narrator to explain why I felt like this. Why did my very existence feel like a problem to be fixed or feared?

I didn't know it then, but pain had already begun weaving itself into the seams of my story. It's the kind of beginning you don't realize is bitter until much later, when you're still chewing on it, wondering why it won't go down smooth.

* * *

Who's Ya Mammy?

Understanding where you come from isn't just necessary for knowing where you are headed; it's vital for understanding who you are at core.

Your history is the blueprint of your being. Without it, you're a house with no foundation, a story ripped from its first page. But what happens when that history is buried beneath propaganda? What happens when the truth of who you are has been bent, suppressed, rewritten by hands that were never meant to hold your story in the first place?

How can a person recognize themselves in a mirror built from lies?

When the mind is flooded with falsities, when the narratives offered to you are poisoned with shame, stereotypes, and deliberate erasure, there aren't many choices left. You either piece yourself together from the fragments they give you, or you disappear trying.

I know what you might be thinking. That's simply not true. It sounds like an excuse. There are far too many resources now, far too many opportunities to educate oneself. If you remain content in your circumstances, it must be your fault, right?

That's the lie we've been fed.
   The truth is: we have been conditioned.

Conditioning (noun)
   The process of training or accustoming a person or animal to behave in a

certain way or to accept certain circumstances.

"Social conditioning"

— Definition from Oxford Languages

We are born into a framework not of our own making. Taught what to value, what to fear, what to aspire to, long before we are old enough to question why. Conditioned to believe that our reflection is too dark, our anger too loud, our hope too naive. Conditioned to adapt, survive, and shrink.

So, when you ask why some of us seem trapped in cycles, know that it isn't always a failure of will. It is often the lingering residue of battles fought generations before us. It is the inheritance of wounds we never consented to carry.

And breaking that conditioning is not as simple as waking up one day and deciding to see differently. It is slow, painful work—the unlearning of a thousand silent lessons etched deep into our bones.

* * *

Inherited Wails

Speak to me,
  I hear the tremble—
  That groan of pain only we can resemble,
  Burning through me.
  Those windows to your soul—

Howling slowly.
I see you!

As vultures dressed as doves
　　Tear at your flesh,
　　nails digging through the dirt,
　　Babies clingin' to your breast!
　　How did you do it?
　　That strength, I cannot process.
　　That spirit, they could not digest.

So, I bear witness—
　　To the lies they nursed our babies with,
　　To the loathing they tried to cleanse us with,
　　To the brutality they tried to defeat us with,
　　To the pain they tried to leave us with.

But I cannot snivel,
　　Not as I listen to your voice tremble,
　　weeping for me to be free,
　　gurgling with blood,
　　Fighting to speak to me.
　　No, I can't stand still;
　　My knees can't go weak!

Ain't no way I'll watch them muzzle you like a bitch,
　　Take your brilliance and silence it.
　　Wail for us!
　　For too long, they have tried to erase the shame,
　　Paint a picture, excuse its broken frame—
　　No more!

I'm ripping the door off the hinges,

tearing with the same conviction,
Ripping apart the false depiction.
Don't care if my hands bruise,
I'm covered in your anointed blood; they tried to misuse.

Your vocals have hummed throughout my soul,
So, I'm digging the way, bearing the toll.
I know this is my role!
I'll beat the drum to every syllable.
I'll beat the drum for every life they stole.
I'll beat the drum through all the hate they spew.

Speak to me!
I'll speak for you.
I'll be the vessel.
I'll carry the torch.
Live for everything you died fighting for!

2

We Called It Normal

Philadelphia PA. November 13, 2012

It was the middle of the night when I was pulled from sleep. My body jolted, instinctively fighting, legs kicking, and arms flailing—until I heard Hope's voice.

"Journee, stop before I drop you," she whispered, breath shaky.

Her voice settled something in me, but my heart still pounded against my ribs.

"What's going on?" I rasped, voice still thick with sleep.

Hope didn't answer. The silence said more than words ever could. She continued to carry me, her freckled fair skin like a beacon against the darkness surrounding us.

I blinked, and the familiar dark of the house melted into the moonlight pouring over the street. My bare feet hit the cold pavement before stepping into the car. Outside, my mother was sobbing, heaving breaths, broken sounds—gripping Serenity's arm until Serenity yanked herself free.

Her long, wavy hair was now matted from sweat as it clung to her ebony skin. Tears stained her cheeks as she briefly turned toward me.

Her eyes—wide, frantic, and full of something I didn't yet understand—met mine for only a split second before snapping away.

Escaping into the refuge of a car, out of the hands of our sworn protector. Her expression stung us all as we sat waist-deep in confusion.

I pressed my hand firmly on the car window and watched as the street, trees, and life as I knew it smeared into the darkness behind us. A thunderous storm began to swell inside me. I wasn't sure what was happening, but something told me it was finally over.

We arrived at my Aunt Andrea's house, and the silence shattered like glass.

"Come on, y'all," Hope ordered. She was steady. Strong. The same way she had always been when life turned cruel.

Inside, all the kids were sent to my cousin's room. We sat like dolls in a row, hushed whispers bouncing back and forth like marbles. None of us said what we feared. But I heard his name—*Mr. Trenton*—and my blood ran cold. He had done something to Serenity.

I pulled my knees into my chest and pressed my face against them. That night, I cried in silence. A skill I had perfected. No sobs. No sniffles. Just soft puffs of breath against skin, and hot tears soaking through my pants. That was how I survived—quietly aching.

In my head, I kept repeating it: *It's over.*

The secret could die with me.

　　Maybe now I'd be safe.

　　Maybe she'd be safe.

　　Maybe we both would be.

But secrets have a way of dragging you back.

* * *

Philadelphia, PA. July 4th, 2016

Time passed, and we went back home. Mr. Trenton was gone—but not for long. I saw him again. In secret. With my mother. With my brothers. In a cheap rented room with one bed, a mini fridge, and a TV too small to distract me from the truth.

Still, I smiled. I said hello. And I died a little every time.

The room was too small to breathe in, too small to hide. But Momma looked happy. My brothers smiled. So I swallowed it and smiled, too.

Lesson number two: Swallow the pain and smile.

The visits continued. Sporadic. Silent. Each one hollowed me out a little more. I didn't have the words back then. Couldn't name what I felt. But every time I saw him, anxiety clawed at my ribs. My stomach twisted. My eyes burned with tears I wasn't allowed to shed.

Not in front of Momma.

Not in front of Mr. Trenton.

Mr. Trenton didn't just carry darkness in his skin—he wore it in his spirit. His calm demeanor was an illusion, a costume that hid the predator underneath. He wasn't a man of God. He wasn't even a man of guilt. Rumors of his violence trickled down from the mouths of careless adults.
Even as children, we heard everything.
The shouting. The drunken laughter. The stale stench of beer and cigarettes was the scent of home.

Dysfunction, dressed as tradition—that was our normal. And like all trauma passed down, we wore it like a second skin. We didn't question it—not out loud. Rose-colored lenses made it easier to mistake chaos for joy. Most of the time, we convinced ourselves we were having fun.

Faith was never as easily fooled. She stood just five-one, but her presence filled any room. Her deep cinnamon complexion only added to the fire in her stare—warm, bold, and unbothered.

She was a natural beauty, like all of my sisters, third in line after Hope, the oldest, and Serenity, the second. Then there was me: the baby. The tag-along.

"Journee, don't you get tired of smiling in people's faces?" Faith teased, refilling my mother's pitcher with ice.

I leaned back against the kitchen counter, grinning.

"Hell no. It's boring when nobody ain't here but us. I love having cookouts."

Faith shook her head, dragging her fingers along the running faucet, waiting for it to turn colder. She was procrastinating, a sensible distraction from what she deemed as madness.

"How cold does she need her tea? There's ice already in it!" I whined, wanting to get back outside to the party, to the noise that made the day feel less heavy. The hectic excitement of people watching and eavesdropping on adult conversations.

Faith cut me a sharp glance before finally filling the pitcher with water.

"See," she said, laughing low, "this is why you're always getting in trouble. You are too easily distracted."

I rolled my eyes, but I knew she was right.

Faith was who I wanted to be— even when she got on my nerves. Everyone praised her for her dependability, a skill I hadn't learned yet.

The kitchen door creaked open, and Jasmine blew in like a gust of wind.

Her presence immediately shifted the air.

Jasmine, my stepfather's niece, loud, reckless, "*too grown*" as most people called it. Too raunchy for her own good. She entered our space, dramatically as she often did.

Faith rarely hid her dislike, and today wasn't different.

Me? I found her fascinating. Like a blazing fire, you couldn't help but watch as it engulfed everything that stood defenseless around it.

"I was looking for you, Journee. Why are you hiding in here?" Jasmine said, laughing.

I turned, laughing too, "Girl, ain't nobody hiding. I'm doing something for my Momma."

Faith snorted. "No. *I'm* doing something for our Momma. You, just following me."

I sighed, giving her a playful glare. She wasn't wrong. I clung to Faith, but I had my reasons.

"Bye, girl. You ain't all that," I shot back, linking arms with Jasmine as we headed for the door.

Jasmine had been dropped off at our house for the summer, she and her two younger siblings—a shipment of wildness we hadn't asked for but somehow made room for. No reason was given, and no one dared to ask.

We stepped outside, the atmosphere thick with the smell of sweat, charcoal, and cheap beer.

Uncle Marlon wobbled down the street, chasing my little brothers, his laughter slurring into the sticky evening air. The sound of their giggles was a balm against the jaggedness of it all.

This was our normal.

Uncle Marlon, drunk, stumbling around.
   Uncle Kyrie, cracking jokes.
   Uncle Raheem, arguing about whatever he thought was destroying the Black community that week.

All actions that made each moment unforgettable.

None of them were my mother's blood brothers, but blood didn't mean much where we came from. In Philly, pain was thicker.

Standing in the doorway, we could hear Uncle Raheem arguing about the music pumping from the speakers.

The same songs we danced to that made the world feel free. The same songs that made me feel like being young was such an uncool thing. I longed to grow up, believing that happiness lived somewhere beyond childhood, a place my young eyes had never seen.

"Y'all young ladies shouldn't be exposed to this garbage," Raheem barked into the crowd, his words falling like pebbles onto water, causing no real ripple.

I rolled my hips to the beat, half-laughing, half-mocking, feeling the power of my own body even if I didn't fully understand it yet.

My new short set clung to my curves; my hair pulled into a slick ponytail so tight it made my forehead shine. The sweet taste of cotton candy lip gloss lingered in my mouth every time I licked my lips. The music enhanced every sensation of the moment.

I felt pretty. And at that age— at that place— feeling pretty was like finding a crack of sunlight in a dark room.

Still, nobody listened to Uncle Raheem. They never did.

I scanned the scene: empty beer cans rolling across the sidewalk, cigarette butts crushed into the cracks, a fight brewing two houses down.

This was love.
  This was family.
  And it was all I knew.

Uncle Raheem shook his head and stormed off, still muttering about how hip-hop and rap music were poison.

At twelve years old, I didn't understand his fear.

How could something made by people who looked like us be *so dangerous* for us?

It would take years before I understood that beauty and destruction could live in the same breath.

Uncle Raheem had lived it—prison, pain, rebirth. But back then, he was just another *nigga* carrying too much regret, talking to people who didn't want to listen. When you have stains on your hands, no one cares what you're trying to wash away. They just see you as unclean.

As the cookout continued, Jasmine elbowed me, snapping me out of my thoughts.

"Don't you see that nigga looking at you?" she whispered, the scent of cheap wine and rebellion on her breath.

My heart skipped, a weird mix of fear and curiosity I didn't yet have a name for.

"What nigga?" I asked, scanning for some boy, someone closer to my age.

"The one over there with Hope and Serenity," she giggled.

I squinted hard. "Bitch, I *know* you ain't talking about Mason."

We cracked up.

Mason— short, brown-skinned, older by at least a decade— leaned awkwardly against a car, his body crooked like his whole life had been tilted sideways. He wasn't hideous. He was worse—he was the kind of man you

17

could tell would make you *feel ugly.*

"Girl, stop playing," I hissed, desperate to change the subject.

"How'd you get that jawn?" I asked, eyeing her red cup.

"I took it," Jasmine shrugged, unbothered.

"But for real, you don't think he's cute in an ugly way?"

I scrunched up my nose. "Not at all."

She laughed harder, and I joined, but the conversation left a bitter taste in my mouth. The way they looked at me made my stomach turn, but it wasn't anything I hadn't felt before.

I was already used to the stares. Already learned how to spot them—the glances that lingered too long, the smiles that weren't kind. David and Mason weren't special. They were just two more men who forgot—or did not care—that I was still a child.

No one asked why my body betrayed me with new curves, why my thighs thickened, and my hips widened without permission.

No one asked if it scared me. Instead, they labeled me—fresh, fast, hot in the pants—like I had chosen this. It didn't matter that I didn't want the attention. It didn't matter that it made my skin crawl. What I now looked like had overwritten who I was.

The older I got, the more I leaned into it. I took the ugly they gave me and made it mine. I swallowed every bitter word, every sideways glance, and let it settle inside me until it felt like something I had chosen. It was the only control I thought I had—and I wasn't about to let anyone take that from me.

Maybe it wasn't power, but it was mine. And for a long time, that was enough. It sounds ridiculous now. But back then, it made perfect sense to a little Black girl trying to survive in a world that looked at her and only saw a woman.

* * *

Fresh or Fast?

Being called by either of those names was never a compliment. In the Black community, they were interchangeable— labels meant to shame a girl for growing up too fast, or at least for being seen that way.

To be too friendly, too open, too seen at an early age was to invite judgment. And judgment came quickly, without warning, without mercy.

I can admit now: I always loved to smile. I adored being the center of attention. That wasn't a problem when I was a little girl, when innocence wrapped my actions in something palatable. Back then, I was praised—a light, a joy, a bright spot. But the moment my body changed, so did the narrative. In a blink, I went from being a ray of sunshine to an attention whore.

The same smile that once made people laugh now made them whisper.

The same lightness they encouraged became a burden I was punished for carrying. It made me start to question myself—how I dressed, how I spoke, how I moved through the world. I became hyper vigilant, taught without words that my existence had to come with restrictions.

Rules I had never agreed to.

Rules I didn't want to follow.

And I didn't always follow them, of course. But that's not the point.

The point is: I learned early that girlhood, for a Black girl like me, wasn't something you got to live in. It was something you had to survive.

* * *

Back to reality

The rest of the night played out with its usual hiccups. Uncle Kyrie and Uncle Marlon grew drunker by the second, their laughter booming through the house. Momma threw her head back laughing with Aunt Andrea, the two of them lost in stories only they could understand. My cousins heaped their plates high with Momma's food, balancing foil trays in their arms as they hugged everyone goodbye.

The house, once bursting with noise, slowly began to empty. Uncle Marlon stumbled his way to the couch, slurring a goodbye no one understood, before collapsing into a heavy, drunken sleep. Within minutes, his snores echoed through the living room, a rough kind of lullaby that marked the end of another long day.

Instantly, my brother darted past me, almost knocking me over.

"Damn, Mir, what the fuck!" I spat, frustrated.

"Move out of my way then!" he yelled back, not even glancing over his shoulder.

A bowl full of mixed chips filled one hand, and a plate stacked with food filled the other as he headed straight for the front room. He knew what was coming.

Not even five minutes later, right on cue, our Momma marched into the house, yelling our names in rapid succession like a broken record:

"Hope, Serenity, Faith, Journee, Miracle, Sincere! Get down these steps and clean up this mess!"

You could hear us all groaning from our hiding spots, huffing and puffing as we dragged ourselves back to the living room.

Our extended family members always left the house in shambles. Half-full cups, soda cans, and bottles were scattered all over the tables and the floor. Unfinished plates of food were left forgotten. Sprinkled crushed chips meshed into the carpet, accompanied by mysterious stains. Half-eaten candy stuck firmly to our glass coffee table, while balled-up used napkins were discarded without care.

Nobody genuinely cared to put effort into helping avoid the aftermath.

My mother would open our home for family gatherings, but to me, it often felt like she was inviting in storms meant to tear us apart. Behind tight smiles and forced laughter, resentment simmered—and it was no secret that many held quiet grudges against her. I remember standing in the hallway sometimes, watching people hug her at the door, their words syrupy sweet but their eyes cold.

While some of our relatives struggled just to keep a roof over their heads, trapped in cycles of overdue rent and public housing, my mother stood as an exception. She owned her home. It wasn't a mansion—the paint peeled in places, the floors creaked under every step—but it was ours. I would hear her sometimes, late at night, running her hand along the walls and whispering, "At least it's mine." She poured her heart into making it a sanctuary, a place where anyone she loved could land when life knocked them down.

Some accepted that shelter with open arms and real gratitude. They cried at her kitchen table, thanked her between heavy sobs, and helped wash the dishes afterward. But others let their jealousy fester. Their compliments were edged with bitterness, their laughter just a little too sharp. What should have been moments of family turned into silent battlegrounds, every smile hiding a wound.

And somehow, even knowing that, my mother still welcomed them—still believed love could heal what pride and bitterness had already tried to destroy. I used to ask her why she bothered.

"They're my family," she would say softly, almost to herself. "And you know we all we got."

Though, as usual, after these elaborate events, Faith and I were left doing most of the cleaning. I slacked off, distracted like always, while Faith, with her endless patience stretched thin, took on the bulk of the cleanup. Jasmine hovered nearby, trying to cozy up to Faith by pointing out my laziness. It didn't work. Faith was a perfectionist with little tolerance for foolishness, and even we, her siblings, walked a fine line.

"Why doesn't Faith like me?" Jasmine asked as I struggled to open a trash bag.

"That's just how Faith is," I laughed lightly. "She doesn't even like me that much."

I continued to struggle, "I really can't open this jawn." I muttered

Jasmine's cheeks were bright red, her hazel eyes glossy from sneaking alcohol. She looked completely flushed. I hadn't realized how much Faith's coldness bothered her. A feeling of pity swept over me as I looked her over. I was used to Faith being standoffish—of course, Jasmine wasn't.

With a softer voice, I reassured her, "Look, Faith just ain't a people person. She doesn't hate you. You just have to catch her in the right mood. Give her time."

Jasmine let out a throaty groan, flagging me off.

"No, she fucking hates me," she insisted loudly.

I furrowed my brows in response. I didn't want to waste any more time trying to convince her not to take Faith's demeanor personally. She wasn't in the mood to receive it.

Slouching down, she grabbed a half-empty can of beer and chugged it to completion. I watched in disbelief. When I first discovered Jasmine was drinking, I was fascinated—it added another layer to her exciting image— but now my initial thrill was swiftly changing to concern.

"Why do you keep doing that?" I questioned.

"Doing what?" Faith asked, brushing past me with a tower of plates in her hands, not even slowing down.

"Nothing," I muttered.

Faith playfully rolled her eyes in annoyance, passing us both quickly in a hurry to finish cleaning. Once Faith stepped into the kitchen, I tried again.

"Why do you keep drinking?" I asked Jasmine, lowering my voice into a whisper.

She gave me a blank stare, almost as if she was looking past me. A crooked smile formed on her face as she burst into wild, shrieking laughter. Her crazed reaction frightened me, causing Miracle to look over, confused and curious.

"Why is she laughing like that?" he asked.

Miracle, younger than me, stood behind us both, naive to the crushed beer cans that surrounded us, alluding to her current condition.

"Boy, mind yo business!" I shot back. "Ain't you supposed to be cleaning up? Instead, you over here being nosy."

Miracle stood there for a second longer, weighing his options, before shuffling off.

I turned back to Jasmine. She'd collapsed onto the floor, her chubby body reeking of beer and sweat, pressed firmly against the wall. As she nodded off, my mother entered the living room with Jasmine's mom, Ms. Nettie. My heart jumped into my throat.

I quickly picked up the rest of the beer cans around her and moved from the living room to the dining room. I did not want to be present when Ms. Nettie realized her eldest daughter was indeed intoxicated.

I waited for the explosion. I waited for the yelling, the threats.

Instead, Ms. Nettie smacked her daughter lightly awake and mumbled through her cigarette-clenched teeth, "Get yo ass up and go sleep that shit off."

No rage. No real concern. Just another night.

I stared, stunned. Was this what having a "cool" mom looked like? Or was this something else entirely?

I retreated upstairs, slipping into the front room where all six of us siblings slept. My Uncle Raheem had claimed the middle room since his release from a long stint in prison. I climbed to the top bunk of the pale green bunk beds, positioning myself as far from the edge as possible. Faith followed, lying on the outer side.

Jasmine tried to scramble up after us, but Faith snapped, "No. First off, you stink, yo feet stink, and it ain't no room."

Jasmine pouted. "Where am I supposed to sleep?"

Faith didn't flinch. She rarely did. She meant what she said and said what she meant—one of the things I admired most about her. I was not naturally strong-willed.

"You can sleep on the dresser for all I care," Faith said, her tone sharp. "But you ain't sleeping up here with us!"

I nodded in agreement, not because I didn't like Jasmine, but because she did, undeniably, stink. The alcohol she'd been drinking all night wasn't doing her any favors.

I tossed her a blanket and pillow as Serenity and Hope entered the room. Serenity immediately wrinkled her nose.

"What the fuck is that smell?" she choked out, climbing into the bottom bunk.

Hope shot her a silencing look—the kind that said, Not right now. Then she turned to Jasmine.

"Take yo shoes to the laundry room and get in the shower."

Jasmine obeyed, sluggish and dazed, her body moving like it weighed a hundred pounds. Hope watched her leave with sharp, narrowing eyes.

"I know y'all wasn't sneaking no damn liquor," Hope said, voice low but dangerous.

Faith and I popped our heads over the bunk railing, shaking them in frantic unison.

"Nope, not us!"

Hope studied us for a moment longer, then relaxed.

"Hmm. Okay."

I collapsed back onto the mattress with a heavy exhale. Faith rolled her eyes beside me. She didn't have to say a word—I knew exactly what she was thinking. Jasmine was spiraling, and none of us could stop it. Still, I wondered why she drank so much. Why her mother barely seemed to notice. I spun questions in my mind, desperate for answers Jasmine wouldn't give me.

I was still lost in thought when Jasmine's little sister, Kiki, clambered up into bed with us. Faith and I made space without hesitation. Kiki curled into the warmth between us and fell asleep almost instantly. Beneath us, Miracle wriggled in between Serenity and Hope. The youngest, Sincere, and Jasmine's little brother, Kevin, slept tucked safely in the back room with Momma.

As the house settled, so did I.

Sleep came easily with the soft rhythm of breathing all around me. I never slept alone growing up. Couldn't sleep peacefully without my siblings beside me.

Some would call it a lack of boundaries.

I called it home.

3

The Cost of Silence

Later that summer...

Despite Faith's clear disdain for Jasmine, she and I became inseparable. We clung close to one another.

She was older and wiser. Every story she shared was expressed in vivid detail. Jasmine knew so much about sex and flaunted her knowledge proudly at the ripe age of sixteen. While I listened, wide-eyed, as she weaved together stories I could barely comprehend. Some of them made me laugh, others made me cringe.

I wanted to tell her stories as well, leave her stunned as she had left me on numerous occasions that summer.

It was my turn to leave her speechless. I told her about the things that had happened to me—the confusing moments I hadn't known how to name. The only experience I had remotely close to the stories she shared. I expected her to cringe as I did, cover her ears as I had done times before, but she didn't.

In that split second, she became the first person I confided in—the first person I allowed to *see me,* even if it wasn't done intentionally.

As I spoke, Jasmine's hazel eyes widened in horror, and my smile faded.

"He... he touched you too?" she asked, the words escaping in a broken whisper.

She reached for my hand, and I snatched away, unable to answer her question.

In that moment, everything inside me clicked into place:

The sharp pricks of fear.
   The night terrors that would leave me gasping for air.
   The dread that sat in my bones every time I was in his presence.
   I wasn't crazy.
   I wasn't overreacting.

All of the memories I hid—buried behind a wall too raw to touch, now sat on my lap like a ton of bricks. Jasmine taught me words I hadn't known before—molestation, abuse. Words that were hidden from my vocabulary under the false guise of protecting my innocence had become a tool that aided in its destruction.

And for the first time, I felt validated.

Up until then, I believed brutal rape depicted on television was the only form of sexual assault. I thought it had to be violent, dramatic, like the scenes I had witnessed peeking through spaced fingers when Momma told me to close my eyes. But what happened to me didn't look like that. There was no kicking and screaming, just silent tears.

My mother warned me about monsters—the ones who lurked in alleyways and dark corners, the ones who prowled beyond the four walls that kept me warm. She taught me that danger lived in the unknown, in the places beyond her watchful eyes and protective arms.

But what she didn't know—what none of us knew—was that sometimes, the real monsters didn't come from outside. Sometimes, they lived among us. Sometimes, they smiled at you across the dinner table. Sometimes, they knew exactly when no one else was looking.

I wasn't violated on a street corner or in some shadowed playground. I was violated in the safest place I knew—my home. The very place built to shield me became the place that deceived me.

I didn't know that monsters could sound like family, that their laughter could lull you into false security. I didn't know that evil could wear a familiar face and move so quietly it left no trace, no proof—only a lingering, choking silence. I didn't know that danger could thrive right under the same roof where prayers were said, where meals were cooked, where love was supposed to live. I didn't know that monsters could hide in plain sight, waiting for the perfect moment to reach out with poisoned hands while the world around you kept on turning, blind.

When it happened, I would float away in my mind. It usually began with me giving him a back rub or a foot rub. He would brag about how good I was at easing his pain. It made me feel talented—special. Then he would insist on returning the favor. His hands would wander, and I would freeze. His body would use mine, and I would lie there lifeless.

Even when my body screamed no, I stayed silent.

Obedience had been beaten into me since I was old enough to walk.

My mother was a God-fearing woman who didn't believe in sparing the rod. "Whoever spares the rod hates their children," she would quote from Proverbs. Disobedience wasn't tolerated, and Mr. Trenton knew that too well. He knew we were raised to comply, to respect our elders without question. And under no circumstances was disrespect tolerated; he used that to his advantage.

Mr. Trenton **hurt me.**

And I never had the words for it—until Jasmine.

But the worst betrayal wasn't just what he did.

It was deceitful store runs with Momma, smiling and pretending everything was fine. Only to drive us in secret to see him, my brothers and I, packed into the minivan, pulling up to that place that made my soul wrench.

I saw it with my own eyes.
Momma, leading us there.
Momma, acting like it was **normal**.

* * *

That was the memory that sat like a stone in my chest as we headed toward Papa's house later that day for Sunday dinner.

Momma drove, her fingers tight around the steering wheel because she hated the highway. Hope sat in the passenger seat, messing with the radio, flipping through stations as static blended with Miracle and Sincere's playful screams. All the rest of us were jammed into the back, sweaty and restless. The summer sun baked the inside of the minivan, and the road stretched out like an endless ribbon of gray.

Papa's house loomed large at the end of the driveway. Big and blue, in a suburban neighborhood. It looked even bigger than I remembered. The grass was trimmed perfectly, the bushes sculpted into neat little domes. Ms. Jean, my grandfather's wife, stood on the front porch, arms crossed, a lit cigarette dangling from her lips, eyeing us with her usual disgust.

"Morgan, your children are here!" she announced as we pulled up, Aunt Andrea parking swiftly behind us.

"Last one in the house is a rotten egg!" My cousin Amy screamed, causing everyone to dash toward the front door.

Everyone but me.

I didn't care.

I was here for two reasons: to eat and leave.

We poured inside the house, and the smell of Pine-Sol and fresh food hit us immediately as we walked in. Ms. Jean barked at us not to touch anything of value, which felt like everything inside the house had become off-limits. Momma instructed us to sit up straight and act right. Papa gave me a rough hug, pulling me close.

"You alright, baby girl?" he asked, squeezing me tighter than usual.

For a second, I let myself melt into the hug, I inhaled the warm scent of his cologne. Letting myself believe he could protect me from the chaos brewing inside my tiny frame. I nodded against his chest, not trusting my voice to answer. After the conversation with Jasmine, my voice clawed at my throat, fighting to be set free. Fighting to reveal truths that I wasn't prepared to speak.

Dinner was already spread out on the table: baked mac and cheese, corn-bread, candied yams, greens, and fried chicken. Papa always went all out for Sunday dinners, but the food tasted like dust in my mouth. Every clank of a fork, every scrape of a chair, made my stomach churn.

I caught Serenity's eye across the room and jerked my head away, I couldn't look at her. I excused myself from the table, holding my breath as I rushed toward the hallway. I made it there and exhaled into the darkness. I prayed to God to turn back time, to make me take back everything I had learned. But God didn't answer, a familiar voice did instead.

Serenity had followed me into the darkness of the hallway.

My heart thudded painfully in my chest.
  Tell her, I thought.
  Please, God, just let me tell her everything.

But when I opened my mouth, fear won.

Instead of the truth, a lie tumbled off my tongue.

"Jasmine told me," I whispered. "She said Momma's still seeing Mr. Trenton."

Serenity's whole face shifted as she examined mine, peering into my eyes for clarity while hers darkened, swelling with pain and rage. I tried to turn away, but the tears had already begun to stain my cheeks. She gripped my shoulders tightly, forcing me to face her. Her eyes searched mine again, digging, desperate for answers—until she found what she was looking for. Serenity didn't say a word. She just released me and turned on her heel, marching back toward the dining room with a deadly kind of determination.

I barely made it to my chair before she exploded.

"You know what?" Serenity said, voice sharp and angry. "I'm sick of sitting at this table acting like everything's perfect. Like nothing ever happened."

Everyone froze. Jean glared at her, face twisted in annoyance.

"Aunt Andrea," Serenity continued, her voice trembling with rage. "Momma's still sneaking around seeing Mr. Trenton behind our backs."

Aunt Andrea slammed her fork down against the table, the sharp clatter cutting through the tension in the room.

"That's a damn lie! My sister wouldn't do that—not after everything..." she objected, her voice trembling with disbelief, unwilling to accept what she was hearing.

Serenity refused to back down.

"Journee heard it. Jasmine told her everything. Did you think you could just keep lying to us? Covering it up, but the truth always comes to the light!" She glared directly at Momma

Ms. Jean finally snapped. She had tolerated enough of this dinner, enough of what she considered "low-class nonsense."

Slamming her wine glass down, she spat, "I knew this dinner was a damn mistake! Y'all bring your hood drama into this man's house, airing dirty laundry at the damn table!"

Serenity tried to speak again, but was interrupted once more by Ms. Jean.

"Sit your disrespectful ass down so we can finish dinner and wrap up this freak show!" Ms. Jean demanded, her voice nasty and cold

"You don't know what you're talking about, Jean." Aunt Andrea stated as she pushed away her plate of food.

Ms. Jean shot Aunt Andrea an ice-cold glare as she persisted in demanding that Serenity be seated.

"I'm not doin' a damn thing." Serenity cried, tears brimming in her eyes. "You don't know what he did to me. You don't know the shit we went through while she is sitting here pretending nothing happened!" Pointing her finger directly at Momma.

"That is enough! You will watch your mouth in this house!" Papa barked.

"Wait, Dad, you don't understand." Aunt Andrea intervened.
Momma's eyes pleaded with her sister to stop.

"What is there to understand? Evidently, Serenity has lost her damn mind. Disrespecting my wife! Disrespecting her mother! Disrespecting my house!" Papa shouted, shooting to his feet. "If you have a better explanation of what's going on here, then share it!"

Aunt Andrea's eyes darted back and forth, from her sister back to her father. As Papa stood there waiting for some kind of explanation of what was happening, no one spoke.

"Y'all just as evil as him, standing there protecting monsters!" Hope declared, breaking the silence as she wrapped her arms around Serenity.

Momma stood up, her expression twisted with shame, sputtering denials. "I swear I ain't seen that man! I swear to God!"

But the damage was already done. The room was heavy with tension. As all the children were instructed by Papa to exit the dining room.

I retreated to the bathroom, splashing my face with water. I cursed myself for all the destruction I had caused.
I hurt Jasmine.

I hurt Serenity.

I hurt Aunt Andrea.

And worst of all, I hurt Momma.
The lie I told had helped no one, not even myself. The truth was still burning inside me, an uncontrollable fire that I had failed to extinguish.

That summer, Jasmine and her siblings were forced to leave. I never asked why. Fear clenched my throat too tightly, but in the pit of my stomach, I knew—it was because of me. After that summer, they were gone, and the hole their absence left never fully closed.

As time dragged forward, the guilt of Jasmine's abrupt departure didn't disappear—it calcified, settling deep inside the marrow of my being. The secret I had swallowed that day festered in silence, birthing a legacy of shame and self-betrayal that would haunt me for years to come.

That moment was the fracture—the shattering of the last fragile layer of normalcy I had clung to. From then on, it felt as though something feral had clawed its way inside me, hollowing me out from within.

I became an impostor even to my own reflection, searching for pieces of myself that no longer existed. I ached to return to a time when ignorance was still mercy, when the dysfunction I lived through could still be disguised by the tender, blinding glow of rose-colored lenses.

* * *

A Soul in Trouble

(For those suffering with internal conflict)

I've got trouble within myself,
   The kind of trouble only God could help.
   The kind of trouble that would make the devil grin,
   From all the pure sin,
   My subconscious keeps on letting in.

Got me sewing transgressions within my heart,
   Bringing me closer to his favorite part.
   I can tell his patience isn't wearing thin—
   Why would it?
   He feels he's bound to win.

Hand firmly on my twisted mind,
   Full of secret acts,
   So foolishly inclined to warped facts.
   I guess I'll figure it out one day,
   If God doesn't forgive me for my sinister ways.

4

Hollow

Three years had passed since that summer.

Each year feeling identical to the last. I tried my best not to draw attention, drifting through life as spring showers watered the earth around me. I stared out my window, expressionless, hollow, but still alive.
Unmoved by Mother Nature, unmoved by the swaying trees. I pressed my hand against the glass as I had done that night when my life changed. But this time, I was wishing it would break, slice deep into my wrist, and end my suffering. Wanting so badly for it to do accidentally what I didn't have the will to attempt.

So much had changed because of one mistake. So much was broken because of one lie.

"Journee, Momma wants you!" Miracle exclaimed, walking into the living room and breaking the silence, pulling me out of my bubble of sorrow.

"The fuck wrong with you?" Miracle asked as I stood from the sofa and walked right past him. A smile crept across my face.

"Want me to tell Momma you in here cussing?" I teased with no real intention of doing so.

Miracle had truly grown into himself. He was still a snot-nosed little brat in my eyes, but he wasn't a scrawny kid anymore. He had put on some weight and height, enough to now stand slightly taller than me, though still my little brother at heart.

"You be cussing too, though!" Miracle shot back in his defense, not wanting to be snitched on.

"And? I'm older," I replied, still standing by the stairs.

"But you ain't grown," he continued, smiling widely.

"I'm grown enough," I giggled, walking up the stairs and ending the conversation at that.

As I neared my mother's room, I could hear her on the phone.

"Yes, Momma?" I pouted, stepping inside.

She held up a finger to signal me to wait, and so I did.

One minute dragged into three, and my frustration began to build. Then, I watched her face change from joy to agony in an instant. She began rocking back and forth on the bed, covering her mouth as my Aunt Andrea's voice crackled through the phone. I could hear screaming on the other end.

A chill climbed my spine.

"Why?" my mother gasped before ending the call.

Her rocking quickened, the bed springs creaking beneath her weight.

"What's wrong, Momma?" I asked, fear creeping up my throat.

"It's your grandmother. She... she's been found... de... dead," she stuttered, each word smashing into my chest like a closed fist.

Tears rolled down my cheeks. I loved my grandmother. She taught me to dance, to sing—always so full of love. I reached for my mother to comfort her, but she recoiled as if I were contagious.

"Don't fucking touch me!" she screamed. "What the fuck are you even crying for? You barely knew her. You ain't seen her since you were little. Get the fuck out my room!"

Apologizing through my sobs, I backed out of the room, devastated and conflicted. It had been years, but not by my choice.

Years ago, Momma and Grandma had a big fight. I never knew exactly what it was about. My siblings and I speculated, but none of us could draw a sensible conclusion.
After that fight, we hadn't seen her again—except for a ten-minute visit to drop off forwarded mail. No one spoke except us kids to say hello. The conversation was dry and awkward. Uncle Mike, who lived with Grandma at the time, barely said a word. Whenever we asked about her, we were told to shut up and stay in a child's place. No explanations. No gossip. Just unusual silence.

As I walked down the hallway, Hope brushed past me. I didn't turn to look, but I heard her cries as she was welcomed into a warm embrace. That wasn't unusual. Hope and Momma shared a bond that none of us others did, born from Momma giving birth to her at just eighteen. I assumed it was because they'd been through so much together.

Still shaking from the rejection, I descended the stairs. Halfway down, I stopped and stared at my clueless brothers playing on the floor, their laughter like acid on raw skin.

"Big Mama passed away," I announced coldly.

"Who's Big Mama?" Sincere asked, wiping his nose on his sleeve.

"Your grandma, dummy!" Miracle snapped, smacking him with a plush toy.

"We ain't got no grandma!" Sincere screamed, flying to his feet and tackling Miracle to the ground.

"Get off me!" Miracle shouted, wrestling back, careful not to hurt him.

Rage boiled over. I raced down the stairs and yanked Sincere off of Miracle by his shirt, stretching out the collar as he squealed.

"Stop fucking around! Y'all don't take shit seriously! Are you so stupid that you don't understand what that means? That means Momma's mom is dead, dick head!" I screamed, tears streaking down my cheeks.

Sincere flinched, his eyes squeezed shut, dangling helplessly above the floor.

I realized what I was doing, then dropped him. He landed hard on the carpet. Both boys stared at me in stunned silence, too scared to speak. Upstairs, fresh wails echoed—Serenity and Faith had just been told.

Everything around me spun into chaos.

More than ever, I wanted to disappear.

"Journee, why—?" Miracle began, his voice trembling.

I didn't wait to hear the rest. I yanked open the front door, slammed it behind me, and stumbled into the storm. Rain pounded against my skin, but I barely felt it. My feet moved on their own, my fist hammered my chest in a frenzied attempt to bang the grief loose.

A crack of thunder roared overhead.

I bawled, but no sound came out. That silent cry, the one I had perfected years ago, stole my voice once again. I begged my throat to open, begged God to hear my agony and bring it all to an end.

The storm began to calm, and so did I.

Completely soaked, I turned around and realized I had barely wandered far. The house stood right behind me, unchanged, unbothered.

I stepped back inside.

Everyone was gathered in the living room. My mother's bloodshot eyes locked onto mine. Without a word, she crossed the room and wrapped her arms around me tightly. Wet and limp, I stood frozen in her embrace, my arms hanging useless at my sides.

I couldn't remember a time when Momma had ever hugged me like this.

I wanted it to feel good.

It didn't.

"Don't ever walk out of my house without telling me where you going again, you hear me?" Momma whispered, kissing my cheek.

My mind stayed blank, my body hollow.

"Yes, Momma," I replied robotically.

It felt like I blinked, and the night was already over.

* * *

A week later, the day of the funeral arrived.

Big Mama's funeral was a lavish celebration, just as she had wanted. The church overflowed with mourners. Total strangers approached us with gifts and condolences. As a key member of the Temple of Worship, she was revered as a beacon of light.

Cries filled every pew as the viewing began.

Momma carried herself with grace, despite the judgmental stares from the church elders who disapproved of her being twice divorced. I never understood why they cared. Would they have preferred she stay married to an addict, or worse, a pedophile?

Uncle Mike appeared wearing an expensive suit and watch, looking like old money as he hunched down to give his condolences. His deep chestnut eyes found mine. He reached for me.

"Do you remember me, sweetheart?" he asked.

Before I could answer, Aunt Andrea slapped his hand away.

43

"Get the fuck away from us," she hissed.

Momma said nothing, but the look she gave him was colder than ice. Uncle Mike straightened his suit and slithered off, pretending to smile.

Later, an old video played on a projector of Big Mama singing in church. At the young age of thirteen. Her voice was an explosion of soul—raw, angelic, overwhelming. I wanted so badly to cry, but couldn't. No tears would come.

All around me, strangers sobbed.

I sat there, fidgeting, hollowed out inside.

What was wrong with me?

Why couldn't I feel it? Why couldn't I even fake it like everyone else?

I blinked—and just like that, it was over.

The funeral. The repast. The long ride home.

Gone.

I lay in my bed, mindlessly scrolling through videos—pranks, makeup tutorials, anything that granted me the privilege of disappearing a little more. Each video flowed into the next. Distractions for an existence that didn't feel like mine anymore.

It was easier than being present in the moment. Easier than just being alive. But not by much.

* * *

The screen blurred in front of me, but I kept scrolling.

Swipe. Tap. Scroll.

I wasn't even watching anymore—just letting the colors flicker across my face in the dark.

Somewhere in the middle of a video about contouring, my mind drifted. My fingers paused.

I was in Big Mama's kitchen.

Big Mama had a skillet full of onions and peppers dancing in grease, cornbread cooling on the stove-top, and her old radio playing Kirk Franklin like the choir was right there with us.

"Journee, baby, pass me that wooden spoon," she called over her shoulder.

I was maybe seven. Quiet and unsure. But in Big Mama's kitchen, I didn't have to be anything more than a girl with clean hands and open ears. I handed her the spoon, careful not to bump the pan.

After giving the food a quick stir, Big Mama stepped out of the kitchen.

From the living room, shouting cut through the gospel music.

"I told you not to let him in here!"

"He ain't got nowhere else to go." Big Mama explained.

"Not after what he—"

"He's my son, Semira, lord knows I ain't done right by the boy his whole

45

life."

"Momma he's a fucking monster, if he's here then I'm gone!"

Big Mama turned the dial up on the radio. "You hush now, Jesus," she muttered with a sigh, as if trying to drown them all out.

She came back into the kitchen, not missing a beat, still stirring like nothing was wrong. Her hands moved with purpose, like she was working something out of her spirit with every fold of the gravy.

"You hungry?" she asked, glancing back at me.

I nodded, but my eyes were glued to the kitchen doorway. The shouting grew louder.

Uncle Mike's voice was slick, but I could hear the smugness in his tone.

"Can't even forgive yo flesh and blood, huh?"

"Forgive you? You should be dead, you deserve a bullet in the head. Not a cozy place to sleep in *my* mother's house!"

"Well, ain't that real Christian of you," Mike replied, smirking.

Big Mama slammed the cabinet door shut loud enough to startle me. Then she caught herself and softened.

"Don't listen to that, sugar," she said, kneeling in front of me. "People lose their minds in pain. But don't you ever let that darkness taint your heart."

I tried to nod, but my lip trembled. "Why's Momma so mad at Uncle Mike?" I asked.

Her mouth pressed into a line. "Because she ain't ready to forgive," she said carefully, "and because he gave her good reason not to."

More yelling.

"Don't raise your voice at me, Mike!"

"You so holy and thou but can't let shit go."

Big Mama placed both hands on my shoulders.

"Journee, I need you to learn something early. Grown folks' pain ain't nothing but old bones and dead memories. You might hear 'em, might even feel 'em, but that ain't your weight to carry round, hear?"

I didn't fully understand it then, but her words sank into me anyway, like seeds buried deep in dirt, waiting for the right heartbreak to bloom.

Then she smiled and tapped my nose. "Now sit down and eat. Cold food ain't no good."

I sat. She served. And for a few minutes, even with the yelling in the next room, even with the air thick with secrets, I knew everything was okay.

Her love drowned out bad noises, and her smile made the worry fade.

Then I was back in bed, phone still in hand.

The memory faded like a song at its final note, and reality crept back in. A tear slipped from the corner of my eye, landing on the bed sheet. I didn't wipe it away. I let it sink in.

Silent sobs crept up my throat, each breath sharp and shallow—my own broken lullaby. My chest rose in tiny jerks as I curled in on myself, the phone slipping from my grasp.

And somewhere between the pain and the quiet, I drifted to sleep.

5

The Lie Between My Thighs

Philadelphia, PA. May 11th, 2022

"Ouch, do you have to yank me like that!" I cried out as Hope gripped the hairs on the nape of my neck. She tried her best to braid neatly, even as I squirmed on the floor beneath her.

"Girl, if you don't quit all that moving, damn." Hope mumbled with the comb clenched between her teeth. I continued to squirm instinctively, the sharp scrape of her nails worked in a rhythm on my sensitive scalp, sending pain striking through me.

"Why can't somebody else do my hair again?" I whined, no longer wanting to subject myself to what felt like torture. "Like, come on, Aunt Stacy owns a salon." I pressed on, jolting as she started the next braid.

"Yo hair is nappy as hell, ain't nobody else want to do it but me, and it ain't my fault you tender-headed." Hope snapped back in irritation.

But deep down, she knew the truth, that after the unsettling dinner at

Papa's house years ago, certain family members wanted no part in anything involving Momma, which also included her children.

Thanks to Ms. Jean, rumors had spread like wildfire. Lies, even more twisted than the truth, were now passed around at everybody's dinner tables. Philly was a small place where everybody knew somebody. Some family members implied Momma knew the whole time. Others insisted that Serenity was a wicked liar. Both left a blot as dark as ink on our family's reputation. That couldn't be scrubbed out, no matter how much time had passed.

That, plus Big Mama's death, caused the church to further ostracize us. We were no longer welcome at a place where my grandma dedicated her last days. Even if no one told us so directly, we could feel the uneasiness in our bones. Every visit to the Temple of Worship felt like Judgment Day. Family members who wanted to knock Momma off her high horse finally had the ammunition to do so. All because of me.

Random phone calls to place false reports to Child Protective Services and gossip had caused my mother to fall apart. A knock on the door from a stranger could ruin a good day in an instant. Social Workers were a common, fearful occurrence inside our home. As frequently as they were called, was as often they would come. Every one of them complimented our mother on her home's decor as they made minor suggestions before they closed the case.

"Gon' head and get up, I'm finished." Hope informed me as I sprang to my feet, eager to stretch my legs.

I walked up to the mirror, smiling, then frowned when I realized two rows of braids were crooked.

"Damn, Hope you did it again, they ain't even parted correctly!" I fussed running my hands through my hair.

She remained seated on the couch, not at all shocked by my observation. "Look, I told you to stay still," was all she replied.

I walked away sucking my teeth, wanting to complain about my hair with no one to vent to about it.

I missed my sister, and I couldn't wait until Faith came back home from down south, she had already started college. I was still in twelfth grade, so close to being done with school but not at the finish line yet. I plopped down on my bed while facing hers, wishing she could just reappear at that very instant. My phone vibrated, I looked down, and it was Karina.

"Hey, girl." Karina sang on the other end of the phone.

"Hey, best friend," I replied dryly.

"Uh-uh, what's wrong? Who I gotta fuck up from fucking with you." Karina teased, and I fought back a smile.

Karina didn't just walk in—she made an entrance. Five-five with curves and confidence, she was a firecracker: bold, beautiful, and unapologetically herself. Her red-bone complexion turned heads, but it was her wild energy that made her unforgettable. A little ratchet, fiercely loyal, and always the life of the party—Karina was sweet, savage, and everything in between. Once you met her, you didn't forget her.

"Girl ain't nothing wrong, Hope just played in my hair. Got me looking all kinds of crazy." I vented, as I lay back in bed, frustrated.

"I can come over and fix it." She offered, already putting on her shoes to head out the door.

"Bet, I damn sure wasn't tryna walk around like this. Like the fuck she thought? I look homeless," I joked, causing her to burst out laughing.

"You mind if I bring my cousin Mia? I don't want to hear my mom's mouth if I leave her here." She asked me, already knowing the answer.

My smile grew wider. "Yeah, come on," I answered, sitting up in excitement.

"Okay, I'm on my way." She let me know as she ended the call.

Mia was coming! My heart fluttered in my chest. I had a crush on Mia ever since I met her. No one knew, not even Karina. I was struggling with my sexuality. I was attracted to boys, but I was drawn to girls too. Back then, I didn't know what bisexual even meant; everything fell underneath the umbrella of gay. A simple label that haunted me. My stomach twisted; even being called 'gay' felt like exposure, so I did everything I could to go unnoticed.

I fought hard to bury my fascination—to not look too long at a girl's lips while she spoke, to avoid locking eyes when their beauty held mine too tightly, to glance away quickly as they walked past. I battled with myself constantly, policing every glimpse, every thought. When my sisters, Serenity and Faith, made gay jokes about me, I never laughed. Instead, I snapped back—too harsh, too defensive—because deep down, I was terrified they'd figure out the truth that I didn't know what I wanted.

Still, Mia made it damn near impossible to keep hiding. She was brown skin and gorgeous, with lips so full they made the most sensitive parts of my flesh ache. Every curve she had messed with my head. I wanted her, and I hated myself for it.

My mind told me to tell Karina that Mia couldn't come, but the yearning desire to see her again made me say yes. I had only ever been around Mia in school. Never in my home, never alone. I had butterflies. I told myself to play it cool. I was just getting my hair fixed, nothing more, nothing less.

Karina only lived six blocks away from me, but their arrival felt like an eternity. When they finally knocked on the door, I calmly walked downstairs to open it. I fought back the urge to dash over in excitement.

"About damn time, what took you so long?" Karina taunted as she walked through the front door.

I brushed it off as I took Mia in from head to toe. Sporting denim jeans and a soft blue crop top. My eyes went straight to her pierced belly button. I gulped.

"Hey Journee," Mia greeted me, smiling with her glossy lips, drawing me further in.

"Wassup, Mia?" I replied, averting my eyes back to Karina, who had just pulled out a chair. I hadn't meant for my stare to linger as long as it did. Mia just had that effect on me.

"We can go upstairs, ain't no reason for us to do it down here." I insisted.

"Oh, my bad," Karina apologized, pushing the chair back where she had pulled it from. "I forgot you got the room all to yourself right now. I'm jealous," she teased as she followed me.

Making it to my bedroom, I grabbed my computer chair and sat down. Karina stood right behind me.

"Now, Journee, why were you being so dramatic over the phone? Your hair ain't even that bad," Karina said, examining my head.

"I know, I just wanted you to fix these two rows," I replied.

I sat back and let Karina work her magic. I didn't know if I was imagining things, but I kept catching Mia looking at me out of the corner of my eye. It was quick, short-lived, but I noticed. After thirty minutes, my hair was done.

"Man, I'm starving," Karina groaned, rubbing her stomach as she sat down on my bed.

"Every time you come over to my house, you hungry," I laughed, spinning around, happy with the finished results of my hair. "You better go get you a plate, before Mir and Sin dog all the leftovers," I warned.

A silence filled the air as Karina left the room. My attention involuntarily went to Mia. She was sitting on the edge of my bed, legs crossed, scrolling through her phone like she didn't have the power to ruin me.

Her laugh broke the silence—low, effortless, hazardous. I sat across from her, pretending to be focused on something else, anything else, but the heat between us made it hard to breathe.

"Why are you so quiet today?" I asked

She finally looked up at me, "Just tired," she shrugged.

I couldn't help it, I tilted my head slightly as I looked at her. We had locked eyes before, but this time was different. The space between us no longer felt far. Instead, it now felt dangerously close.

She grinned at me, "See something you like?" she asked, pulling me out of my haze.

Clearing my throat, "No," I lied.

My body tensed up. Was it that obvious? I thought to myself as I parted my lips, but no sound escaped them. My throat tightened, and I was losing grip on the last strand of control I had. I wanted to kiss her, and all she did was smile at me.

"Then why are you staring at me? Are you mad at me or something?" she asked, her voice softer than usual.

I paused, leaning back into my seat. "No, I'm not mad at you, Mia."

I was mad at myself for feelings I didn't have the pride to discuss. For wanting something that I could never have. My confusion showed all over my face.

"Come here," she instructed as she patted the space beside her.

What was she trying to do? In my mind, I couldn't dare move closer. If I did, there's no telling what I would do. But my body had other plans, I sat next to her like she instructed. I was a puppet, and she was controlling the strings.

She leaned toward me, slow, deliberate. My stomach tightened as she got close, close enough for me to smell her. A hint of sweetness with something warmer. Her lips brushed mine, and I lost all control. Fueled by lust, our tongues danced. A river began to flow between my thighs as our hands explored each other's bodies. Until we heard the creaking of someone climbing the stairs, we both jumped back.

Karina had burst through the door of my bedroom, squealing as if she had won the lottery. "Yo Momma said we could stay the night since it's gettin' late."

Mia and I locked eyes with one another awkwardly.

Her lips were still glistening from the gloss. That I now knew tasted like cherries. The silence between us wasn't empty—it was charged. My heartbeat was thunder in my ears.

Karina flopped down on the bed between us, oblivious.

"I'm about to crash so hard after all the food I just ate," she said, kicking off her shoes. She examined us.

"Y'all good? Sitting here lookin' weird as shit."

I forced a laugh. "Sis, you always sayin' somebody's weird."

"True," she shrugged, already pulling up a video on her phone.

The brightness lit her face, but all I could see was Mia in my peripheral vision—still, silent, trying her hardest to act normal.

I stood up. "I need to take a shower."

Mia glanced at me, just once. But her eyes said everything.

I leaned against the wall in the hallway, trying to steady my breathing. My body shuddered, and my hands shook. I felt like I was unraveling.

What the hell just happened?

That kiss wasn't supposed to happen. I wasn't supposed to feel like that. Not with her. *Not with a girl.*

I adjusted the shower head and water sprayed down on my face, hoping it would wash away the heat that still burned in my cheeks, in my chest, between my legs.

* * *

When I returned, Karina was under the covers on the other side of the room in my sister's bed, turned away, already snoring. Mia was on my bed. Lying comfortably as if she were waiting for me.

I sat slowly, heart still racing. There was barely a few inches of space between us.

Mia whispered, almost too low to hear. "What took you so long?"

I looked around anxiously, "I didn't know I was gon be that long." I whispered back.

The light from the window hovered over us, casting a soft glow in the darkness of the room. I lay beside her, barely breathing, my heart still pounding loud enough to shake the stillness between us. The space grew thin—too thin.

Mia propped herself up on her elbow and looked down at me. Her eyes glimmered in the dim light, catching every secret, everything I tried to keep hidden.

"Have you ever kissed a girl before?" she asked, her voice hushed, like it didn't want to disturb the quiet that engulfed us.

I swallowed hard. My lips parted, and I missed the feeling of hers touching mine.

"No," I finally whispered. "You?"

She didn't answer right away. I could tell other things occupied her thoughts.

She just kept staring at me, studying every detail of my face. Her eyes lingered on other places.

"Yeah," she said, soft and certain. "Nothing that has ever felt like that."

My heart raced faster.

She reached over and touched my stomach—light, careful. Her fingers traced me. I felt a feverish chill run down my spine. She traced her way to the waistband of my loosely fitted pajama shorts. Stopping immediately there.

My chest rose and fell faster, each breath sharper than the last. Is this real? I asked myself.

"Can I?" she murmured. "Taste you." Her breathing, just as ragged as mine.

I nodded as she slipped her hand beneath my waistband. Her fingers stroked between my inner folds. Causing a soft moan to escape my lips. I covered my mouth instantly.

Mia smiled at me, dragging her hand from between my legs to her lips. She swirled her tongue around my sticky juices that now coated her fingers.

"Mm mm...Tasty," she moaned directly in my ear.

I could only whimper in response.

I needed to feel her, taste her, watch her face contort with bliss like mine. I reached for her jeans under the covers to discover she had already taken them off. Her soft panties clung to her moist mound. Our kiss had ignited a fire that had been slowly simmering from the moment we met. I couldn't hold back any longer. I grabbed her chin, kissing her more ferociously than

I had done before.

We whimpered and moaned softly into each other's mouths. Hidden within the dark of night.

"Take these off," I breathed into her neck, needing more than just a kiss.

Mia complied as she removed her panties, and I removed mine. The covers hide our secret as my hands found her love button. She bit down on her bottom lip in ecstasy. I watched her face, drunk with my own pleasure as we pushed each other closer to the edge. My eyes fluttered. A wave began crashing over me, but then it stopped.

"I have something so much better to show you," Mia breathed, the words brushing against my skin like a secret.

And just like that, Mia straddled me. She lifted my leg with care, guiding it until it entangled with hers. Our sacred, secret springs flowed into one another as her body rocked gently.

Sticky, soft, wet.

A sensation I had never felt before rippled through me. A rush of warm waves hit as I thrashed beneath her. Feeling our pussies collide repeatedly.

"Mia," I whimpered as the core of my belly tightened.

One shudder, then two, three. I felt moans daring to escape my lips, and I pinched them shut with my teeth. My body went limp, and Mia collapsed. Our bodies meshed, covered in sweat. The smell of our secret had broken free throughout the room.

Exhausted, I rose, putting my pajama shorts back on. I cracked the window, hoping the night breeze would carry away the heat, the breathless scent of what we'd just done.

As the tides of pleasure left my body, guilt began to creep in. The shame of what I had done quickly replaced the waves of pleasure that had clouded my mind. Mia reached for me, but I shamefully pulled away. I didn't want to touch her; even looking at her now was just too painful. I was no longer confused about whether I was gay; I now knew it. The evidence now sat painfully, a few feet away.

"Journee, you okay?" she asked reluctantly, grabbing her panties from off the floor.

Growing up in church, I was taught that homosexuality was a sin. I remembered lowering my head as the preacher bellowed from the pulpit, calling gay people an abomination, while those around me nodded in agreement. Sitting among them, I always felt like an outcast, a liar. Now, those memories swarmed my thoughts, drowning me in guilt and fear.

Had I just committed a grave sin?
  Was I now going to *Hell*?

My mind was a cobweb of remorse, "I don't...know," fled my lips before I could muster up a lie.

Mia lifted her bottom, sliding her panties on without even sitting up. "Did you not like it?"

I sat back on the bed with my back still facing her. I wanted to turn around and embrace her. Express how good it felt to feel her touch. Describe the pleasures she had made me feel, but I couldn't.

"No, it's not that," I reassured her, my discomfort not allowing me to soothe her any further.

"Then what is it? she pressed on, digging for a reason.

Why did she even need an answer? She had done this before. Not me, she had been gay all along. Way before I even stepped into the picture.

"I ain't never did nothing like that before," I reminded her, still facing the window, "You've kissed girls before, I haven't. I'm not gay." My tone was sharp, and it sliced deep.

"Then explain what we just did," she voiced frankly, her tone no longer pleasant. "Don't tell me that's all you wanted from me," Mia's voice cracked, her hurt seeping through despite her effort to hide it.

What we did, all I wanted.

Those words sat on my mind like a ton of bricks. What did I want? That was a question I hadn't asked myself. I was more focused on morality than my mortal existence. I wanted to be free. Free of the lies, the dark twisted secrets. I wanted more than this. But what did that even mean? Was I going to do it again, use another person to relieve my burden, then discard them? Push away another person who learned one of my secrets, another person who *saw my ugly*.

What was wrong with me?

"Mia, please don't." My words came out in a sniffle.

I was tired of hiding, exhausted with pretending everything was okay, while inside my body, I suffered an internal purgatory.

"You just don't understand. I can't remember the last time I genuinely smiled. Or the last time, I just existed freely within my own skin. It's deeper than being gay, Mia. I'm ashamed that I don't know who I am." I confessed, trembling, filled with a whirlwind of emotions.

Every word spilled out of my soul as tears rolled down my cheeks. This time, my cries weren't so silent. The bed squeaked as I rocked back and forth, sobbing into my hands. Wondering if God would ever forgive me.

Mia wrapped her arms around me, squeezing me tight. I felt the tension leave my spirit.

"It's okay," she whispered as she pulled me under the covers. I snuggled into her warmth, feeling saved, feeling seen. No longer living a lie.

* * *

I awoke early that Sunday morning, slipping out of Mia's arms.

I headed for the bathroom to shower—to wash off the stench of regret still clinging to my skin.

Her words still chewed at me. **Was that all I wanted?**

Last night, Mia and I had sex. It was raw. Intimate. But honestly? Meaningless. It wasn't what I wanted. I craved something more.

It felt good in the midst of the touching and thrusting, but outside of lust, there was nothing. No connection. No emotion. Just flesh.

I couldn't even name anything I liked about Mia that wasn't rooted in physical attraction. How could it ever flourish into more if all I wanted was the stimulation she provided? I knew I could milk this opportunity, use it to explore all my deep desires—but I also knew that would be wrong.

As the water ran down my back, I made up my mind. I wasn't going to keep feeding my inner purgatory with another lie or betrayal. It was time to dismantle, time to be who I truly was. What happened between us was a moment of weakness—an impulsive decision that should've never happened. And I was going to make that clear as soon as possible.

I stepped out of the shower, wrapping a towel around myself as I faced the mirror.

Buzz.

A text from Karina sent my system into full-blown panic.

'I heard everything.'

Shit.
   I rushed back to the bedroom. For once, couldn't something just be simple?
   I pushed open the door—
   They were both gone.

Still frantic, I texted her back:

'I don't know what you're talking about.'

I silently prayed Mia hadn't confirmed anything. Maybe we could chalk it up to a wild dream cooked up by Karina's imagination.

'Girl, why you cappin'? You know damn well I don't give a fuck about whatever y'all did. I'm just glad you finally did something, lol. I was beginning to think you were asexual.'

'What the fuck is asexual?'

'People who don't get horny.'

'What lol?!?!'

I couldn't help it—I busted out laughing. My hands still trembled as I typed, but it felt good knowing another secret wasn't choking the life out of me.

And more than that, I had Karina.

A best friend who didn't ask if I was gay, who didn't care that it was her cousin. She just poked fun. And I couldn't appreciate her more for it.

Mia called, and I declined it. I didn't want to say what I needed to say over the phone.

'Damn, bitch. How much did you hear? lol'

'Enough.'

I shook my head in disbelief. I thought I heard her shift in bed last night, but I was too lost in the moment. A FaceTime call interrupted me mid-text, but I rejected it.

'And you didn't say anything?!?!'

'Nope.'

'OMG! Rina!'

I looked around my room. I was caught—but I knew she wouldn't say a word. We held each other's secrets.

Karina had her share of fun with niggas. She liked them older, generous, and she loved telling me every detail. I didn't dare to skip school and chill at older niggas apartments out of fear of being caught by Momma, even though I wanted to. Still, I admired her boldness. Every story she shared lit me up inside. I wanted to be in the mix. But I wasn't there **yet.**

I yanked the sheets off my bed, tossed them in the hamper, and jogged to the laundry room. I needed every trace of last night gone. Not out of shame—at least, not anymore—but out of fear of getting caught by someone else.

* * *

The rest of the day, I floated in uncertainty. What would tomorrow look like? How would Mia react when we saw each other again? Ideally, we'd walk away cool—no drama, no beef, no hard feelings. She wasn't my girlfriend. It was just a one-time thing.

I washed clothes, played the game, scrolled through socials—used every distraction within arm's reach. When dinner came, I ate, cleaned up, and brushed my teeth. Then I lay in bed, hoping tomorrow would come with answers.

The next day, I zoned in on finishing up my school assignments. Between class periods, I lounged in the halls. I was searching for her, waiting for her anxiously.

The bell rang, signaling the end of another period, booming through the hallway like a warning shot. Students flooded past me, phones in hand, laughs and chatter bouncing from all directions. I didn't walk, I floated down the halls looking for her.

I spotted Mia's long, silky hair disappearing into the girls' bathroom.

Without thinking twice, I followed.

Inside, the floor was tracked with muddy footprints. The click of flickering fluorescent lights buzzed in my ears. Mia was at the sink, fixing her makeup like it was just another Monday. Like we hadn't blurred every boundary between us less than 48 hours ago.

"Mia."

She glanced at me in the mirror briefly, "You good?"

"Yeah," I answered, tugging on my hoodie sleeve. "But we need to talk."

Mia capped the gloss and turned to me, expressionless as she leaned against the sink. "Talk about what?"

"The other night."

This time, she glared at me coldly. "What about it?"

"It was a mistake."

Silence.

I could feel my heartbeat in my hands. I hadn't intended to be so blunt. After hours of tension building, I just wanted it all to end. The words rushed out before I could buffer them.

Mia's jaw tightened. "Wow. So that's what we callin' it now?" She shook her head as she turned back to face the mirror. "A mistake," she laughed.

"I'm just being honest," I persisted. "It didn't mean anything. It was... it was a moment of weakness."

Mia spun back around to look me dead in the face, like she was searching for something—truth maybe, or hesitation.

"Nah, don't do that. Don't fuck me and then pretend it was some kinda accident."

"I'm not pretending," I erupted, instantly regretting the fierceness of my tone. "I just—I didn't mean to lead you on. Yes, I like girls, but I like boys too. I'm still confused, okay?"

She laughed, bitter and low. "Confused or ashamed?"

I withdrew. Just like that, she used my vulnerability to cut me, and the knife sank in deep.

"I don't care what you are," Mia continued. "But don't play with me. I was there too, Journee. I felt what you felt."

"No, you didn't, all I wanted was to fuck, Mia. That's it, damn." I barked, voice smashing into hers. "You think I felt something?" Snatching her hand, I placed it on my chest. "I haven't felt shit in years. It wasn't real. It wasn't love. It was just a fuck."

Mia stared at me for a long second, hurt displayed all over her face as she stepped back, brushing by me, pausing before she exited the bathroom.

"Maybe, that's all it was for you," she said softly. "But for a second, it felt more real than anything else in this fake-ass school."

The door screeched open and slammed behind her.

I stood there, alone, blinking at the cracked mirror. My reflection staring back—torn, guilty, and still trembling with rage.

I walked into the bathroom, uncertain, and left it in shambles. Nothing had gone like I thought it would. Mia was pissed, and I still had to face Karina. I could no longer predict what was coming next.

I barely made it to lunch before Karina cornered me at our usual table in the lunchroom.

"I saw Mia, what happened?" Karina asked, tearing open her pack of Skittles like she hadn't been blowing up my phone from the moment she woke up this morning.

I sat down slowly, looking over my shoulder before I spoke. Mia was nowhere in sight.

Karina couldn't wait for an update. "So, Wassup? Y'all talked?"

I nodded. "Yeah. In the bathroom between the second and third period."

"And?"

"I told her it was a mistake."

She raised her eyebrows, as she winced as if I had said it directly to her personally. "Damn. That's Cold."

"I had to, Rina. I made a promise to myself that I wouldn't lie anymore."

Karina chewed on a piece of candy, then shrugged. "You sure you not just scared of what you are?"

I looked at my best friend—really looked at her. "Nah, I was but I'm over that shit. I'd rather be a bitch and honest than nice and fake."

Karina balled the empty candy wrapper up and shot it in the trash.

"You know I don't care what you are, right? You could love this damn table and I'd still ride for you."

I cracked up, just a little. "This table, really Rina?"

"This sexy-ass table," Karina smirked. "With me and you on it!" She teased, slapping it like she was giving it a spanking.

We both laughed, the tension dissolving between us from our witty banter.

"Thanks, Hoe."

"Anytime, bitch." She beamed, bumping my shoulder. "Just don't make it weird next time I invite y'all both somewhere."

I sighed, giggling, "Trust me, I'm off that shit, but I can't say its the same for Mia."

* * *

The rest of the day just felt off.

I arrived home from school, relieved to finally be back. The old air conditioner wheezed through the living room, cutting through the heavy, humid spring air.

Sweat clung to my brow as I scrolled aimlessly through Netflix. I was already worked up from everything that had happened today. I just wanted to relax and watch a movie, but nothing held my interest.

"If you're not gon to pick anything, hand it over," Serenity said, snatching the remote from my hand.

I sank into the couch and watched my siblings argue back and forth over what to watch.

I wasn't in the mood for any of it, so I slipped away upstairs.

Everything had gone wrong—the conversation with Mia, the way things ended between us. It all left me anxious and guilt-ridden, the weight of it pressing against my chest and clouding my thoughts.

Even when I received a certificate for my academic achievements, I couldn't enjoy it—I was too distracted. The pride I was supposed to feel was swallowed by the tight knot in my stomach. I stood on stage, smiling at Karina as she cheered loudly in the crowd... but beside her sat a stranger.

Where was Mia?

Still, I reflected on yesterday. **I promised myself:** I would stop pretending to be happy and being with Mia, though it felt amazing momentarily, it didn't make me happy. The aftermath was too heavy to digest.

In less than 48 hours, I had grown violent toward the purgatory inside me. The loneliness, the shame, the guilt—they had lived in my heart for too long. I wanted them gone. I was actively trying to purge them, but they wouldn't die easily. Not without effort. Not without a fight.

That also meant deception was no longer welcome. Still, even as I told myself that, I kept a smile plastered on my face. Unable to rewire my brain from what I had beaten into its subconscious. I was drowning in despair, desperately trying to evict every dark feeling festering inside me.

My Senior year was coming to an end, and with a flicker of newfound self-worth, I wanted to make the best of what was left.

But bad habits don't just die overnight.

I walked into my mother's room seeking guidance. Sitting on the edge of her bed with my back to the television, I forced the words out.

"Momma... I think I'm suffering from depression and anxiety."

I couldn't keep it in anymore. After stuffing it down for so long, the least I could do was let it out—just once.

Without even looking at me, she turned up the volume on her TV.

"Depression is a sin, Journee," she said flatly. "If anyone should be depressed, it's me. I'm the one dealing with all of you alone. You ain't got no kids. You don't have to take care of anybody but yourself. You ain't got nothing to be depressed about."

Her words were loaded like a gun.

"How is depression a sin?" I asked, fidgeting nervously as I picked at my skin.

"God blessed you with life. He didn't have to. So yeah, it's a sin to waste it being depressed."

"But Momma, I—"

Before I could finish, she hurled the remote at my face. It cracked against my nose and lip, splitting both. My eyes instantly filled with tears.

"Bitch, don't you see me watching TV? Don't I do enough for y'all? Can I not have one fucking minute to myself?" she screamed, charging toward me until her face was inches from mine.

"Now get the fuck out my face before I whoop your ass for real this time! Asking me all these dumb-ass questions!" she yelled, spit flying from her mouth, landing on my cheek.

I ran out of her room, covering my face as blood poured through my fingers, soaking my wrists. My siblings were gathered near the banister, their eyes wide with fear. They parted as I ran past, some of them following behind me.

Once again, I found myself looking in a bathroom mirror. I barely recognized my reflection. Blood oozed down my lips, painting my teeth a bright red. My busted lip had already begun to swell rapidly.

Hope rushed in holding a hand towel wrapped around a bag of frozen peas.

"Here. Put this on it before the swelling gets worse."

I took the towel from her and pressed it to my face, wincing.

"What happened?" Hope asked as she stepped inside, closing the door behind her.

"I was just talking to her," I mumbled through the fabric. "And she threw the remote at my face."

Serenity slipped in next. Her eyes examined the scene.

"She's getting worse," she whispered, stepping closer. She reached for the towel and gently pulled it down. Her eyes widened.

"Oh shit. That's bad."

I took a deep breath, trying not to panic.

Hope pinched Serenity's side, making her jump.

"Ow! Don't pinch me! It's not my fault, Momma's gon crazy," Serenity snapped, rubbing her side and avoiding Hope's gaze.

"Look, Momma's gonna be cool. I'm picking up her medicine tomorrow," Hope said, taking control. "Stay clear of her until then. And Journee—don't talk to her about nothing. I mean it. I don't want her flipping out again. You hear me?"

I nodded.

My mother hadn't been the same since everything that happened all those years ago.

Maybe it was the mounting pressure of overdue bills. Maybe it was the guilt of failing to shield her children from the same misfortune that once swallowed her whole. Or maybe it was the merciless whispers from relatives, judging her for a second marriage gone up in flames, leaving her with even more children than the last. Whatever the reason, something in her broke.

She spent most of her days in bed, angry at the world and paralyzed by her circumstances. She no longer cooked. She no longer cleaned. She no longer hosted family gatherings with the pride she once carried.

My mother was battling her own inner purgatory. The smallest inconvenience could send her spiraling, lashing out with anything within reach, striking whoever stood too close.

With no father to call and no way out, we were all trapped in the same hell together. Some days, we tried to understand her suffering. Other days, we blamed her—because there was no one else left to blame.

Occasionally, we'd hear rumors about our father still out in the streets, dancing with his demons. The rare times we saw him, he was stumbling to our doorstep, drunk and slurring apologies. Sometimes, we'd come home from school to find him sprawled out on the steps, too high to stand, too detached to greet us.

As a child, it was hard to feel anything but resentment. I didn't see addiction as illness—I saw it as abandonment, as a selfish performance disguised as pain.

The best version of my father I ever knew was the one captured in a single photograph, tucked beside my grandmother's obituary on the living room shelf. He had been handsome then, with a smile that looked genuine, warm, and inviting. Sometimes, I'd stare at that picture and daydream about what it must have been like: him and my mother before the heartbreak, before the addiction. Before everything.

Momma would share memories of that time in pieces. Some recollections lit her up, her face softening into a smile we rarely saw—certainly not the one she wore with Mr. Trenton. But other times, her eyes would go vacant as if she were watching everything fade from the inside out.

From them, I learned that love gives people the power to make or break you.

It was a lesson that etched itself into me without permission. In my mind, love became synonymous with power, and the day my father walked away, my mother lost all of hers.

Every time I saw her cry, I made a vow: **I would never be that weak.**

Every time she flew into a rage, I made another: **I would never lose control like her.**

And above all else, I promised myself—**I would never fall in love.**

As Hope left, Faith walked in, having just gotten back home for spring break. She sat on the closed toilet lid, a smirk tugging at her lips.

"What did you say to Momma that made her bust you like that?" she asked, holding back laughter.

"I told her I was depressed," I muttered, rinsing blood from my mouth.

Faith scoffed. "Why the hell would you tell her that?" she asked, genuinely baffled.

Not in the mood to explain myself or my emotions, I kept it short. "I wasn't thinking."

She slapped her knees, stood, and shook her head in disbelief. "You never learn."

"I thought maybe I'd finally get a warm welcome home—but this was what I got instead." She complained, stepping behind me to get a better look at my face from the reflection in the mirror.

Still, through the pain, I smiled at her, blood staining my teeth.

"Well, I'm happy to see you," I said with a grimace.

Faith erupted in laughter "you're one crazy bitch." she stated as she slipped out the door.

I looked at my reflection. My hair was sweaty and mangled. My beautiful brown eyes, bloodshot from crying. A messy mix of blood and snot streaked across my face and white t-shirt. I looked deranged... and I was smiling.

Maybe I was insane. I damn sure felt like it. Every thought in my head went quiet.

Something disappeared inside me that day. The last part of me that still gave a fuck... melted away.

Something irreparable shattered as I began to laugh at myself in the mirror.

The sound of my own laughter echoed throughout the bathroom, but it didn't feel like mine. It leaped out of my mouth, bouncing off the walls— empty, hollow—almost like someone else had taken over. I didn't recognize that version of me, but I didn't stop her either.

A knock tapped softly on the bathroom door.

"Journee?" It was Hope again, her voice small. "Are you okay?"

I didn't answer.

I didn't know what *okay* even meant anymore.

She hesitated, giving me a weak smile. "You want me to get you something from the store? I can head out and grab it now, be back in less than fifteen."

I almost laughed again, but it came out more like a sigh.

"I'm good," I smiled back, even though I wasn't. Not even close.

I locked the door, turned the faucet on, and splashed cold water on my face. It stung where the skin had split, but the shock helped pull me out of my trance.

This couldn't be it. This *couldn't* be all my life was going to be—getting hit for opening up, mocked for trying to heal.

I grabbed a washcloth and scrubbed the blood from my shirt, even though I knew it would stain. Some things never come clean.

My eyes flicked back to the mirror, and for the first time, I didn't force a smile. I just stared at myself, swollen and trembling.

"Mission accomplished," I whispered.

* * *

Blame Momma

(For children raised in broken homes)

Momma, I'm still hurting.
   I don't understand why nothing's working.
   No pills, no spirits—just short-lived chills
   From thrills that leave my temple empty.
   Yet all I do is feel.
   So mentally broken.

Who did this to me?
   I wanna blame Daddy,
   But that's a nigga I hardly ever see.

So, Momma—it's you.
   You made me like this.
   Brought me into a world where I'd be treated like shit.
   My mouth held open to drink the lemonade,

But all I taste is piss.

Fuck all of this.
    You gave me these eyes,
    This nose I can't even recognize,
    And lips that can't do anything
    But repeat fables and lies.

But Momma—why?
    Please tell me why I'm still hurting.

See, my heart told my chest the reason that it heaves
    Is nothing, short of the blame
    For the reason, I breathe.
    Then my thoughts told my head.
    The reason why it pains—
    Is you!
    The one who gave me this one-track-ass brain.

But I don't use it.
    If I did,
    My heart wouldn't have all these bruises
    From those who abuse it.

Now look at me.
    I'm so damn short on fuse.
    To light this temple, you said to worship—
    While all it ever seems to do is accumulate hope
    Only to turn around and lose it.

I've been violated by plenty,
    Subjected to many,
    But somehow—

Unlovable.

Damn, Momma.
   I've been so empty—
   Of empathy, even sympathy—
   For those who don't remember me.
   But I can't forget them.

Lost after lost—
   When will I win?

So much has ravished my soul,
   The only passion I had to hold—
   The one thing about me that was completely whole.

Now look at me,
   Alive only by obligation,
   With pain the only thing remaining.
   All this so-called life is
   Unnaturally draining.

To the point where it's actually straining
   Just to remind myself, I'm barely twenty.
   So, what the hell am I actually even saying?

When I say—
   I don't wanna live no more.
   Don't wanna feel no more.
   Don't wanna try to heal no more.
   Waiting patiently
   For the last part of me
   To not wanna build no more—

So I can finally
  End this fight in me.

Momma, I'm still trying to breathe...
  When I fear
  There is no life in me.

II

Two Black Birds

"A generational curse is like an anchor—stuck and sunken in a place it was never meant to stay. It cannot rise on its own; it needs the very hands that cast it down to lift it back to light."

— *Dajaha Dior Halliday Blair*

6

It Gets Cold In Winter

One year later...

The school year slipped away before I could grasp it, and my graduation came and went with little celebration. Summer blurred into autumn, each season passing like pages in a book I barely remembered reading. The trees shed their last golden remnants, and the wind grew sharp, sweeping the Philly streets clean with a chill that announced winter's arrival and the year's impending close. I chose to take a gap year, a pause to breathe before pursuing my dreams at N.Y.U.

The weekend started pretty normally, just my brothers and I making our way to get their hair cut.

I clung tightly to Sincere's hand as I guided him across the street, even though he insisted on walking on his own. Eight years old was not old enough for me to allow him to do so.

Miracle walked close beside us. The sky hung rigid with fog, making it hard to see an ideal path. We walked aimlessly until the bright red neon *OPEN* sign of the barbershop pierced through the gray.

I pushed on the door, despite the faded letters that clearly said 'pull'—making Miracle and Sincere chuckle as we stepped inside.

A tiny Christmas tree stood next to a gumball machine, instantly catching Sincere's eye.

"Wow, Miracle, look! Gumballs!" he shouted, releasing my hand.

Miracle, not nearly as impressed, shrugged.

"Journee, give me a quarter," Sincere demanded, holding out his hand.

"After I pay for y'all's haircuts," I replied, reaching into my pocket to check that I still had the money.

You know you didn't have to come, right? You could've just gave me the money." Miracle fussed, sitting back in his seat.

"I know, but I don't like y'all walking around this way by y'all selves," I explained, adjusting myself.

"Which one of y'all is going first?" the barber asked, shaking his cape clean as the last customer excused himself.

"I'll go," Miracle said, walking over to the barber's chair.

I blew warm air into my freezing hands, rubbing them together, to adapt to the warmth inside. I placed them between my thighs and watched as Sincere knelt in front of the gumball machine, determined. I sighed. He wasn't going to let it go.

"Here, Sincere," I called, holding out the quarter.

He leapt up excitedly, crashing into my legs as he snatched it.

"Dang, Sincere!" I giggled, leaning back—bumping into the person sitting beside me.

"My bad," I said, still laughing, as I turned to face him.

"We good," he replied with a smile, sizing me up.

He was sitting, but I could tell he stood at least five-ten. Slim build, golden honey complexion, and eyes—soft, light brown—framed by lashes that made me a little jealous. I blushed, glancing away. It felt awkward, being this close to someone I barely knew. Close enough to hear his breath, feel the tension, and wonder what he was thinking.

"What's yo name?" he asked, flashing a grin and chewing gum.

"Journee," I replied, trying not to smile too much. "What's yours?"

"I like that, it's different. My name's Khalil. How old are you?" he asked as he stuck out his hand.

"I'm nineteen," I answered, shyly accepting his touch that lingered longer than necessary.

"I'm twenty," he replied, eyeing me down.

I kept stealing glances, admiring the details of his face. Thick, reddish-brown curls framed his head, matched by a light mustache and a neatly trimmed beard. His teeth were perfect—pearly white, the kind that made his smile hard to ignore. He was undeniably attractive; any woman would see that. But it was the subtle twinkle in his eye that held my attention, like he knew something I didn't, and I wanted to find out what.

I sat quietly, unsure of what to say next, silently hoping he'd continue from there since I wasn't yet comfortable flirting with a stranger.

"So, you from around here?" he asked, gently tapping my knee.

"Yeah, not too far. You?"

"Oh, for real, me too," he said as the barber finished Miracle's cut.

I stood and directed Sincere to the chair. Glancing over my shoulder, I noticed Khalil was watching me. Wanting to give him more of a show, I switched my hips with extra purpose, tossing him a smile as I walked back toward him.

He couldn't take his eyes off me. His gaze moved from my brown eyes to my glossy pink lips, then down to the bit of cleavage exposed from my low-cut top.

"Damn, you pretty as shit. Why I ain't been seen you around here?"

"I don't go out much," I replied, trying not to sound boring.

We flirted until Sincere's haircut was done. As I reached into my pocket to pay, I realized I was a quarter short.

"You're short. I'm missing twenty-five cents," the barber said flatly, sliding the cash I'd already handed him into his apron.

"I'm sorry, I gave the quarter to my little brother for the gumball machine," I explained.

The barber looked like he was about to fuss, but Khalil stepped over and handed him a quarter.

I breathed a sigh of relief. "Thank you so much," I said gratefully.

As we exited the shop, Khalil followed us.

"Can I get your number?" he asked, holding out his phone.

"Yes," I replied, smiling as I entered my number and saved it under Journee.

"Oh, so it's Journee with two E's? That's cute. I'ma hit you up after I get my shit cut."

"Alright," I said as we went our separate ways.

I was in such a good mood, I didn't even notice I had missed three calls from my Momma. I called her back quickly.

"Why the fuck weren't you answering your phone?" she barked, picking up on the first ring.

"I'm sorry, Momma. It was in my coat pocket on vibrate," I rushed to explain.

She paid my apology dust as she spat, "Bring yo ass home!" into the phone speaker before ending the call.

* * *

I walked home with the weight of Momma's words at the forefront of my mind.

Sincere started whining, exhausted from walking.

"I don't wanna walk anymore!" he whined.

Without saying a word, Miracle picked him up and carried him on his back.

Even though I was older, Miracle was taller and stronger. Built like a football player, people always assumed he was the older sibling. At just seventeen, he already looked full-grown.

We slowed down as we reached Point Breeze, a notorious stretch filled with fiends and addicts.

I warned Miracle to stay close. The fog had lifted slightly, revealing the sidewalk littered with needles, trash, and broken glass. People stumbled around, some moaning in pain, others lying on the cold concrete.

As we passed a row of poorly pitched tents, a man suddenly reached out and grabbed my pants leg.

"Get off me!" I screamed, horrified.

Then I saw his face. My father.

He was sprawled out in filth, reeking of vomit and calling my mother's name in a daze. The horror on my face turned to deep sadness.

I helped him to his feet, and we slowly made our way home.

When we got there, my mother met us at the door.

"Fuck no! Who told you to bring him here?" she yelled as I let go of him and he collapsed on the love seat.

"We found Daddy passed out on Point Breeze. He ain't looking so good. I think he's sick."

She walked over, covering her nose as she tapped him lightly.

"James… James, wake up."

Concern slowly overtook her fury.

"Faith, go upstairs and run the shower," she ordered. "Miracle, Journee—help me get him up the stairs."

My father drifted in and out of consciousness.

"Semira… Semira, uh…"

He could barely speak.

"Hurry!" my mother urged as we reached the top of the stairs.

We placed him in the shower. As the water ran, blood and feces mixed with it and flowed down the drain. My father gripped my mother's arm and looked her in the eyes.

"What happened, James?" she asked, fear in her voice.

His eyes pleaded with her not to make him say it.

"Please… don't make me say it."

She unbuttoned his shirt, revealing bruises across his chest and a deep, infected wound. She unfastened his pants and recoiled.

Blood. Feces. Pain.

"What the fuck..." she gasped.

"Don't..." was all he could say before his arm went limp.

"James! Please stay with me! Oh God, please!" she cried.

"Hope!" she screamed.

Hope ran in, panicked. "What's going on?"

"Call 911! Now!"

Hope dialed, speaking into the phone. "We need an ambulance."

The rest blurred into the background of the panic that spread around the room.

Then she paused and asked my mother, "Did he overdose?"

My mother held my father tightly, shaking her head.

"No..." she inhaled sharply, "Tell them he's been raped."

* * *

Don't You Tell 'Em

(For silenced men and boys)

Don't you tell 'em what they did to you—
    Better hush now. Don't speak.
    Part yo lips to share that shit,
    They'll question yo sexuality.

What did you do to entice that fool?
    Why'd he want a piece?
    You ain't fight back 'til yo bones cracked?
    Oh, you ain't man enough—I see.

Death ain't invite you to the table?
    You just accepted—willing and able?
    Don't you dare look sideways at me.

'Cause you a man,
    Like I'm a man.
    We can't be victims of each other's hands.
    That don't make no sense to me.

Either you fight 'til the death,
    Or don't waste your breath—
    That's just the way it's supposed to be.

Some secrets kept can save yo rep—
    You feel me, my O.G.?
    Ain't no point in tradin' truth
    For bags of misery.

Boys don't feel.

Real men? We kill.
That's just the way it's supposed to be.

You got me now?
Gon' fix that frown.
I'm just tellin' you the truth—
But what you do is up to you.
Listen... I don't make the rules.

7

Semira's Heart

I want to stop loving you so fucking bad that it hurts, but I can't. And that's why I hate you.

I've prayed countless nights, begging the Lord to take this agony from me, to heal this wound you left behind. I've asked Him to bring you back to me, to fix what's broken between us, to remove the weight of this hate that's crushing my chest. But nothing ever changes.

If I could return to that first moment, when you smiled at me like I was the only thing that mattered, I would erase it all. You always told me I was the best thing that ever happened to you. I disagree. Maybe I was the worst.

I can't help but wonder—*if we had never crossed paths, would you still be this lost?*

My heart can't fathom a life without you, but my mind already knows that I have to. And I've done it! Every waking moment of hell, I've lived it without you. I had no choice. It's too late for us to change the past. Take back the pain that was already inflicted.

When I look at these beautiful babies we created, all I see is you. And yet, I can't hold you. I can't touch you. My love for you is suffocating, it's bleeding me dry. Still, even as it kills me, I can't stop.

Half the time, I feel like I'm losing my mind, imprisoned in the past of all the dreams we let die. All of it, everything has driven me mad. I'm fragile, I never knew I could be this unstable. I didn't choose to feel this broken, but now these pieces are my life.

I've tried to get help. I've begged for someone to listen, to understand, but instead, I've been handed more pills. Another prescription to swallow. Another dose stronger than the last, stretching the nights out, each one feeling longer than the last, each one leaving me more vacant.

What else am I supposed to do? I'm left alone to raise our children, even as I spiral, even as I teeter on the edge of insanity. There's no one to help save them from the chaos of my mind, from the wreckage of my episodes. It's just me, trapped in the hell I never intended to create, left to deal with the guilt and the fallout.

I don't want to be bitter, but I'm so fucking tired. Tired of feeling like I've failed you. Tired of feeling like I'm failing as a mother, as a wife. Tired of feeling like I've failed at everything. I know deep down that I failed—I failed us. And I wish I could take it all back, wish I had never brought you into this misery. I wish I could've shielded you from the darkness that devoured us both.

Life did nothing but break us apart, and once you were hooked on drugs, nothing could stop you. Not me. Not our children. Nothing was more important than the next fix. And for that, I've hated you. For the pain that consumed you, I've hated myself. I never thought loving someone could come with so many consequences. I never imagined that losing you would hollow me out like this.

You're still here, haunting me, even though you're gone. I'm still so deeply in love with a ghost that every day feels like I'm drowning in your absence. I've tried to mourn you, to bury this love, to put the past to rest so I can finally let go. But you keep coming back, showing up in my mind, in my dreams, in the spaces between breaths, on my doorstep. You're always here, a reminder of the monster I helped create.

I'm sorry, James, for everything.

* * *

Philadelphia, December 3rd, 1982

"Semira! I know your ass ain't leave my shit like this?! All trifling and dirty— get yo ass down here, bitch, before I drag you down!" Imani screamed up the stairs loud enough to startle her daughter awake.

Semira forced herself to sit up in bed.

"Bitch, I know the fuck you heard me!" she shouted as she barged into the kitchen.

"You've got to the count of ten. One... two... three!"

Groggy and panicked, Semira yanked the covers off her body. From upstairs, she could still hear her mother's angry tirade echoing through the walls.

"Here I come," she answered, her voice riddled with fear.

"Damn, I got to come home to this fucking mess? How many times do I have to tell you to keep my shit clean?!" she continued to shout as she took a mental note of everything Semira didn't do.

Cursing herself, Semira darted into the narrow hallway, nearly slipping on the puddle collected from a ceiling leak as she rushed downstairs. She entered the kitchen with her head lowered, shoulders slumped—physically and emotionally drained from school, endless chores, and caring for her younger siblings. She barely had the strength to absorb her mother's fury. Every few words, Imani called her a bitch, lacing each insult with venom as she laid them on thick.

A thought crossed her mind to protest, and it was immediately abandoned. Semira knew better; the consequences of such actions would be dire.

"You really are an ungrateful bitch. Ain't no way I would've left my mom's shit like this," Imani sneered, pointing in disgust at the pots and pans still full of the dinner Semira cooked earlier that evening.

"Come clean this shit up," Imani demanded standing directly in her path.

Semira pressed her body against the refrigerator, wishing she could dissolve into the cold tile beneath her feet. She closed her eyes and inhaled sharply, holding her breath as she squeezed by her.

Taking the lack of eye contact as disrespect. Imani stepped closer, she loomed over her daughter, causing Semira to flinch and shift toward the counter, bracing herself for a blow that didn't come. Imani only smirked.

"Scary bitch," she muttered, rolling her eyes as she picked up a pot and flung it toward the sink.

Her aim was completely off. The pot hit the counter=top, splattering the rice everywhere as it spun in a spiral, clinking rapidly and filling the once-silent room with even more noise.

"You just gonna stand there, dummy? Fix it!" Imani barked, dragging a chair out and plopping onto it with a loud, exhausted exhale. "Whew!" she huffed, launching into another rant.

"Sorry, Momma," Semira said softly, stepping over the mess to start packing up the leftovers. She scraped the uneaten food into old butter containers, repurposed as Tupperware.

"You just hell-bent on being a nasty bitch, huh?" Imani kept prodding, her voice full of bitterness.

"No, Momma," Semira replied, her tone low as she placed the containers in the fridge and ran hot water into the pots.

Then, as always, she poured her mother a drink—a ritual whenever Imani returned home from work at three a.m. The flick of a match sparked a flame, and soon the kitchen filled with the familiar stench of a Newport cigarette.

"I work all fucking night to come home to a dirty fucking kitchen," Imani spat, pausing to take a long sip of her gin.

She waited for a retort she could strike down, but Semira stayed quiet. She knew better, she knew silence was safer.

Whenever her mother came home drunk, which was every night, she knew any action, no matter how minuscule, was still enough to be deemed as disrespect. Suspected disrespect was all that was needed to initiate an ass-whooping.

Imani sat there stewing in her own frustration. Displeased with her daughter's avoidance. She twirled a finger around the rim of her glass, unsatisfied. She craved release as she shrugged but she would not be humored with any tonight.

After hours onstage, singing for her regulars, Imani returned home sunken. She lacked the self-awareness to name the emptiness growing inside her. The joy she once felt from performing had long since vanished.

In her youth, raised in a Baptist church, Imani's voice had carried across pews and city blocks. People crossed neighborhoods just to hear her sing on Sundays. Back then, she'd been radiant, filled with hope and the kind of purpose that only dreams can promise. But all that faded after she got pregnant. Having a baby had clipped her ambitions at the root.

Still, she held onto the fantasy that her big break would come. But now, pushing forty with two daughters and three nephews left in her care after her sister's untimely death during childbirth, she was drowning. Five kids she never asked for. Five lives she couldn't afford—emotionally or financially.

Every year, she swore her stardom was coming. And every year it didn't. Newer, younger girls had started to grace the stage she once lit up, and reality began to set in. Her once beautiful face had aged. Her body, worn from years of gin and cocaine, was breaking down. What once felt like euphoria had turned on her—now the high was the predator, hunting her every night, warping her mind and robbing her of control. But still, she denied she had a problem. It was her little secret.

Semira finished the dishes quickly and slipped out of the kitchen. She held her breath once more until she was back in her bed, where she finally exhaled.

Another night survived.

As she lay there, her mother's laughter echoed in her mind. Every insult crawled under her blanket and lay beside her. She clutched her pillow, the word bitch gnawing at her spirit. Quietly, she began to hum a lullaby—one her mother used to sing when Semira was still her darling baby girl:

"*Birds flying high,*
  You know how I feel.
  Sun in the sky,
  You know how I feel.
  Breeze drifting on by,
  You know how I feel…"

Tears slid down her cheeks. She sobbed into the fabric, heaving like a newborn. Her fists gripped the bedding as emotions overwhelmed her.

Why didn't her mother love her anymore?

Those once warm eyes were now cold with contempt.

What changed? What did I do wrong? The questions ran in circles inside her head, restless, unanswered.

* * *

Philadelphia, December 31st, 1985

"Semira, come on, girl—wake up!" Andrea whispered, her voice urgent but playful as she leaned in and gently shook her sister's shoulder.

Semira's eyes fluttered open to a world of darkness.

"Huh... What?" she murmured, her voice thick with sleep.

It felt like she'd only just closed her eyes. Her body ached with exhaustion, the kind that clung to her bones.

"It's the big New Year's party tonight. You didn't forget, did you?" Andrea asked, her face practically glowing with excitement.

Semira blinked against the sudden light as she reached over and switched on the lamp. The golden hue cast across the room revealed Andrea already dressed to impress—hair done, makeup light but confident, and a gleam in her eyes that only the anticipation of something magical could bring. Semira's gaze drifted to the outfit she recognized all too well: her own black blouse, fitted just right on Andrea's growing frame, paired with blue jeans and a cropped denim jacket.

A tired smile crept across Semira's lips. Her little sister wasn't so little anymore.

"Is that mine?" Semira teased, poking Andrea playfully in the stomach, prompting a burst of giggles.

"Maybe," Andrea replied coyly, spinning on her heel into a full dance routine. She swayed and twisted, letting the rhythm in her head take over.

"Come on, get up!" she sang, her joy infectious.

With a soft laugh, Semira threw back the covers and slipped out of bed. She crossed the room, retrieving the white dress she'd set aside days ago—the one she saved for special occasions, moments that might become memories. As she stepped into it, Andrea hurried over, helping zip her up in the back.

Then Andrea slipped off her jacket, revealing that her blouse was still unfastened. She turned and pointed, silently asking for help.

"This is the only part I couldn't do," she said with a sheepish smile, glancing at their reflections.

For a moment, both girls were still, captivated by the resemblance. The mirror didn't lie—they were their mother's daughters.

"We finally get to go out together. I can't wait," Andrea said, her voice laced with wonder. "I ain't never been to no real party before."

Semira reached under the bed and pulled out her white sneakers—the clean ones she rarely wore unless the night mattered.

"Girl, we've been to plenty of parties."

"Church lady parties at the T.O.W. don't count," Andrea quipped. "I'm talking about the kind that Marlon goes to—with a DJ, lights, dancing... freedom."

As her sister danced again, Semira headed into the bathroom to remove the curlers from her hair, each twist falling into soft curls. She reached for the red lipstick tucked away in her cabinet, a rebellious little treasure she'd hidden weeks ago.

"Here," she said, offering it to Andrea. "Put this on."

Andrea's eyes widened. "Where did you get this? Momma, don't let me wear no bright makeup."

"She doesn't let me either," Semira said with a smirk. "I swiped it from my job."

Andrea attempted to apply it, but smeared it crooked across her lips.

"Girl, give me that," Semira chuckled, taking over. With delicate fingers, she painted Andrea's lips just right, then capped the lipstick and returned it to its hiding place.

"Now rub your lips together like this," she said, demonstrating.

Dressed and glowing, Semira grabbed her denim jacket. "Let's go," she chimed, nudging Andrea playfully onto the bed before racing downstairs.

Andrea laughed as she scrambled after her, both girls bounding toward a night that promised something more than just music—it promised a kind of freedom neither of them had tasted before.

The music thundered as they stepped into the pulse of the party. Lights flickered across the walls, and the air was thick with heat, perfume, and bass. Andrea stood in awe, her eyes drinking in every detail like a scene from a dream.

Marlon appeared through the crowd, flashing a grin. "Y'all finally made it!" he shouted above the beat.

Neither Semira nor Andrea heard him clearly, but their faces said it all—they were exactly where they wanted to be. Semira clutched her cup, trying to ease her nerves. Crowds had never been her thing, and yet tonight... something felt different. The air hummed with promise.

"Dance with me!" Andrea yelled, grabbing Semira's hand. They slipped into the crowd, their laughter spilling between beats as they swayed and spun under the strobe lights.

Song after song melted into each other until the music suddenly cut off, and the crowd erupted.

"Ten... nine... eight... seven..." the countdown began.

Semira felt time slow, the world narrowing to her sister's beaming face, the warmth of strangers, the weightlessness of joy.

"Three... two... one—Happy New Year!"

Cheers echoed. Confetti rained. The music roared back to life.

Andrea pulled Semira deeper into the crowd, their bodies moving freely with everyone else, as if the rhythm had stitched them into a collective heartbeat. Then, just as Semira twirled mid-dance, she felt a tap on her shoulder.

She turned.

And time stopped.

A man stood before her, tall and handsome, with a slow, smoldering smile that made her breath catch. His eyes met hers—curious, confident, warm. There was something in his gaze that didn't demand attention, but invited it.

"Happy New Year," he said, his voice rich and steady despite the noise around them.

Semira blinked, the rest of the party fading to a blur behind him.

"Happy New Year," she replied, heart thudding as if she'd stepped into something she couldn't quite name—but already felt.

* * *

James's Letter to Semira

I will never forget the night I saw you standing there.

The room was loud, packed with bodies swaying and people screaming "Happy New Year!" But all I saw—was you. In that white dress, glowing like an angel. Your kinky, coiled curls framed your face like a halo, your red lips parted in laughter, and then you smiled.

That smile—Lord, that smile—sealed it for me. I swear, Cupid must've hit me dead in the chest before I even knew your name.

I was never supposed to be at that party. The only reason I crossed the tracks that night was because Marlon wouldn't let it go. If I'd known his sister looked like *you*, I would've made it a priority to run, not walk.

You were dancing with Andrea when I first saw you move—so free, so alive. And I just stood there, frozen. Shy, nervous, unsure. But something about you made me brave. I tapped your shoulder. You turned around, so quick and defensive, I thought I'd ruined my shot. But then our eyes met—and you smiled.

"Happy New Year!" I shouted over the music, smiling as you did the same.

"What's your name?" you asked.

"James," I answered, heart damn near pounding out of my chest.

You just kept dancing. And even though I wasn't much of a dancer, I danced with you that night. When the party thinned and the music faded, you finally told me your name.

Semira.

I felt like I hit the lottery.

Meeting you marked the beginning of the best years of my life. I just wish I'd been strong enough to give you all the things I promised. I made so many promises, Semira. And broke more than I care to count. Maybe you hate me for it. I wouldn't blame you.

We fought hard for each other. Even harder to stay together. But some love stories are made of fire, and ours kept burning us both. Your mother hated me. No matter what I did, I was never good enough in her eyes. But I think, deep down, she hated that I saw through her lies. That I saw the truth in you, she spent her whole life trying to bury.

And you? You defended her—even when she dishonored you, you honored her. I respected that loyalty, even when it tore you apart. Your parents were your compass, even if that compass pointed you straight into a storm. You followed it.

I fell in love with a proper church girl from South Philly. A girl raised to wear the mask, to play the part, to smile through pain. And I was just a broke boy from the other side of town who didn't even have two pennies to rub together. But I loved you with everything I had, I made that nothing into something.

At first, I thought you had it all—fancy clothes, a nice house, the illusion of security. But the closer I got, the more I saw the truth. The nasty, gritty nature of it all.

Your father played the role of provider, but he gave you money instead of love. Your mother was a ghost with a wine glass and a powdery high, inviting strangers into the house like it wasn't filled with children. You cried out, and no one came. The man who should've protected you—your uncle—used that silence to feed his own evil. Your father showed up only to drop off envelopes and pretend he didn't see a thing.

And you? You took care of everything. The house, the bills, the siblings. You cooked, cleaned, and held it all together while you were still a child. I saw it, and it tore me up inside. Your mother gloated about your maturity but I knew better. You weren't living—you were surviving.

So, I made a choice. I chose to help you carry that weight. Not because I pitied you, not because I felt obligated, but because I loved you. Deeply. Fully. And I never, not once, saw you as a burden.

But love, as strong as it was, wasn't enough.

I was carrying my own pain, my own rage, my own brokenness. And sometimes, without meaning to, I let that spill into us. I didn't always listen when I should have. I tried to be your savior instead of your partner. I thought if I could protect you from the world, that would be enough. But what I didn't realize was—you also needed someone to protect you from yourself, from the guilt, from the need to please those who didn't deserve you.

I failed you there.

I know now that love isn't loud declarations or grand rescues. Sometimes, it's just holding space. Being gentle. And I didn't always give you that. I let my frustrations speak when I should've softened my tone. I let pride become a wall between us when we needed a bridge. I left you nothing but a blanket to snuggle with at night when you needed my warm embrace.

And for that, Semira, I am sorry.

Deeply.

If you ever wonder—if any of this was real—know that it was. Every dance, every fight, every stolen moment in between. You were the brightest light in my life. And even when that light dimmed, even when your spirit was breaking under the weight of everyone's expectations—*I still saw you*. The real you, the beauty trapped inside the ugly of terrible situations.

You were never invisible to me.

I carry your memory with me. I still see that girl from the party in my dreams. I still remember how it felt to hold your hand, to hear your laugh, to whisper dreams of a future we never got to build.

And even though I didn't live up to everything I promised you, I'll never regret loving you.

Never.

– James.

Bruised Hearts

(For lovers crying together)

"I love you,"
   He leans sideways to say,
   In the midst of all the pain.
   He can feel the thunder rumble in his chest—

the blank stare,
The dryness in his breath.

Waiting for a reply,
  just one single move.
  Nothing.

She just sighs, inhales,
  and finally says,
  "I love you, too."

And here comes the "but" —
  a quick flash of déjà vu,
  accompanied by:
  "I've been hurt too many times
  to be loved by you."

Though he never asked,
  it's not like he didn't know.
  He's seen her at her worst—
  With fake smiles in happy photos.

He raises his eyes to meet hers,
  filled with so much pain.
  Fractured. Shattered.
  She stood—
  a broken heart remained.

"I thought love was supposed to repair it."
  She says,
  glancing at her lifeless marriage
  With a quiet gasp.

He leans back,
   tilting his head to the sky.
   Tears rush forward,
   but never meet his waiting eyes.

He clears his throat, begins to speak:

"You claim to love,
   but throw it away so easily.
   I don't complain—
   Unless it's too cold inside.
   I'm a man;
   I swallow the hardest of pride.
   I humble my words
   when I talk to you.
   And yes,
   I know my tone
   bounces around this room."

Before he can finish,
   She interrupts—
   With yet again, another "but."

He can't lose or win.
   With every move,
   She's too convinced
   to be somebody's fool.

She was a fool for her mother,
   a pocket for another,
   a watchdog,
   to tame her wild-life brother.

And all he asked
   was for a piece unused.

As he questions himself,
   Was she always this abused?

Philadelphia, June 24th

"One, two, three, push! That's it—take a deep breath. When I say three, we'll start again," the doctor instructed as Semira gripped the nurse's hand tightly beside her hospital bed.

"I can't breathe! Stop, please! It hurts—I need to sit up!" Semira screamed.

Panicking, fighting to sit up, but the doctor didn't listen. Pushing her back down, he insisted she lie flat on her back. Forced into such an unnatural position to give birth, her body screamed in protest.

The epidural hadn't been administered properly, and no matter how many times Semira pleaded that she could feel everything, the hospital staff dismissed her. Her cries fell on deaf ears as they urged her to keep pushing.

"Ah! Ahhh! I can't—God, please help me!" Semira sobbed, trying to convince herself it was all worth it. She was alone, surrounded by strangers, giving birth to what she believed was her first son.

"One more time—give me a big push!" the doctor instructed again. Semira took a deep breath and pushed with everything she had left. At last, her baby emerged.

"Finally, my baby boy," she coughed, struggling to catch her breath.

"Oh my," the doctor said, shocked as they cleaned off the newborn.

"What's wrong?!" Semira asked frantically, panic rising again in her chest.

"Congratulations—it's a girl."

Semira blinked.

During the ultrasound, they hadn't been able to confirm the baby's gender, but the doctor had guessed a boy based on the size. Still, she smiled. Another girl—her fourth. She always believed being a mother was her true purpose. It didn't matter what she had hoped for—this was all part of God's plan.

"Ten pounds, fourteen ounces," the nurse announced.

Semira was pleased, but the joy quickly faded as she looked down to find a pool of blood soaking the sheets beneath her. Her vision blurred as she lost feeling in her legs and quickly slipped into unconsciousness.

She awoke in a different hospital room. James was asleep in a chair beside her. Her first instinct was panic.

"Where is she?! Where's my baby?!" she cried, jolting James awake.

"Calm down, she's fine. They're just runnin' some tests—checking her lungs. That was the doctor's main concern," James said, standing to his feet.

Semira exhaled in relief. She remembered they'd given her steroid shots during the pregnancy, anticipating she might need to be induced early.

"How long ago did they take her?" she asked, trying to sit up, but collapsed back in pain.

"Ouch!" she cried, tears springing to her eyes.

"Not long. Less than five minutes," James said, his voice tight. He had been trying to remain sober for less than two weeks and was silently struggling to resist the urge to use again.

"If you don't wanna be here, you don't have to be," Semira snapped, her voice cracking.

James picked up the cup of water from her bedside table and gently placed the straw at her lips. She took a few sips, then waved him off.

Staring into his eyes, she asked, "Where have you been?"

"Don't start," James muttered, avoiding her gaze.

"You missed her birth."

"Ain't no different from the last three," he replied, rubbing the back of his neck.

"I almost died, James. And you weren't even here."

"What the fuck was I gonna change by being there? You alive, ain't you? Don't start your shit, or I'll walk the fuck out of this hospital."

Just then, the nurse entered, wheeling in the newborn in a clear bassinet. A pink sign with no name sat at the head.

"You didn't name her?" James asked, his eyes lighting up as he looked at the baby.

"No, not yet. I didn't get the chance," Semira said, forcing herself to sit up completely.

James stood silently, guilt rising in his soul. He hadn't meant to miss her birth. He hadn't planned to get drunk. But he had. He'd chosen a beer to quiet his cravings, to keep from using—but that decision cost him yet another irreplaceable moment. Still, looking at his daughter now, he couldn't deny he felt blessed.

"I was too busy fighting for my life to think of girl names," Semira muttered. "We thought it was a boy, remember?"

James nodded slowly, then said, "How bout Journey?"

"Journey? What made you think of that?" Semira asked, cradling her baby's chubby face.

"Because... it was a journey to get her here," James replied.

"I like that. But let's spell it differently. With two E's—Journee."

"That's perfect," James agreed, smiling as he sat beside her on the bed.

The nurse exited the room, leaving a quiet behind. Semira's smile faded.

"We can't keep doin' this," she whispered, breathing in her baby's scent.

She was beginning to lose faith in James. Every promise he made, he broke. Every vow to be there, he abandoned. Her eyes locked onto him coldly. How could I love this man?

"I'm fine, baby. Look at me—I'm kickin' that shit. I promise," James said. But it sounded more like he was trying to convince himself. His sniffles, the way he shivered—he was lying, again.

"You know it's always cold in hospitals," he added with a weak smile.

Semira didn't respond. She knew she should leave—but she didn't want to. As she looked down at Journee, her eyes welled up with tears.

"James... if you can't get it right this time, I don't think—"

"I will, baby. I will!" James cut in desperately.

The silence that followed was thick with unspoken words. The joy of new life was drowned beneath the weight of old pain. Since that night, their whole life had been slowly falling apart.

8

The Company You Keep

Philadelphia, February 9th, 1988

"I can't believe you did it, nigga," Marlon exclaimed as he dapped James up and handed him a beer.

"I told you I was gon do right by her, dawg. She means more to me than anything in this world," James said, smiling down at his hand, admiring the wedding ring that now fit snugly on his finger. He and Semira had decided to elope—despite her father's disapproval.

"I'm proud of you, too," Greg joined in, handing both James and Marlon a beer.

"Well, the nigga had no choice. Wasn't she knocked up?" Mike questioned knowingly as he sparked up a rolled joint he had pulled from his shirt pocket.

"Hell nah, nigga, my sister ain't pregnant, punk," Marlon spat back, annoyed as he took a swig of his beer.

James looked at Mike and shook his head. He didn't understand why his cousin always had something foul to say out of his mouth. Noticing James's hostility, Mike pivoted.

"I'm just playin', my bad, nigga," he smirked, taking a huge puff before passing the joint to Greg.

Greg shook his head as he grabbed it, took a puff, and passed it to his left. "Ignore him. He just mad 'cause not even his own Momma could love that face," Greg chuckled as he lay back on the sofa.

The room erupted in laughter.

Mike laughed it off, but he didn't find the joke funny. He watched as James laughed so hard he couldn't catch his breath. Mike couldn't understand how James could find it funny, after all they had been through.

Both of their mothers had abandoned them to be raised by their aunt. All they ever had was her and each other.

He hated his mother. He hated Aunt Kim, too. He felt all women were the same—worthless whores. He had pleaded with James not to get married. He knew, deep down, Semira was just another nasty bitch pretending to be a good woman, just like his mother.

"All they do is lie, cheat, and use you," he had told his younger cousin. But James never listened.

Now he was married. Moving into a new place, leaving Mike behind for her.

Lost in thought, Mike didn't notice the joint had finished its rotation and was now in front of his face.

"Yo, you good?" James asked, noticing that Mike had gone quiet again.

"Man, I'm cool," Mike muttered, grabbing the joint.

Sensing the tension, Greg tapped Marlon. "We're about to head out. I'll see y'all niggas tomorrow—congratulations again," he said, reaching for his jacket.

"Aight, catch y'all later," James replied as he walked them out, shutting and locking the door behind them.

Walking back over to the sofa, he shook his head.

"What, nigga?" Mike asked, already agitated.

"What do you mean 'what'? Why you gotta talk about Semira like that—especially in front of Marlon? That's her brother. We just got married, and you're causing problems already," James said, rubbing his forehead.

"So? I don't care if that's *that nigga* sister. He playin' you like a sucker! Probably laughin' at you right now for marryin' a hoe," Mike spat back, his anger flaring.

"You better watch your mouth when you talkin' bout my wife!" James shouted, stepping in close, nose to nose.

"Oh, so you think you a big nigga now, huh?" Mike gritted his teeth.

His once smaller cousin now towered over him, looking down with a threatening gaze.

"I don't think a damn thing, Mike—you do," James spat, stepping away and into the bedroom they shared in their tiny cramped apartment.

Mike's rage boiled over as he sat down. *This nigga thinks he better than me?* It played in his mind like a broken record. His heart pounded as he snatched his jacket off the hook and stormed out the door, slamming it behind him.

James heard the commotion but didn't budge.

Instead, he lay in bed as the fire in his chest slowly settled into a dull ache. He used to be so close to Mike. They were like brothers in more ways than anyone dared to speak aloud.

James had once hated his own mother, too, until he found out the truth. The real truth. A truth he had learned to live with, unlike Mike.

He remembered the whispers at family gatherings. The sidelong glances. The silent judgment from people who knew but never spoke. The horrible things Aunt Kim's late husband had done. How he and Mike were actually blood brothers—ashamed of the same man, disgusted by the same name. Even though they'd grown up together as such, they never dared to call each other anything other than **cousins**.

James's mother was only twelve when she gave birth to him. Mike's mother was only thirteen. Their father, Pastor Eric Harris of the Temple of Worship, repented publicly for his sins while their mothers bore the shame. The girls were called whores. James and Mike were labeled bastards.

James was the spitting image of Eric—tall, broad-shouldered, with rich, deep, dark skin. Mike, on the other hand, favored his mother: fair-skinned, sharp-featured, and high yellow like the women Eric preyed on.

In vague memories, James recalled how their mothers used to visit them together, whispering plans about running away, starting over. They dreamed of taking a train to New York City and never coming back. James and Mike would listen, excited and full of hope. Now, James could barely remember their faces.

They lived for Sundays. Until Sundays stopped coming.

Two hot summer nights destroyed it all.

The first night was chaos—screaming, crying. James had crept out of his bedroom and peeked downstairs. He saw his mother and Mike's mother, standing over Aunt Kim, who was on her knees beside Eric's lifeless body. Paramedics tried to revive him, but it was too late. He was pronounced dead at the scene. A heart attack at sixty-four. He lived a long life and died a natural death. More than what a man of his vile nature deserved.

Aunt Kim wailed like an infant. James had never heard that kind of sound from a grown woman's mouth. Their mothers stood there, silent. Stoic.

The second night came weeks later. A tearful goodbye.

Aunt Kim cursed their mothers, hurling insults about how they had seduced and killed a holy man. She called them demons as they fled, clutching the last shreds of their dignity.

James and Mike ran into the street after them, grabbing at their skirts, pleading. But the women pulled away, tears in their eyes. They vanished into the night air, never looking back.

James was six. Mike was nine.

After that, Aunt Kim stopped pretending to care. Some winters came without jackets. Some days came without food. She locked the fridge and counted every can of beans. If even one was found out of place, they were sent to the basement.

James was terrified of the dark. So, Mike had pried the boards off the window so light could sneak in during the day. At night, they sat close, leaned on each other, and waited for the creak of the door before bolting upstairs. That damp, moldy basement became their home more times than they could count.

The last time, James had an asthma attack. He remembered Mike hoisting him up the stairs, gasping for breath, and dialing 911 at just twelve years old. James always said Mike saved his life. Mike never acted like it was a big deal. He just nodded, like it was nothing.

But James never forgot.

Now, years later, to see the current state of their brotherhood left James stumped. He couldn't understand how they got to this point. Was it because he found love? Or was it because he simply got married? James's mind cycled through the past and present for answers as the last sip of beer consumed him, easing his mind and body into a deep slumber.

* * *

Meanwhile, Mike continued to walk as the cold winter air nipped at his hands. Shoving them deep inside his pocket, he gripped the needle tightly. His mind raced with thoughts of rage that seemed to be never-ending.

How could James look down on him after all that he'd had done for him? Mike reflected on all of the things he sacrificed so that James wouldn't have to.

Days he wouldn't eat because there wasn't enough for both of them. The times he took the brunt of the abuse because he understood that James couldn't handle it. Those early morning showers with that nasty old bitch so James could just be free and innocent. Never becoming subject to the taste of a woman at the young tender age of ten.

Mike endured the unspeakable so James wouldn't have to. He could still remember the musty taste of Aunt Kim's private parts that lingered on his breath.

That last thought made Mike stop in his tracks. His breath came in sharp gasps, and his body shook. All he had done for him, just for James to look down on him, and worse than that.

Leave.

How dare James leave him after he swore he never would?

Mike fought back tears as he punched himself repeatedly in the head.

"Don't cry like no bitch," he muttered, pacing in the snow. "Don't cry like no bitch."

He stormed back into the house.

This was the only way.

The only way to make James stay.

He moved through the kitchen and into the bathroom, gathering supplies. His hands trembled as he heated the substance in a silver spoon, the flame blackening its edges. He filtered it through the butt of a cigarette, drew it into a syringe, and capped it.

He stepped into the bedroom. For a moment, Mike's heart tried to reason with him, but his mind was already made up.

He stood over James as he lay there slumped, arms dangling, as his fingers curled around a bottle of beer that he still clung to even in his deep sleep.

Mike found a vein in James's arm and slid the needle in.

"What the fuck..." James mumbled, stirring drunkenly, attempting to shift himself awake

Mike pushed the plunger down. The warm fluid entered his bloodstream. James's eyes widened as the burn hit. He tried to sit up, but his limbs went numb. His vision blurred as he looked up at Mike, who peered down at him in anguish.

James's lips parted. His body fell limp...

"Shit, shit, shit," he whispered, yanking the bathroom drawer open and tossing everything inside. Regretting it the moment after he had done it, but it was too late.

He sprinted to the front door in a failed attempt to make a run for it, crashing straight into Marlon, who was just about to knock.

"Fuck, What the fuck are you doing here?" Mike hissed, his forehead glistening with sweat.

"I left my wallet," Marlon said, eyes narrowing. "Shit must've fell in the couch again," he explained but he couldn't help but notice how frantic Mike appeared causing him to assume the worse. He's seen Mike angry before, but this time was different; his intuition was telling him something was off.

"Man, I know y'all niggas wasn't in here fighting," he stated as he brushed past Mike and entered the house.

Mike remained silent.

Marlon reached the couch and dug between the cushions but found nothing. He knelt to check underneath the couch.

Mike slipped the wallet out of his pocket and shoved it deep into the corner.

"You sure you ain't left it somewhere else?" Mike asked as he walked around pretending to help him find it.

"I'm telling you I had it right here." Marlon insisted as he began digging deeper inside the couch, sliding his hand back and forth before he felt something familiar.

Looking up, Marlon shot Mike a smile, "I told you." He boasted as he pulled his wallet from the couch.

Mike smiled back at him for an entirely different reason.

Just then, a low groan was heard throughout the apartment. Mike's smile vanished.

Marlon froze. "What the fuck was that?"

"You got your shit. Time to go," Mike demanded, quickly ushering him toward the door.

Another groan.

Marlon pushed past Mike, heading toward the bedroom.

Mike lunged, but Marlon punched him in the face. Blood gushed from Mike's nose as he fell back.

"What the fuck you got goin' on?" Marlon barked, throwing open the door.

James lay on the floor, unconscious, barely breathing.

"What the fuck did you do!?" Marlon grilled as he looked at James, who appeared lifeless aside from his groans of pain.

Mike didn't answer; he just stood there, tugging one side of his beard, unable to provide a reason that wasn't his fault.

Marlon's eyes filled with rage and fear, not just for James but also for his sister. He darted toward the kitchen, the only place in the house that had a phone. Quickly, he dialed 911, requesting an ambulance before hanging up and rushing back to James.

When he returned to James's side, Mike was already gone.

* * *

As the ambulance arrived on the scene, Marlon tried his best to answer all of their questions. He rode with them as James was transported to the hospital.

The hospital was bright and sterile. Marlon paced the room, hands shaking, mind reeling. He didn't know what Mike did, but he felt it in his gut that he was responsible for whatever had happened to James.

As he continued to pace back and forth, two detectives lifted the curtain and entered the room.

Marlon froze instinctively.

The older one eyes went directly to James as he laid in bed rigged up to several devices. While the younger one locked eyes with Marlon.

"I'm Detective Davis. This is my partner, Anderson," the older one said, extending a hand to introduce himself. Nudging his younger companion, prompting him to follow suit.

Anderson fumbled with his badge clumsily in one hand as he extended the other, "Nice to meet you."

Unfolding his arms, he shook both of their hands. "My name's Marlon, sorry about that," he apologized wiping his sweaty palms on his jeans.

"Can you walk us through what happened?" Davis asked as he made himself comfortable in one of the hospital chairs.

"I... I don't know," Marlon answered. "I just found him like that."

Davis nodded but didn't believe him.

"Have the doctor given you any updates?" He inquired further, fishing for information that Marlon didn't have.

Again, Marlon stated that he didn't know anything, causing the detective to massage his temples.

Rising back to his feet, Davis dug in the side pocket of his suit to retrieve his business card and handed it to Marlon.

"If anything changes, call us."

Grabbing the card, he gripped it tightly.

Even as the steady rhythm of the heart monitor pulsed in the background,

Marlon couldn't hear anything but the echo of his sister's laugh, the way it had sounded earlier that day as she appeared in her wedding dress, the way she looked at James like he was her safe place in a broken world.

Now he was broken too.

Davis and Anderson exchanged a silent glance, the kind that said this wasn't over.

And Marlon, hands clenched at his side, the card becoming crushed within his palm as he also shared the same realization.

Whatever Mike had done, whatever darkness he'd let in—Marlon was going to find him, and when he did, he'd make sure Mike never hurt anyone he loved again.

* * *

Tolerance

"Omertà:
  (as practiced by the Mafia) a code of silence about criminal activity and a refusal to give evidence to authorities."

— Definition from Oxford Languages

Once a sacred oath whispered among Italian Mafiosi, *Omertà* found its way into the mouths of Black boys on street corners, reshaped into a hardened commandment: *no snitching.* A borrowed silence, now stitched into our communities like scar tissue—protecting not honor, but horror.

What was once a criminal code has become a cultural curse. Fearful of being labeled a snitch, many in our community have chosen silence, even when their loved ones bleed for justice. The killers of children, the violators of women, the destroyers of families walk among us—unbothered, untouched, and in some cases, even respected. That silence has become the soil in which our pain grows roots.

We've built a tolerance for terror. We celebrate our scars in songs, reenact our traumas in films, and dance to the rhythm of our own suffering. Crime has become fashionable. Pain has become profitable. And somewhere along the way, we began to romanticize the very things that are killing us.

What we call art is sometimes just a pretty lie—one that tells our children there is pride in the pistol, power in the silence, and justice in revenge. But there is no honor in letting monsters sleep peacefully while mothers cry themselves to sleep. There is no strength in watching from the shadows as our sisters and brothers are buried without answers.

This silence is not noble. It is a betrayal. One passed down like an heirloom.

III

NO ANGEL

"Baby, you understand me now
If sometimes you see that I'm mad
Don't you know, no one alive can always be an angel?
When everything goes wrong, you see some bad
But I'm just a soul whose intentions are good
Oh Lord, please, don't let me be misunderstood."

— Nina Simone

9

Hurricane Karina

Back to the future...

"Stop playing with me, Journee, before I come around there. Pick up your motherfuckin' phone!" Khalil spat through the speaker, his voice sharp with frustration.

That was the fourth voicemail he'd left today. I played them all back, stretched out on my bed with a smile creeping across my face. I wasn't mad at him. In fact, I was enjoying this—all of it. I'd been ignoring Khalil for two days. Not because I didn't want to talk, but because the moment things got calm between us, I got bored. Peace didn't excite me. His anger did.

There was something about knowing how to press every one of his buttons that gave me a rush. A twisted thrill I couldn't resist. I'd push just hard enough to make him sweat, and no matter how pissed he got, he always came back.

Today was no different.

Dodging his calls was my favorite game—an easy way to send his temper through the roof. But it wasn't just about him. I had someone else on the line—another man who, at the moment, seemed more worthy of my attention.

Darren.

Thirty-five. Fine as hell. Brown skin like melted chocolate, standing tall at six-two, muscles packed beneath every inch of him. His beard stayed fresh. Low cut, faded, and clean. Tattoos painted his body like art, but the bible scripture with the fallen angel down his forearm? That one did something to me.

He texted, asking what I was doing, and I wasted no time. I hit FaceTime.

"Wassup, sexy?" he answered on the first ring, smiling.

"Nothing. I'm bored," I pouted, giving the camera my best come-play-with-me look. "Entertain me."

He laughed, nervous and flustered. "What do you want me to do? Talk to me."

I licked my lips slowly. "I don't know... show me something. Impress me."

"Say less." He grinned, already moving.

"Check yo Cash App," he voiced, arrogantly.

Darren sent you $3,500 lit up across my screen.

"Awe... Daddy, thank you," I purred.

He went back to twisting up his grinder, shirtless in just his boxers, standing proudly in front of his phone. The fat blunt, already held between his lips. His vibe, unbothered. He knew I was watching, and he liked it.

Then, Khalil's name flashed across my screen—for the tenth time. I rolled my eyes and sent him to voicemail again, still smirking.

"Who's callin' you?" Darren asked, raising an eyebrow.

"My girl Karina," I lied smoothly. "She's been going through it with her dude."

"Aight… you better not be cappin', I'd hate to have to show you why niggas call me a demon," he teased, but heat was behind it.

This wasn't Darren's first money drop. Hell, it wasn't even the second. He wasn't a trick—at least not the kind that just threw money for a quick fuck. Darren wanted me badly. Wanted to claim me as his. He tried hard. Sent gifts. Played nice when I insisted I was too busy to see him. All for a taste of something he still hadn't touched.

And that's exactly how I liked it.

Serenity had taught me the game. Once I gave it up, I'd lose control. I liked keeping them just close enough to hope, far enough to chase. I played innocent, kept my legs closed, and let them think they had a chance. Took them for everything they were desperate enough to give.

It worked every time.

I already made up my mind—my virginity wasn't up for sale. Not for stacks. Not for sympathy,' I wasn't fucking for brief moments of pleasure, I had done that before. I wanted more.

"Anything for you, baby girl. When I'm gon see you?" Darren asked, his voice dripping with lust.

"Soon. I'm gonna need a ride to spend this money," I said, teasing.

"That's your way of asking me to come scoop you?" he chuckled, clearly picturing my soft tits bouncing in his passenger seat.

"Yes, Daddy," I said, sweet and spoiled, knowing he was already wrapped tight around my finger.

"Yeah, I got you, baby girl. Just hit me when you're ready for me to slide," he said before hanging up.

Keeping a roster of men had become my routine. Each one gave me something different. I didn't love them. Hell, I didn't even like them. But I enjoyed them. Enjoyed the compliments. The heart-eye emojis. The flame reacts. The money.

The attention?

That was the drug.

Every like, comment, and message hit like a rush of electricity.

Being wanted made me feel powerful, untouchable.

It was my favorite escape from the wreckage of real life.

* * *

It had been seven months since we found my father on Point Breeze, beaten and raped. It seemed as though the whole family had taken an oath of silence. No one spoke of the night my father was rushed to the hospital. Life went on very differently from before that incident. The state of Pennsylvania had funded my Dad to go to rehab and therapy, which resulted in him finally getting clean, so for the first time in years, he was home.

Most days, my dad sat in silence in a room with no television, just a radio. He listened to music, mainly jazz, and when he would tire of that, he turned the knob to listen to the news.

Today, my dad was seated in the living room. He had brought the radio downstairs and pulled a chair over to sit in front of it. He had been home for a week now, sober and sulking.

My dad never said a word about who attacked him. I don't know whether it was fear or shame. Momma would bring him a cup of coffee or tea every morning. Something about that night had given her the nudge she needed to get out of bed.

"Did you drink any of it?" my mother asked, as she picked up a cup of coffee still almost filled to the top.

"Wasn't thirsty," my father replied vaguely, as he turned down the radio.

"How are you feeling?" my mother asked, placing her hand on his shoulder. My father leaned into her, holding her fingers with his hand as he rested his head on her stomach.

"I don't know." Those were the only words he spoke.

I watched them from across the room, trying to understand. How could two people who had done nothing but argue for as long as I could remember now start being so caring toward one another?

"It's okay, James, you don't have to talk about it right now," my mother reassured my father, as a new jazz song began to play on the radio.

Still confused, I got up to walk down the stairs. It was too much, I didn't understand about my mother and father's relationship. Plopping down on the bed beside Serenity, I tugged at the charger cord.

"What percent are you on? let me use that jawn." I asked, as she sat up, annoyed by my barging into her room.

Hope had been kicked out of the house after a big argument with Momma involving allowing Daddy to live in the house again. No one knew more about how bad arguments could get between my mother and father than Hope. Because she was the oldest, Hope remained hell-bent on not being involved in what she considered a "toxic ass situation." After a huge blowout, she had given our mother an ultimatum, threatening to leave, which led to her being kicked out. She now lives with our Aunt Andrea, leaving the basement as Serenity's new room. The middle room was given to me and Faith, while the back room went to our little brothers.

"You need to learn how to knock," Serenity said, as she unplugged the charger from her phone.

"You know Momma's up there holdin' hands with Daddy," I said, stuffing my mouth with Serenity's chips she had open on her bed.

"They are doing what?" Serenity asked, baffled, as she snatched her bag of chips away from me.

"Bitch, they up there looking like they're about to kiss and shit," I pressed on, still trying to get more chips.

Faith came down the stairs, plopping next to me on Serenity's bed.

136

"What the hell is this, a fucking family reunion?" Serenity huffed, annoyed by the growing number of siblings in her private space.

"Bitch, don't start with me," Faith responded, annoyed by Serenity's attitude.

"You know they're up there dancing with Sincere?" Faith informed us, and our jaws dropped open.

"You a fucking lie?" I said, on the verge of tears from busting out in laughter.

"Nah, y'all, I'm bein' for real," Faith clarified, as she gave a straight face. "The universe's vibrations are shifting."

"Don't start that weird spiritual shit in my room." Serenity announced loudly, "What Big Mama used to say, it ain't nothing but the blood of Jesus." She imitated, making her voice low and shaky.

We all cracked up in unison.

"Shit, I don't know Hell must be freezing over," I voiced, shaking my head.

We all just couldn't believe it. How the hell was any of this happening? We all thought they hated each other.

Just then, Miracle came walking into Serenity's room, crashing onto her bean bag.

"Tell me what the fuck is going on?" he said, twisting his hair between his fingertips.

"Bro, we don't even know. We're just as lost as you," I replied, pushing decline yet again on another call from Khalil.

We all sat in the basement, conversing freely about the foolishness that took place upstairs. We couldn't wrap our minds around our mother and father loving one another, which, in hindsight, sounds sort of insane. After all, they had six children together, including our brother Sincere, whom my father treated no differently than his own flesh and blood.

"Hope, would you let it the fuck go!" We heard our mother yell, and we all sprang to our feet, running to see what was taking place upstairs in the living room.

"What's going on?" Serenity chimed in, making it up the stairs first.

"Momma doesn't want me here anymore! She's choosing yet again another nigga over me!" Hope shouted back through tears, accusing my mother of putting my father first.

My mother raised her hands, trying to explain herself. "That's not what I'm doing. Why are you so upset that I allowed your father to come back home?" My mom asked, trying to calm Hope down.

"He wasn't here all this time, and all of a sudden, he wants to come back after he was violated on them streets. What about when *you needed him*?" Hope cried, pointing her finger at Momma

"What about when *I needed him*?" Hope screamed, becoming completely hysterical as she pointed her finger toward herself.

Momma walked over to Hope and grabbed her hand, pulling her close to hold her as Hope bawled like a baby in our mother's arms.

I had never seen my sister cry like that before. It was heartbreaking to watch her sob as she clung to my mother's robe.

"I'm sorry, Hope, please forgive me," my father pleaded, dropping down on his knees. The wall my father built up came crumbling down as tears flowed freely down his face.

"I swear to you, I tried so hard to kick it. I don't blame you if you hate me. I don't blame any of you if y'all decided to never forgive me," he said shamefully, as his voice cracked.

Just then, Hope let go of my mother's robe and looked at my father as he remained remorseful on his knees. We all walked over to him, reassuring him that we did not hate him. We loved him.

The number of times I had wished my father would get clean and come home was immeasurable. Never did I ever imagine it would happen this way. So much pain and forgiveness filled our home as we all stood in it, comforting one another.

The day went by as quickly as it had started. For the first time since his arrival, I watched my father smile as he engaged in conversation. Part of me was still in disbelief about the day's events, while my inner child sat in awe. Never having experienced a family dynamic where my mother and father sat at a table together left me in a rare state of emotional satisfaction. I wasn't happy about the events that led to this unusual reunification, but I couldn't have been happier with the result. Something about it filled a void in my aching heart—a feeling that stirred a new fear inside me.

What if none of this lasts? I thought to myself.

* * *

Then I was pulled back to reality when Khalil texted my phone:

'Come outside.'

Submerged in my good mood from my newfound happiness, I walked downstairs to the door and opened it. There, Khalil stood—angry and fine as hell. I crept out of the house, shutting the door softly behind me.

"Why the fuck ain't you picking up the phone, Journee?" Khalil asked, trying to stay calm.

"My Dad just came home this week from rehab. I've been busy helping him get comfortable," I answered, while I reached for his jean jacket, yanking it softly and pulling him close to my body.

Khalil stood over me, looking into my brown eyes as I watched him dial back his anger.

"You couldn't even text me? You don't know what goes through my mind when I don't hear from you," Khalil stated, as he leaned into me.

I could feel his hard dick through his jeans, making a smile creep across my face.

"Thank you for worrying about me, babe," I replied, planting a kiss on his lips. Khalil gripped my ass hard as we fucked each other with our tongues.

This was all a part of the game for me, just a harmless tease.

"I missed you," he mumbled into my mouth, not wanting to break our kiss. I reached down and rubbed his manhood through his jeans, giving it a soft squeeze.

I loved teasing Khalil, even though I had no intention of fucking him. He was already too clingy for my liking. I couldn't imagine how he would act if

I gave him some pussy. I just enjoyed the attention, but even so, at times, it became too much for me.

"When you gonna let me taste you?" Khalil groaned, reaching down to put his hands in my pants, as I grabbed his wrist, stopping him.

"I'm not letting you play with my pussy in front of these nosy-ass neighbors," I said, pulling away.

"Damn, I can't even touch it? You got my shit bricked," Khalil complained, as he kept a firm grip on my ass.

I was enjoying him all over me, but I wasn't trying to get caught slipping by any of my other niggas that could be driving by.

"Babe, I know I'm sorry. I just wanted to show you how much I missed you," I moaned in his ear, knowing I was making it even harder to resist me.

"It's alright, you coming to see me tonight or what?" Khalil asked.

I looked him up and down for a second. Something about the way he spoke to me always kept me blushing. Maybe it was simply the chase, whatever it was, I found it exciting.

"I can't. I have to be up early, you know schools out and somebody's got to watch these kids." I lied.

I didn't want to be alone with Khalil at this point. He was always trying to have sex with me, and it occasionally killed the vibe. I was only twenty, and I remembered the way my sister went crazy after she lost her virginity to the wrong man. I couldn't afford any accidents like that, even though I knew I wouldn't, I just didn't trust how pushy Khalil was. Being the youngest girl allowed me to turn my older sister's mistakes into lessons.

I kissed Khalil goodbye. He hopped in his cousin's truck, and they sped off, the music blaring through the speakers.

Before I could open the door and walk into my house, Karina came walking down the street. She was known for popping up at my house uninvited, but I didn't mind since we treated each other like family.

"Hey, Bitch!" Karina greeted me loudly as she walked only halfway down the block.

"Hey, Hoe!" I joked back as I opened the door, waiting for her to make it the rest of the way down.

"Why were you standing out front?" Karina asked as we both walked into my house.

"Girl, Khalil's ass popped up because I wasn't answering my phone," I giggled, shutting the door.

It was still hot and humid as the sun started to set. I put my hair in a ponytail, no longer wanting it to fall on my back and shoulders. Karina was already sitting on the couch, scrolling through her phone and watching funny videos, as I sat down next to her.

"I saw what you were doing out there," she mentioned as she continued scrolling through her phone.

"And?" I replied, taking off my Gucci slides.

"You know you shouldn't be playing with niggas like that," Karina said, as she put her phone face down.

I raised an eyebrow. "Playing with niggas? Like you give a fuck about it," I laughed, ignoring her attempt to try and make me feel guilty.

"You're crazy if you think he's been waiting for me to fuck him faithfully for seven months. I guarantee he hit a few bitches. I ain't no dummy," I said, defending my actions.

Karina averted her eyes from looking at her phone to looking directly at me.

"I'm just saying, he's a good guy. I don't understand why you are playing him," she replied, rolling her eyes.

I don't know if it was her demeanor or the fact that she and Khalil barely spoke to each other, but for some reason, I found it completely odd of her to draw that conclusion. Something about the way Karina was acting toward the situation felt completely off.

"Look, I'm not doing anything to him that he wouldn't do to me. It's not like I'm trying to marry the nigga," I snapped.

Karina shook her head in disapproval, which made me roll my eyes.

"If you don't like him, maybe you should just break up with him," she said calmly.

I blinked in disbelief. Was this the same girl who played men like a deck of cards? I was just getting started, and now I was catching judgment?

Karina and I had been tight since the fourth grade, getting closer as the years passed, especially after what happened between me and Mia.

We ran the streets together, playing in niggas faces. We also were close in age, both summer babies. My birthday was in June and had just passed. Hers was coming up now that it was August—less than two weeks away—but I still hadn't gotten an invite to her infamous birthday party. When we were kids, I understood missing out because my Momma was strict. But now? I had no curfew, no restrictions. So why was I being left out?

Everything about her lately was off, and I couldn't figure out why.

"Did Ms. Semira cook anything?" Karina asked, continuing her usual routine when she came to my house.

"Yeah, girl. Go fix yourself a plate," I replied, watching her get up from the couch. She left her iPhone face down on the table as she walked into the kitchen.

Her phone started buzzing—back-to-back vibrations. I flipped it over out of curiosity. No contact name, just a plug emoji. Then it started ringing. Same number. I answered but didn't say a word.

"Wassup, ma? You free? I'm tryna' get my dick wet."

I didn't need to ask who it was. I recognized that voice.

Khalil.

I hung up and nodded to myself, lips tight.

I wasn't even mad about Khalil—he did exactly what I expected. I never cared for him like that anyway. But Karina? That betrayal cut deep. She was supposed to be my best friend. Even more than that, my sister.

Karina walked back in just as I set her phone back exactly how she left it— face down.

"Wanna watch the *Baddies* reunion? I saw some clips of it earlier I know that shit gon' go crazy." she asked, chuckling oblivious already chowing down.

"Yeah, put it on," I replied with a fake smile.

* * *

While she laughed at the TV, I was working behind the scenes. I dropped a few thirst traps into my private story, removing both Karina and Khalil from it. Then I scrolled my likes, looking for one name in particular. When I saw it, I smirked and added it to my close friends list.

Omar—Khalil's first cousin, the one he called his brother.

I had wanted Omar for a long time, but stayed away out of respect. Not anymore. Not after this.

I liked a few of his photos, then went back to the show, waiting. Just like clockwork, not even thirty minutes later, Omar viewed my story.

Got him.

I switched our DMs to vanish mode. The trap was set, and numbers were exchanged quickly. And now, I was planning to rip that bond apart—not out of spite, but out of principle.

I texted Khalil, telling him to come get me. Karina eventually left, and I walked her to the bus stop. The moment her bus pulled off, I answered Khalil's call.

"What time do you want me to slide?" he asked.

"You can come at one, park two houses down, I'll meet you," I replied before hanging up.

It was already set in stone—I was going to ruin them both.

The clock struck one a.m., and I slipped out of the house, heart pounding but face calm.

"Shit, I been waitin' for you all day." Khalil greeted me with a wide smile as I slid into the back seat of the truck.

"Oh, really," I replied, pecking his lips before leaning forward between the front seats.

"Hey, Omar," I purred, letting my stare linger as I took in just how damn good he looked behind the steering wheel.

"Wassup, Journee," he replied, glancing at me, eyes roaming from my face to my chest before looking back at the road.

I leaned back, resting my head on Khalil's shoulder.

"I'm hungry. Can we stop at a Chinese spot?"

"Yeah, what do you want?" Khalil asked, hand sliding up my thigh.

"Same thing I always get," I answered, but my attention was still locked on Omar in the rear-view mirror.

"Yo, bro, let's make a stop at Lucky Sevens first," Khalil announced, still caressing my curves.

"Bet. I'm hungry anyway." Omar replied, a loaded statement that made my mind wander.

Still, I was putting on a show, moaning over Khalil's touch like he was doing something. My eyes were fixated on Omar as he watched through the rearview mirror. Our early text messages already confirmed this was all an act.

Omar shook his head, a smirk remained on his face.

When we pulled up, Khalil got out, but I stayed put.

"I'm tired, just bring it out," I said.

Now it was just me and Omar.

"You gonna keep watching me through the mirror or you gon say something?" I teased.

Omar let out a throaty laugh, "Journee, why you playing with me?" he asked, turning to face me. "You know how bad I want you."

I leaned in, face inches from his lips.

"Remind me again," I whispered, then pulled away, eyes still locked on his.

"You staying the night?" he questioned, adjusting himself.

"Nah. You're driving me home."

"And what if I don't?" he teased, checking for Khalil.

"We both know you will."

Moments later, Khalil returned and pulled the car handle, but it didn't budge.

147

"Damn, nigga, you tryna lock me out?" He shouted, knocking on the window.

"My bad, bro," Omar snickered as he unlocked his car.

* * *

Back at Omar's house, I stepped out into the breeze. My curly hair whipped in the wind, my crop top clinging to my chest, nipples hard. My shorts were short enough to tease but not enough to give it all away. I knew they were both watching.

Inside, Omar turned on his Bluetooth speaker before he started rolling up.

"Let me pick the music." I asserted as I grabbed the phone out of Khalil's hand before he could protest.

I clicked on his Spotify app and searched for a playlist, clicking the best one I saw.

As Lil Durk's song played through the speakers, Omar handed Kahlil the blunt.

Nodding his head along to the music then he sparked it, taking a deep pull before puffing it again.

"You want parts?" Khalil questioned, attempting to pass it to me.

"No, I'm good, I got stuff to do tomorrow, and it's already two in the morning." I declined.

I wasn't trying to get too high and end up falling asleep. I never went through Khalil's phone before. The obvious reason was I never gave a fuck to check it. I did my dirt and had no interest in knowing his.

Well, that was until today. I pretended to look for the next song as I opened his text messages. Scrolling through them I saw nothing but his group chats and random friends. Then I looked in his recently deleted and there it was, 800 plus messages saved under a single letter "K".

I restored it and I scrolled through all of them, occasionally stopping to switch the song and engage in conversation casually to not raise suspicion. I got halfway through the flirting and sexting. Stopping briefly on the ones talking about me. Until I found videos and pictures confirming they had fucked.

I airdropped them all to my phone, checking to make sure I received them. I restored his apps the way he left them. Re-deleted the text messages and remained calm regardless of the disgust that teetered under the surface.

By now, I was just biding my time. Khalil tried to get me upstairs, but I shut it down with fake fatigue. At three a.m., I asked Omar to take me home.

Khalil stayed behind, frustrated, unwilling to ride with me back.

He was so predictable.

He always threw these tantrums. I was over it completely, he would soon be taught an unforgettable lesson.

* * *

As we arrived at the car, Omar opened the door for me. I loved how much of a gentleman he was. I got in slowly, letting him enjoy the view.

"Thank you."

"You don't have to thank me. It's my pleasure," he replied as he got in as well.

As we drove off, I sat there anxiously thinking of a way to break the silence.

"Honestly, how come you wanna fuck with me now?" he asked eyes locked on the road. "When I came at you before you curved me."

I paused. Time to drop the act.

"Can we go somewhere and talk?" I asked softly.

Truth be told, I developed feelings for Omar; it wasn't intentional, but I could still remember the moment it started. That was the main reason I had begun avoiding him. Whenever we were around each other, the vibe was different.

Omar was tall, with a rich, dark coffee complexion, smooth skin, handsome, and strong. His soft, kinky hair was kept short while his beard, though neatly trimmed, flourished around his full lips. He had deep brown, piercing eyes that always seemed to look straight through me, instead of at me. He didn't call me sexy like the other guys instead, he always referred to me as beautiful. And his bright smile made me melt. He was dangerously seductive, and I could barely resist.

When I first met Omar, I couldn't take my eyes off him. Kahlil had invited me and my girls out to the movie theater the week after I gave him my number. He brought his group of friends along as well, all of them loud, rowdy, as well as me.

All except Omar.

He remained laid back quietly sitting behind everyone else. While I put on my usual dramatic act to blend in with the crowd. He sat there watching me, occasionally looking at his phone like he had better places to be. I couldn't stand it. I was used to reading niggas like books. With him, I couldn't even tell if he liked me.

That was until he approached me from behind while I stood at the concession stand *alone,* in an attempt to break free from the constant performance that I called "being myself".

"Why did you come if you ain't want to be here?" I asked, not looking fully in his direction.

"I was merely transportation, why did you come if *you* ain't wanna be here?" was all he said staring directly at me before he paid for both our items and walked away.

He said so much without saying anything at all, and that's how I knew he truly saw right through my charade.

"Aight, I'll pull over."

He pulled into an empty parking lot and turned the car off. Taking the keys out of the ignition.

"I always liked you," I admitted.

"From the first day we met, before I even knew you liked me. I wanted you too."

"Then why, Khalil?"

"Because you intimidate me," I said honestly.

"Listen, I'd never hurt you—"

"That's not what I meant," I said, cutting him off.

"You make me feel open every time I get close to you. No matter how much I try to fight it, all I wanna do when I'm around you is tell you everything. I don't like it."

He reached over, grabbed my hand. The walls around me crumbled.

"Are you saying I make you feel vulnerable, Journee?" he chuckled lightly.

Staring me down, the truck felt as if it was shrinking. The space between us began to dissipate.

"Yes. It's not funny."

"I don't think it's funny, I think it's adorable."

Before I could say anything else, he kissed me, slowly, deeply. His hand cradled my cheek, then slid to my neck, choking me gently before pulling away.

"Why'd you stop?" I asked breathlessly.

"So, I don't go further than you're ready for," he said, starting the car.

"I wasn't going to stop you."

"I know," he replied, pulling off.

"When are you going to tell Khalil it's over?" he asked.

"After I expose him and Karina at her birthday party," I replied truthfully, no longer holding back.

He nodded.

"Oh, so you know about that. I told him, he might as well leave you alone if he wasn't going to treat you right after he told me about that shit."

"Why didn't you tell me?" I asked with a hint of annoyance in my tone.

"You know I'm not on that snake shit." He answered nonchalantly, not fazed by my attitude.

"So, what's this, then?" I asked, pointing between us.

Omar chuckled.

"After I told him to leave you alone if he couldn't treat you right, I told him I wanted you."

"What did he say?"

"He didn't think I could pull you. Told me to shoot my shot."

We both laughed. Khalil's arrogance was blinding. I never understood why he thought being light-skinned made him irresistible.

"We honestly have better chemistry. I don't know why he thought you couldn't pull me."

"Then why give him a chance?" Omar asked as we pulled up to my street.

"He felt like the safer option. I couldn't see myself taking him seriously."

Omar cut the engine, stepped out, and opened my door. I slid out, cheeks flushed.

He walked me to my door, kissed me on the forehead, and whispered:

"Goodnight, beautiful."

* * *

Two weeks had passed, and the night I rode with Omar in the car replayed in my mind like a movie I couldn't pause. His lips on mine, hands exploring my body, the way he choked me just enough to send my senses spiraling—I was high off the memory.

While Khalil kept calling like clockwork, I answered only to keep up appearances.

Karina's party was tonight. Because she wanted Khalil there, she made it a point to invite me. I knew I was only invited to ensure he and his boys showed up. She played it off like she was excited to see me, but I knew better.

I smiled and lied right back.

"You sure you coming, bitch? I know if you don't come, Khalil and his friends won't come. I want this party to be lit," Karina said, her eyes glued to her phone.

"Bitch, I told you I got you," I replied, giggling to mask my disgust. "Besides that, which one of them niggas got you so jumpy?"

"Girl, ain't nobody," she said, brushing me off. "I'm just excited. My best bitch gon' be there, and we gonna look good as fuck." She leaned in to hug me.

"Right. I can't wait either, bitch. I got you the best gift ever," I said, faking a hug and smile.

But truthfully, I didn't even want her to touch me. I wanted to beat her ass up and down the street. It wasn't because I loved Khalil—I barely even liked the nigga. He was a distraction, something to pass the time.

Karina was my best friend. If she wanted him, all she had to do was say that. But no—she crept behind my back, aired out my business, and talked about me like a dog. I loved her. That love turned to hatred the moment I saw who she truly was.

"Girl, what are you wearing to my party?" Karina asked while I laid out a few dresses.

"I was thinking this one," I said, holding up my least favorite, something I knew she wouldn't even wear to a party. I paused, waiting for her reaction.

"Yeah, that's cute. I've been thinking of wearing something like that too," she lied.

That's when it hit me—love isn't just blind in relationships. It's blind in friendships, too. I ignored every sign. The jealousy in her tone. The shade in her compliments. I was so wrapped up in the idea of who she pretended to be that I refused to see the snake right in front of me.

She left my house a few hours early to finish party prep.

Darren wouldn't stop blowing me up on FaceTime—call after call, all rejected. I had no reason to entertain him anymore. I got what I needed, and he had served his purpose. It was pathetic, really—how a grown-ass man could be so weak over someone he barely knew.

"You want me to come with you?" Faith asked, walking into our room with a bowl of ramen.

"Nah, I got it," I said, pressing mousse into my fingers to slick down my edges.

"You sure you wanna do it like this?" she asked mid-slurp.

"Absolutely."

Only Faith and Omar knew I was planning something. They didn't know the details—just that I was going to expose Karina.

Faith looked worried.

"Journee, I know she did you dirty, but do you really want to put her on blast like this? Her family gon' be there."

"I thought I *was* her family," I said, barely looking up.

"You know what I mean. Ain't no coming back from this," Faith warned.

"I know. That's why it has to be this way."

I made sure my new iPad—paid for with Darren's money—was fully charged. I had already edited the footage into one smooth video using iMovie. I looked stunning in my black mini dress, clear platform heels, and matching Telfar bag. I wasn't just dressed to kill. Tonight was Karina's funeral.

Khalil had asked Omar to drive us, and Omar had already agreed. As I stepped outside, my thirty-inch bundles swayed in the breeze. Omar bit his lip when he saw me. Khalil hopped out of the passenger seat and climbed into the back, leaving the door open. No chivalry. No surprise.

"You look good as shit. You wore that for me?" Khalil asked, grinning.

Smiling back, I said, "You know I do this for me."

I leaned between the front seats. "Hey, Omar," I said, locking eyes with him.

"Wassup, Journee?" he replied, not breaking the gaze.

I wanted to stay there, but I leaned back, keeping my plan intact.

When we pulled up, the venue was packed. Karina's mom had booked it months in advance. It was beautiful.

Before I could open my door, Omar was already there, helping me out.

"Damn, I see that dress got all the niggas simpin' already'," Khalil joked.

I rolled my eyes. I wouldn't be dealing with him much longer.

Inside, I took my seat at Karina's table, catching glares from her other friends. Their stares screamed envy. Karina approached, clearly surprised I wasn't wearing the dress we agreed on.

"You look really good, sis," I said with a forced hug.

"You too," she said, smiling through her disdain.

Khalil walked up and hugged me from behind. Karina turned away quickly.

The nerve of her. Acting betrayed when she was the one who crossed *me*.

As the night dragged on, I mingled just enough to play my part. Finally, the DJ paused the music. It was time to sing Happy Birthday.

"Everybody! We got a special montage for Karina. Turn your Airdrop on!" her mom announced.

I tapped Omar and told him to get the car ready.

I slipped my iPad out of my Telfar bag, hiding it carefully. Everyone was ready—phones out, waiting.

Perfect.

I hit "Share" and airdropped the video to every available device.

Gasps. Whispers.

"Yo, what the fuck..."

"Damn, that's crazy."

"Send me that jawn."

On every other screen, Karina was getting exposed—fucking Khalil, sucking his dick as he busted a nut directly on her face. Her betrayal was now public knowledge.

Her mother screamed. "Please, delete that! Delete it!"

Karina ran to Khalil in tears. "Why would you do this to me?!"

"I ain't do shit!" he shouted, backing away.

I packed up my iPad and walked toward the exit.

"Journee, wait! Let me talk to you!" Karina chased after me.

I didn't look back.

I got in the car, and Omar drove off.

* * *

"Tell me where you wanna go," he said calmly.

"The lakes," I answered.

We rode in silence. He reached over and rubbed my thigh.

"I know, baby," he said as my tears fell.

"This is why I don't let people in. I never thought Karina would do me like that."

"There's nothing wrong with letting people in—you just have to choose the right ones," Omar replied.

At the lake, he opened my door. I took off my heels and walked toward the water.

"Wait for me," he called, laughing.

I stopped at the edge. "You never asked me what I did," I said.

"Did you want me to?"

"No. I don't think you'd look at me the same."

"I'm not an angel, Journee. I've done shit too," he said, pulling me close.

"I airdropped her nudes," I whispered.

"I know. I was by the door watching," he admitted.

I looked up. "Why?"

"To make sure you got out safely. I don't care what you did," he said, kissing my cheek.

"I have one last thing to do," I said, pulling out the iPad. "Can you break this and throw it in the lake?"

He smashed it and tossed it into the water without hesitation.

"Done," he said.

I kissed him.

He wrapped his arms around me, his hands tracing down my spine stopping right above my ass before pulling back to look me in the eyes.

"Don't stop," I whispered.

He nibbled my ear, trailing his tongue lower before planting a kiss on my neck.

"Please." I whimpered

He continued licking his way down to my breast, biting one gently, yet hard enough to make me shudder.

He stopped again to look at me as I whined from frustration.

"Why do you keep doing that?" I huffed, playfully hitting his chest.

"Doing what?" he chuckled. "I'm just controlling myself. We've got time. We can take it slow."

I kissed him again, then rested my head against his solid frame, and both of us stood there gazing at the lake.

For the first time in a long time, I felt like I belonged.

10

After The Hurricane

Karina

"Fuck! Fuck! Fuck!"

That was all I could manage to say as I tried to wrap my mind around what the hell had just happened. I picked up my phone and dialed Journee again. Straight to voicemail.

"Damn, did she fucking block me?" I muttered under my breath, pacing inside the bathroom, hiding while my mom cleared the guests out.

No way I was going back out there, pretending everything was fine. My birthday was ruined, and I had no idea how I'd explain it to my mother, let alone my entire family.

I locked myself in a stall, and I sat on the toilet feeling the room spin as I replayed everything in my head. How did it get to this point? I didn't deserve this. I'm not a bad person. I just got tired of always being overlooked.

Didn't I deserve to be happy, too?

Why is it always about Journee?

Even on my goddamn birthday, it's still all about *fucking* Journee.

I was the best friend she ever had. Always there, no matter what. Now, look at how she did me—won't even answer the phone after I got exposed in front of everyone.

This bitch didn't even want Khalil. She never gave a fuck about him. I did. And now, everyone's going to judge me anyway, so why should I care? I don't feel like I was wrong. Okay—*maybe* how I went about it was messy, but I wasn't wrong.

Khalil and I had been messing around on the low for a minute now. It all started when he messaged me on Instagram, asking about Journee. She was pulling one of her disappearing acts again—ignoring him for days, only texting back when she felt like it.

He asked me, *"You heard from her?"* And for once, I didn't lie for her.

"Yeah," I replied. *"She's just ignoring you."*

I didn't care how it would affect anything. I was over it—over her, over how she always had everyone wrapped around her finger, that ungrateful bitch.

She didn't even *fuck* him, and yet he stayed chasing her. I hated that. How the fuck did she always manage to get the guy I wanted?

Whenever she curved them, they'd try their luck with me. And Journee would laugh it off, telling me she "didn't want them anyway."

Like that was supposed to make me feel better.

Like, I should be grateful for her leftovers.

Was I not worth being chased? I would've done anything to keep a man—or secure the bag. I'm beautiful. I've got a body. I know how to please a man. And still, I was always second best.

I didn't always feel that way. I used to *love* being her friend. Me and her were like sisters but over time, I realized Journee only cared about herself.

She couldn't even follow through on hooking me up with Khalil's homeboy, Omar. Left me out here dating these broke-ass niggas while she shopped like she had a sponsor—which she did. Khalil stayed putting money in her pocket, and I acted like I didn't notice. I did.

Shit, me and this bitch used to run the same game, I always included her on double dates with niggas. We'd get a free meal, some gas, and a bottle every time, then she became boujee overnight. Looking down on the way that I did things. Fucking with niggas with real motion.
Yeah, she'd buy me little things here and there, like I should be thankful for the crumbs. But I could've been doing the same exact shit if she just would've put me on. That's how I new she was a hating ass bitch. Journee didn't want us to be equals. She liked having the upper hand. She always looked down on me, like I wasn't good enough to do what she did.

If she had been more solid, I wouldn't have done what I did.

I've never had a problem sharing a man—I don't owe no bitch any loyalty. If your nigga cheats, take that up with him. As long as I'm getting everything you get, I don't care.

So, that day, I took an Uber to Khalil's spot. I smiled when he told me how fucking sexy I was. We spent the afternoon fucking. I gagged on his dick to make him feel good, slurped loud enough for him to *hear* I wanted him.

I moaned with intention when he fucked me—because I know what niggas like.

I had him nuttin' back to back. He loved every second. And afterward, he broke me off a few hundred like it was nothing.

Felt like Christmas.

From that day on, every time he hit me up, I came through. I sucked him off, let him take me however he wanted. And he kept the money flowing.

Enough to keep my hair slayed, my nails done, and some cash in my pocket.

I loved the arrangement.

But I couldn't tell Journee. And if I'm being honest, I didn't want to.
  I loved that shit.

Knowing I could fuck her man whenever I felt like it turned me on.
  He didn't deserve how she treated him anyway.

I should've known better than to let him record anything, though.

That part? That's on me.

I kicked off my heels and yanked out my earrings, heart pounding, tears stinging my eyes. I still couldn't believe it all came out like this.

I called Journee again. Still no answer.

This bitch really didn't give a fuck about me.

I felt humiliated—sick, even. My image was done.

Everyone knew Journee was my best friend.
Now I'll forever be the girl who fucked her best friend's man.

I sobbed harder, chest heaving, snot mixing with tears as I hunched over the toilet.

Then I heard the door creak open.

I looked up.

And there he was.

Khalil.

Standing in the doorway, quiet for a second before he finally said:
  "Can you let me explain?"

* * *

Khalil

The whole party was on some nut shit—I didn't even wanna come.

Being in the same room with *two bitches* I was involved with felt like a setup. But Journee insisted Karina wanted us to come. I should've known better.

After somebody leaked the video, the party was over. Karina stormed off, and I searched everywhere trying to find Journee, holding my phone to my ear while rapping with my mans.

"Yo bro, you outta pocket for doing that shit at Karina's birthday party," Tyree said, putting me on speaker so the rest of the crew could hear.

"If I wanted to leak her shit, I would've been done that shit bro, I keep tellin' y'all niggas that!" I barked back, frustrated.

Laughter exploded on the other end of the line. Niggas dying laughing like it was funny.

That shit pissed me off.

I hung up without another word—no longer in the mood to defend myself. No matter how many times I denied it, everybody assumed I did it. A nigga couldn't win.

My phone kept buzzing back-to-back. Calls. DMs. Texts. I finally put it on *Do Not Disturb*. I didn't have time for none of that shit right now.

The only person I owed an explanation to was Journee.

I made my way through the crowd, ducking Karina's mom, who was yelling for everybody to leave. Slipping past the buffet table, through the side hallway, I headed toward the back of the dining hall, assuming Journee ran off crying, probably hiding in the bathroom. She had to be too embarrassed to face anybody after all that happened.

I pulled out my phone and called her again as I walked. Still no answer. Straight to voicemail.

Despite what it looked like—I fucked with Journee.

She was top-tier.

She was everything I wanted: a thick brown-skin jawn with a pretty face, good energy, and real ambition. She carried herself different—wasn't like the rest of these bitches.

Even when she avoided me, I knew she was just scared to open up.

My only issue was that she wanted to wait. She wanted to give her virginity to me at the "right time." And don't get me wrong—I respected it.

But I wasn't about to sit around celibate either. Sex wasn't something I just wanted—it was something I needed.

I don't even remember how life felt before I started fucking.

I had sex for the first time when I was eight. It was with my mom's girlfriend, the one who used to babysit us after school.

At first, it was weird. I didn't like it.

It didn't feel like how my older cousins said it should feel. I ain't even know what I was doing—she taught me everything.

When I told my uncle, he just dapped me up and said, "You a man now." And let me smoke my first blunt.

From then on, I stayed chasing that feeling.

Whenever I felt lonely—I wanted to fuck. Sad? Same shit.

Sex became the only way I knew how to feel close to somebody.

Except with Journee.

Something about the way she treated me... it made me want to be better.

She didn't gas me for clout. She wasn't a dick-eater. Journee kept it real. She called me out on my bullshit. She never let me get away with shit.

So yeah—I know I fucked up when I fucked her best friend.

The truth is, I didn't even plan to smash Karina. She just made it too easy.

Karina was just as bad as Journee—light-skin, thick, and freaky as hell. Only difference? She was a known whore.

I could never take a bitch seriously who fucked for a fee. Karina had a rep all through the P—she'd already messed with a few of my niggas before I ever touched her.

Journee believed in all that spiritual sex, soul-tie shit. Me? I didn't buy into all that.

To me, sex was just fucking. If we both got off, no harm done.

So, the situation seemed perfect: Journee for the image, Karina for the release. No strings.

We both agreed Journee could never find out. Karina was paranoid as hell about it, and so was I.

I made my way to the bathroom, my stomach twisting with guilt.

All I could hear inside was somebody crying. Heavy sobs echoed off the tile.

"Damn," I muttered to myself, shaking my head. I felt like a whole dickhead walking into that moment.

I took a breath, stepped up to the stall door, and opened it slowly.

"Can you let me explain?" I said, voice low and remorseful.

But to my surprise...

It wasn't Journee.

It was Karina.

* * *

The Aftermath

"Can you let me explain?"

"What the hell is left to explain, Khalil? You played me," Karina cried, her voice shaky as tears streamed down her face.

"Look, I keep tellin' you—I didn't do shit. I ain't want that video to get out. What the fuck do I gain from exposin' you?" He shot back, his voice rising with each word.

Karina reached for the stall door to shut it in his face, but he gripped it firmly, refusing to let it close.

"Where's Journee?" he asked, the frustration now overriding his patience.

"That's all you give a fuck about, huh?" Karina said, swiping at her smeared makeup with the back of her hand.

"Karina, I don't have time for this shit. Where the fuck is Journee?" he demanded, still holding the door open.

"She left in the car with Omar," she finally answered, her voice low but bitter. "I told you that bitch doesn't give a fuck about you. Why can't you see that? Journee only cares about herself."

She stood up from the toilet, shoved past him, and headed toward the mirror. Yanking a few paper towels from the dispenser, she tried to clean the mess off her face.

Khalil stood there, stunned. "Journee left with Omar?" he repeated, trying to connect the dots.

"Yeah, what?" Karina snapped, still unable to see what he was putting together.

"Nothing," he muttered, shaking his head and letting out a humorless laugh. He pulled out his phone.

"What the fuck is so funny?" Karina asked, her patience gone.

"Nothing... Omar was my ride home," he said flatly.

That was far from the truth.

Khalil had a sinking feeling that Omar told Journee everything—that he was the one who exposed him for fucking Karina. Why else would she leave with him?

He thought back. The way Journee acted last time they saw each other... how she barely wanted to kiss him. She stayed on his phone longer than usual, too. At the time, he thought she was just putting on music—but maybe she saw something.

The only part that didn't make sense was why she hadn't confronted Karina. That's the piece that didn't fit.

Did she plan all of this from the beginning? Khalil thought, staring down at his phone, waiting for Omar to pick up.

"Yo, Wassup?" Omar answered.

"Where you at, bro?" Khalil asked, trying to keep his voice level.

"I'm not far."

"Journee with you?"

"Yeah, she's right here. Wassup?"

"Can you hand her the phone?"

Khalil waited as Omar looked over. Journee must've nodded, because a second later, her voice came through the speaker.

"What, Khalil?" she asked, already annoyed.

"Where you at?" he asked, jaw tightening.

"Didn't Omar just tell you we ain't far?" she replied, sucking her teeth.

Before Khalil could respond, Journee cut him off. "Look—it's over. You and that bitch can have each other." Then she hung up.

Khalil stared at the phone in disbelief. Karina watched him, trying to read his face.

"What did she say?"

"She said it was over," Khalil replied quietly, stepping back and leaning against the wall.

His thoughts spun, heart thudding in his chest as a slow-burning anger built inside him. Karina stepped toward him and reached out to touch his face.

Khalil caught her wrist.

Then he started pulling up her dress.

Karina bent over the sink without hesitation, but her eyes darted toward the door.

"What if there are cameras in here?" she asked nervously.

Khalil didn't answer. He pulled her panties to the side and shoved himself inside her.

Karina moaned softly, pushing back into him as he gripped her hair roughly. Somewhere in the back of her mind, she was glad—it was over between him and Journee. Maybe now she could finally have him to herself.

Kahlil pumped faster, fucking her with a mix of rage and heartbreak. He wasn't making love. He was trying to escape.

Karina begged him to go deeper, and he did. Her eyes rolled back as her body gave in, her walls gripped his dick as she reached her climax. He kept going until his own release approached, pulling out and letting his cum hit splat right on the bathroom floor.

"You think I'm gonna keep letting you just fuck me on the low?" Karina asked breathlessly.

"I don't plan on it," Khalil replied coldly as he turned to the sink and washed himself off.

"What do you mean?" she asked, voice softer now, concern creeping in. She didn't want to lose him—not like this.

"I'm single now," he said, staring into the mirror while pumping soap into his hands. "So what's stoppin' us?"

"You saying you want me to be your girl?" Karina asked, trying to contain the smile tugging at her lips.

"Yeah. Why not?" Khalil replied with a half-hearted smile.

But the truth was—he didn't give a fuck about cuffing Karina. He just wasn't trying to walk away empty-handed.

Karina leaned in, drying his hands with paper towels, then kissed him softly on the lips—While he was already planning his next move.

* * *

His Fool, Forever

(A Confession)

There was a moment I realized you were using me—
   The second, I identified as your fool.
   Etched into my mind:
   "To be his tool...
   until he has nothing to do with you."

That moment nearly drowned me in spit.
   My heart—heaviest it had ever been.
   I was willing to live like swine
   If it meant a chance
   to make him mine.

Live on all fours.
   Neglect my feet.
   Eat sloppy scum—
   wholeheartedly.
   Be his sideshow freak.

Yes...
   And I'd probably do it all again.
   Can't pretend—
   his love,
   I still desire to win.

11

What's Yours Is Mine

I hung up the phone on Khalil, not the least bit upset. I was ready to let go of the headache that came with being his girlfriend.

For seven long months, I dealt with his bullshit—random girls having beef with me that I never even met, the lies, the pressure. It was time to let it all go. I didn't care about his status the way everyone else seemed to. The fact that he was still living off the clout from high school was corny to me. Life moves forward, but he acted like his best days were already behind him.

No, I wasn't in love with him, but I did care for him, as a person. He had the potential to be a great man if he ever stopped lying to himself. There was so much pain hidden behind his image. And even though we both did our dirt, I never intended to let him face his demons alone. But once you betray me, there's no coming back from that.

Omar was still holding me as he stared out at the lake.

"Are you gon' to talk to yourself all night, or are you gonna talk to me?" he asked, tightening his arms around me.

It was as if he always knew what was going on inside my head. I didn't know how he did it, but no matter how much I tried to suppress my feelings, he always pulled them back up to the surface.

"I'm thinkin' about karma," I said softly, nuzzling my face into his chest.

"Karma?" he repeated, chuckling, and I cracked a small smile.

"Yes, karma. You don't believe that whatever you put out into the universe comes back to you?" I asked, inhaling the scent of his Dior cologne.

Everything about Omar put my soul at ease—even the smell of him was calming.

"I believe in playing it even," he said, resting his chin on top of my head. "We are the universe, Journee. We create the balance."

I tilted my head and looked up at him, admiring the glow of his skin under the moonlight. When our eyes locked, I looked away shyly.

"Do you know you're beautiful?" Omar asked, still gazing at me.

"I'm beautiful?" I echoed, unsure.

I'd been called sexy, bad, thick, and pretty—but none of that compared to hearing Omar call me beautiful. When he said it, it was like he was looking through me, into me—searching for something sacred.

"You are beautiful in every way... beyond your eyes," he whispered, softly kissing my eyelids.
"Beyond your smile." He kissed my lips gently.
"Your mind and soul are beautiful," he said as he pressed a kiss to my forehead.

Tears began to fill my eyes, and I didn't understand why. Before I could wipe them, he reached up and swiped them away with his thumb. I turned from him quickly, trying to collect myself.

"Journee," he said from behind me, pulling me into his embrace. "I promise."

That was all he said—but it was everything.

How could he think someone like me was beautiful? I thought about all the wrong I'd done, the things I continued to do. I didn't deserve this softness. I wasn't the woman he thought I was.

"Omar," I said, my voice trembling, "I don't think we should do this. I'm not the kind of woman you think I am. Tonight doesn't compare to the things I've done."

He stayed quiet for a moment, then spoke with a calm certainty. "No matter what you've done, I've most likely done worse."

Still holding me, he continued. "I don't define myself by what I've done, but by what I will do now that I've learned. It's never too late to do better."

His hands moved gently along my arms. I turned to face him, needing to see his eyes for my next question.

"And are you doing better?" I asked, genuinely curious.

"I've been trying to," he admitted. His smile faded slightly, and a distant look crept into his eyes.

"Now who's talking to themselves?" I teased, touching his cheek softly.

"I don't want you to think any less of me either," he confessed.

We stood there, wordless. I felt emotionally exposed, like he could see all of me and still didn't turn away.

"I have an idea," Omar said suddenly, taking my hand. "Come with me."

He led me back to his truck, lowered the back seats, and opened the trunk. "What are you doin'?" I asked, my heart fluttering as he helped me climb in.

"I'm helping us see each other," he replied, climbing in after me.

It was dark in the back of his car, lit only by moonlight. He lay on his back and beckoned me closer.

"It's just you and me. No one else. No judgment," Omar said, pointing from his chest to mine. "I want to tell you everything. Ask me anything—I'm yours."

He helped me straddle him, and I sat atop him, feeling his warmth beneath me.

"Why do you want me?" I asked, fingers interlacing with his.

"Because I can't help it," he said with conviction. "I feel drawn to you, like I've known you before this life. From the moment I saw you, I knew I needed you."

"My turn," I whispered, trying to look away.

He held my chin gently. "Look at me. Don't run," he said softly.

"What are you really afraid of?"

"Every time I let someone in... I hurt them," I admitted, my voice cracking under the weight of my truth.

My heart pounded. My body trembled under his touch. This wasn't just lust. I had felt that before. I couldn't explain it, but it was something deeper—something spiritual.

"Do you plan on hurting me?" he asked.

"Never," I said, barely audible.

I could feel him growing hard beneath me, but he remained composed, focused on me. The intensity was unbearable. I leaned in and kissed him, reaching to undo his pants.

"Journee, don't," he whispered.

I ignored him. We kissed passionately, his hands roaming my body as I melted into him.

But once again, he broke our kiss.

"You're gonna make it hard for me to say no," he said, sitting up.

"Me?" I laughed, still breathless, still wanting him.

"It's too soon. We have forever," he said with a smile. "I promise we won't wait long."

"Don't act like I'm trying to take it from you," I teased, giggling as I rolled off him.

"I don't know... I keep havin' to stop, and you keep trying to convince me not to," he joked, checking the time on his phone.

"What time do you have to be home?" he asked, a hint of sadness in his voice.

"I told my family I'm staying at Tameka's house for a few days," I answered, grinning.

Omar laughed and shook his head. "You skippin' steps. I'm supposed to take you out, ask you to be my girlfriend, and then you spend the night."

"You can still do all that," I said, playfully. "But first, we gotta get my overnight bag."

I climbed into the front seat. "Come on, let's go."

Omar climbed in after me. We exchanged a look—one of those rare, glowing smiles you only share when something real is beginning.

And just like that, he started the car and we drove off.

* * *

That morning, I woke up in Omar's bed. My head rested on his chest as I listened to the steady rhythm of his heartbeat while he slept, his arm loosely wrapped around me. Even in slumber, he looked devastatingly handsome. I watched the slow rise and fall of his chest, wondering what he might be dreaming about—wondering if I was in that dream.

His phone buzzed on the nightstand, breaking the silence and stirring him from sleep. He blinked slowly, then looked at me with a sleepy gaze that made my stomach flutter.

"What time is it?" he asked in a raspy voice, his arms tightening around me.

"I don't know... but it's morning," I replied, drawing slow circles with my fingertip across his bare chest.

A drowsy smile crept across his face as he kissed my cheek.

"Then good morning, beautiful."

I blushed, returning his smile.

"Good morning."

I sat up to stretch, arching my back as I slid toward the edge of the bed.

"How'd you sleep?" Omar asked, shifting closer, his voice softer now.

"Peacefully," I said, reflecting on how safe and held I'd felt wrapped in his arms all night.

"Good," he said, sitting up. "I made plans for us today."

I turned slightly to look at him over my shoulder. Everything about him was magnetic—his posture, his voice, even his sleepy smirk. He caught me staring, and I quickly looked away, feeling heat rush to my cheeks.

"What kind of plans?" I asked, rising and reaching for my overnight bag.

"You'll see," he teased, as I made my way into the bathroom.

I was grateful Omar lived alone. It meant I could move freely in his space, and that kind of freedom—of—safety was rare for me. It made this intimacy even more special. I undressed, peeling off the dress from the night before, standing in just my lace bra and panties. I paused in front of the mirror, taking in my reflection—puffy eyes from yesterday's tears, lips still warm from Omar's kisses, and curves I was still learning to love.

I heard the door open, and it startled me, quickly tried to cover myself.

Omar stood there, taking me in. "Wow…" was all he said as he stepped closer.

There was a shift in the air, a silent gravity pulling us together.

"Why are you hiding?" he asked, gently moving my hands from my body.

"Let me see you."

My heart pounded. I hadn't expected him to come in. My mind raced, but I didn't stop him. I let my hands fall away.

"You want to shower first?" I asked breathlessly, feeling his hard dick press against me.

"No," he murmured, his voice thick with desire.

"Then… what are you doing?" I asked, already knowing.

"You make me want to risk it all," he whispered, his lips brushing the back of my neck. Goosebumps erupted across my skin.

"Are you mine?" he asked, holding me against him.

"Yes," I breathed, trembling.

"Then can I have what's mine?" he whispered, licking from my earlobe down to my collarbone.

I bit my lip, my eyes falling to the floor.

"I thought you said we had forever," I teased, my voice cracking under the weight of wanting.

"We do," he replied, his kisses igniting a fire that spread through me.

"What are you doing?" I asked again, barely able to think.

"Do you trust me?" Omar asked, releasing my hands and placing his on my breasts.

I nodded, breathless.

"Say it," he whispered, unclasping my bra.

"I trust you."

He spun me around, his mouth capturing my neck, trailing kisses to my breasts. He cupped them gently, then took one nipple into his mouth, swirling and lightly biting until I moaned, melting into his hands.

He knelt, pulling down my panties. I stepped out of them, my thighs already slick with arousal. Omar kissed down my body, pausing at my navel, then lower.

"So pretty," he murmured, placing soft kisses on my inner thighs before finally tasting me.

My body buckled as his tongue swirled around my clit, and a soft cry escaped my lips. A finger slid inside me, and the pressure was perfect—his rhythm deliberate.

"That's it, baby," he hummed, his breath vibrating through me. My climax hit like a wave crashing over a dam, and I gasped as pleasure consumed me.

He caught me as my knees gave out, lifting me in his arms and carrying me back to the bed like I was the most precious thing in the world.

Lying me gently down, he undressed, his thick length standing proud. I swallowed hard, nervous but burning for him. He smirked, as if reading my thoughts, then went back to pleasuring me with his fingers and tongue until my second orgasm pulsed through me with intensity.

I cried out, tears streaming down my face from the overwhelming sensation. He paused, wiping my cheeks and kissing me gently.

"You taste so damn good," he said with a grin.

"You're amazing," I whispered back, breathless.

Then he was above me, gazing into my eyes.

"I love you," he said. "I know this feels fast... I've tried to slow it down, but I can't. I ain't never felt this way."

His words disarmed me. My heart cracked open in the best way.

We kissed, slow and deep. I could taste myself on his lips. I moved against him, my body aching with need. Reaching between us, I stroked him, thick and hard in my hand.

"Can we?" I asked, pleading with my eyes.

"I need you inside me," I whispered.

"You sure?" he asked softly.

"Yes. I love you, too," I said, meaning every word.

He slid the tip of his length into me, and I inhaled sharply. The stretch was intense. My body tensed, adjusting to him.

"You okay?" he asked, pausing.

"Yes," I whimpered, biting my lip.

He moved slowly, giving me time to adjust, his thrusts deep and gentle. I rocked with him, meeting each stroke as heat pooled in my belly.

"Let it out for me, baby," he said, rubbing my clit as my walls clenched around him.

"You can do it."

Another orgasm tore through me, and I cried out, body throbbing. Omar kept going, his pace patient and steady, coaxing me into release after release.

"That's it, baby."

I bit down on his shoulder, and he groaned.

"I'm so proud of you."

My body shook involuntarily.

"Cum again for me beautiful."

I wrapped my legs around his waist, clinging to him as he rubbed my clit again. My body tensed, and I squirted, gasping at the unfamiliar yet incredible sensation.

"Please... I can't," I whimpered, overwhelmed.

"Yes, you can," he murmured, thrusting deep and slow, until my body gave in again and again.

With a final groan, he sank fully into me, and I felt his warmth flood inside me.

He kissed me as he pulled out gently, then cradled me in his arms. I lay there dazed, my body humming, feeling high.

Nudging him with my elbow, I pouted, "You came inside me."

He chuckled, unfazed. "So?"

"What do you mean by 'so'? You lucky I'm on birth control," I giggled.

"Wouldn't matter. I'm going to marry you one day, Journee," he said with calm certainty.

Marry me?

The thought lingered in my mind as I melted into his arms and drifted into sleep, still floating from the way he made me feel—seen, loved, and completely his.

* * *

Her Mind

(A Reflection)

Inside her beautiful mind
    Was a puzzle I longed to complete—
    a jigsaw of imperfections,
    All so perfect for me.

I'll piece her together,
    no matter how hard the task.
    Time could slip away,
    and I'd savor each moment as it passed.

Her mind is just *that* beautiful—
    An art show I'd be a fool to miss.
    Each splatter of passion,
    Every stroke of risk,
    paints a world where thoughts of me exist.

Within that elegant brain
    lives an extraordinary gift:
    understanding and reason,
    enlightenment she emits.

She is bliss—
    free from ignorance, untouched by lies.
    An endless pattern of dyes
    shifting before my eyes.

And I find myself falling deeply
    for her...
    Inside her beautiful mind.

12

Transgressions

Khalil

I waited for my Uber, jaw tight, heart thudding in my chest. I dialed Omar for the seventh damn time that day. Straight to voicemail. Again.

"This nigga keep duckin' me," I muttered under my breath, standing up from the edge of the sidewalk.

The night at the hotel with Karina had been cool, just us getting lost in fucking and drinking, but none of that shit dulled the ache burning in my chest. I couldn't stop thinking about Journee. About how I lost her. And worse, who I lost her to.

Omar.

Of all people.

That shit stung more than I wanted to admit.
I never thought he'd snake me. Omar was my brother. Not by blood, but by

everything else. We've bled together, fought side by side. That nigga used to swing before I did, just to protect me. He was loyal—at least I thought so. Now, all I could see was betrayal.

My Uber pulled up with a soft double honk. I climbed in, slamming the door harder than necessary. The ride felt like it took forever. I sat in silence, staring out the window, fists clenched in my lap.

My thoughts were loud. I kept telling myself to chill. Don't go over there on no hype shit. Don't assume the worst until I hear it from him. But the image of Journee in his bed wouldn't leave me.

That shit boiled in my chest.

The car finally pulled up in front of Omar's place. I stepped out before the driver could even fully stop, slamming the door behind me. I walked up to his front door, jaw tight, breath shallow. My hand trembled as I pulled out my phone and called him again.

To my surprise, this time, he answered.

* * *

Omar

My phone rang again, the vibration pulling me out of a dream I didn't want to leave. I sat up, groggy, reaching for it on the nightstand.

Khalil.
The name flashed across the screen, bold and insistent. Seven missed calls.

"This nigga drawlin'," I muttered under my breath, rolling my neck to release the tension before stretching my arms overhead.

I turned to look at Journee—still wrapped in the sheets, her bare back peeking from beneath the blanket like some kind of masterpiece. She looked peaceful, untouched by the chaos waiting outside this room. Mine. Finally.

I pulled the blanket down just a bit, my fingers tracing the curve of her hip. Her skin was still warm from what we'd just done, and soft like velvet. Every inch of her called to me. The memory of being inside her—her moans, the way she gripped me like she never wanted to let go—played in my head like a loop I never wanted to end.

My dick stirred again at the thought.

Damn, I never expected to feel like this. Not about anybody. But Journee? She was everything I never knew I needed—beautiful, broken in all the right places, and brave enough to love through the pain.

My phone vibrated again—this time, a text.

'We need to talk. Now.' – **Khalil.**

I ran a hand down my face, the weight of it all creeping in. I knew Khalil was heated, and maybe he had every right to be. But I didn't cross him—not really. We both knew what it was. He told me himself how he wasn't really feeling her like that, just wanted to hit and move on. Like she was some easy conquest.

That shit never sat right with me.

Because Journee wasn't just some girl. She was layered, guarded, and stronger than she let on—but I saw through it. I saw the softness beneath the steel. The way she laughed when no one was watching. The quiet in her eyes that begged to be understood.

She didn't need to be played—she needed to be protected.

And I wanted to be that for her. I was that for her.

No matter what Khalil said, no matter how this played out, I wasn't backing down.

My phone rang again, cutting through my thoughts like a blade.

"Wassup?" I answered, already knowing it was Khalil.

"Can you open the door? I'm out front."

I clenched my jaw, sucked in a breath, and shook my head. "Yeah... gimme a minute."

Journee stirred beside me, still wrapped in sleep. "What's going on?" she mumbled, rubbing her eyes.

"Khalil's at the door. Don't worry about it," I said, already pulling on my boxers and shorts. My tone stayed even, but inside, I was coiled tight—like a spring wound to the edge.

She sat up, more alert now. "Do you have anything I can wear?"

I opened my closet, yanked out a pair of my ball shorts and a T-shirt. Handed them to her gently. My mind drifted to how she would look so damn good in my clothes, even like that—barefaced, raw, mine.

"You can come downstairs if you want or stay here," I said as I slipped on a tank top and turned toward the door. "You straight either way."

But really? I wanted her far away from this shit. Just in case Khalil said something reckless. And knowing that nigga, he would.

As I headed downstairs, my pulse pounded in my neck. I had to force my hands to stay open. Every part of me wanted to be ready to swing from all the reckless messages that flooded my phone, but not with Journee watching. Not with her sitting there, soft and exposed in my space. I had to stay solid for her, not just tough. Solid.

I opened the front door, jaw set tight.

"Damn, nigga. It's late as hell," I fussed as Khalil walked in.

"My fault, bro. I just needed to rap with you real quick," he said—but then he froze as soon as he saw her.

Journee was already on the couch, curled up in my shirt like she belonged there. And she did.

"Yeah," I said, closing the door behind him. "I need to rap with you, too."

He stepped inside like he was walking through fire, finally landing on the love seat across from her. His stare dragged across her face like he wanted to rewrite the past.

"Looks like I ain't gotta ask where you been," he said, voice already coated in rage.

I moved to the couch and sat down beside her, real close, resting my hand on her thigh. She was tense—I could feel it—but she stayed quiet. That's when I knew I needed to show her she wasn't standing in the middle of this alone. I rubbed my thumb against her skin. My touch said *I got you*. Even if I had to burn for it.

"I told you last night she was with me," I said, my tone cutting sharply.

"I know. I just needed to see it," Khalil snapped. Then he leaned forward, cocked his head sideways like he was feeling bold.

"I ain't even here to fall out with you over no bitch."

My whole body locked up. That word echoed in my ears like a trigger pull.

"Don't call my girl no bitch," I said, leaning forward ready to rise to my feet in an instant. "Don't disrespect her. Don't disrespect me, nigga."

My voice was calm, low—too low. The kind of low that only comes before the explosion.

Journee tensed beside me again. I felt her shift, barely. I slid my hand under hers, steadying her. Steadying me. She didn't even know—she was the reason I hadn't already blacked out on him.

Khalil stared me down. I stared right back. The room went silent, thick with everything we didn't say.

Then Journee spoke.

"I made a decision a while ago, Khalil," she said, voice cutting through the fog.

"I didn't want to be with you anymore."

He jumped up, full of bark now. "You decided that before or after he told you I was fuckin' Karina?"

I stood too. Instinct.

"Nigga, what the fuck are you talking bout?" I growled, my hands flexing like they were ready to ball into fists.

"I know you said that snake shit'."

"I ain't tell her none of that shit," I barked, stepping in. My voice smashed into his.

"Don't put your bullshit on me nigga."

"Don't fuckin' play with me, Omar!"

"I ain't playing, nigga," I said, stepping in even closer. "But you better watch your fuckin' mouth. Especially when you talkin' bout mines."

I felt Journee rise behind me. Without thinking, I shifted just enough to block her. I didn't even look—just knew I had to put myself between her and whatever could come next. That was instinct. Not bravado, not ego. Just love. Real love—the kind that protects at all costs.

* * *

Journee

Omar and Khalil were squared up, energy crackling in the air like static. I sat there, caught in the middle of two storms I had created, watching them both ready to go to war over me.

For a second, I thought about staying silent. Letting the tension snap. Letting Omar take the hit for something **I** did. The petty part of me—the one that once thirsted for revenge—wanted that. Wanted Khalil to feel that sting, wanted him to suffer. But the part of me that had grown, the part that currently **loved Omar**, couldn't let it happen.

I thought back to our late-night talks, his promises to do better, be better— not just for me, but for himself. I saw the change in him, and I wasn't about to let that be undone by a lie I let live.

I stood up, heart thudding, body tight with nerves. My voice cut through the air.

"Nobody told me anything," I said, stepping between them, shoving Khalil back into his seat before either of them could throw a punch. "I figured it out myself."

Khalil looked up at me, confused.

"Karina was with me when you called her phone, asking if you could 'get your dick wet.'" I said, staring down at him, my throat dry, my heart pounding in my ears. "I was the one who answered and hung up on you."

Silence hit the room like a punch.

Khalil sat there, eyes blinking slowly as the memory clawed its way back to him. It was there, faint, murky, but real. He remembered calling Karina that night. He remembered her hanging up. He didn't even think twice about it back then. She had told him before to stop talking to her like that, but he never listened. Just shrugged it off, like it was nothing.

Now it was something.

He looked dumbfounded, eyes distant like he was rewinding time and coming up short. His pride lay crumpled at his feet, bruised from every careless move he'd made to get to this point.

"You gonna say something?" I asked, voice softer now, scared that opening that one door might swing wide enough for him to see the rest of the truth. The parts I wasn't ready to admit to. Not yet.

But Khalil didn't speak.

He just sat there, stunned. Swallowed by silence.

And for once, I couldn't tell if that was a win... or the beginning of something worse.

* * *

Khalil

I leaned back on the love seat, baffled. My chest felt hollow.

It was me.
  I fucked up everything.

The truth hit like a gut punch—I was the only one to blame. All the wild swings, the accusations, the mess... that was on me.

I glanced up at Omar and Journee. Their faces mirrored the same pissed-off expression, though Omar looked like he was holding himself together by a thread. I ran a hand over my face, trying to center myself, but my pride was still bleeding out.

My voice came low, tight. "Who leaked the video?"

I locked eyes with Journee, trying to scan her expression, hoping to catch a twitch, a flinch—something. But she stood there cold, arms crossed like armor.

"I don't know," she said flatly.

She didn't even blink.

I watched her, studied her posture, her tone. Everything screamed that **she did it.** The timing, the coldness, the way she looked through me instead of at me. But I couldn't prove a damn thing. And honestly? I didn't care about the damn video. Not really.

It was just the last string I had left to pull on, the only excuse I had to get her to look in my direction. To talk to me. To feel something.

I turned to Omar, and yeah, he was still grilling me like he wanted to knock my head off. Rightfully so.

"Look, bro... my bad for accusing you and shit," I said, my voice heavy with something I wasn't used to—humility. "All that shit last night, you dippin' on me... it fucked my head up."

The words tasted bitter coming out, but I wasn't gonna destroy our bond over my bruised-ass ego. Omar and I had been through too much.

And I felt it—that ugly shame crawling up my neck when I thought about what I called Journee earlier. I wasn't proud of it. I was just pissed, out of my mind, running on spite and confusion.

Omar looked at me long and hard, then slowly reached out and dapped me up.

"It's cool, bro," he said. "But don't disrespect me or her again."

His tone was calm, but it carried weight. A warning wrapped in brotherhood. I nodded. No words needed.

Then I looked at Journee.

That's when I saw it—his clothes.
   She had on Omar's damn clothes.

Ball shorts. T-shirt. Hair slightly messy like she just rolled out of his bed. Reality started punching me in the ribs.

Damn... she spent the night.

All those times she told me she would and never did—lies, empty promises. But she did it for him.

The silence buzzed between us, and my tongue got ahead of my brain.

"What the fuck?" I snapped, rage leaking out. "You fucking this nigga?"

The question hit the room like a grenade.

Omar's whole body tensed. Journee froze, eyes wide. She didn't even get the chance to respond.

"Journee, go upstairs," Omar said, voice low but sharp. "Let me talk to this nigga. He trippin'."

She looked at me, hesitated, then turned and quietly walked off, leaving her silence hanging behind her like smoke.

And just like that, the room felt smaller. Hotter. Meaner.

And I knew Omar was about to say something that might change everything.

* * *

Omar

I was losing patience.

This nigga was acting brand new—like I'd crossed some sacred line when he'd made it clear a dozen times that he didn't give a fuck about Journee. Now he was in my house, salty as hell, walking like I stole his prize.

"Yo," I said, voice hard, "what the fuck is goin' on with you?"

Khalil's jaw clenched. "Did y'all fuck?"

I stared at him, gave it a beat before I answered. I wasn't hiding anything. Not now.

"Yeah," I said flatly. "That's my girl now."

I dropped onto the couch, cool and calm, even though the air between us felt like it could explode at any second.

"I was gonna tell you," I added. "We made it official this morning."

I watched the heat rise in his face, red creeping up his neck, eyes turning glassy.
"That's fucked up," Khalil muttered, trying to hold it together, but his whole aura shifted. He looked like a dude trying to keep his pride from bleeding out.

And for a moment, I truly felt something other than anger for him. Sympathy.

"I love that girl," I said, and my voice didn't shake when I said it. "She ain't just some random bitch I'm fucking bro."

That was the truth, and he needed to hear it. If he'd ever acted like he gave a damn about Journee, this might've played out different. But he hadn't. He treated her like a body, not a person. I never caught wind of it being more until now.

"How you gonna make it official the day after we break up?" Khalil shook his head. "Talking 'bout you in love. Nigga, you barely know her."

I laughed, couldn't help it. That made him flinch.

"Nigga, I talk to her more than you ever did," I chuckled. "You was just too busy tryna fuck. That was it."

He didn't like that truth, but he couldn't deny it. Journee would come to me every time he got mad and ghosted her. When she didn't put out, he dipped. But with me? We stayed up talking. Learning from each other. Feeling something real.

Khalil dropped his gaze, head low, and that's when it hit him. The truth slapped him hard.

He didn't feel the way that I did about Journee. He didn't love her. He just wanted to have her.

"Man... I fucked up," he sighed, voice almost too soft to catch.

I looked over at him. "Nigga, we straight. I knew how this was gon' go."

That was real. Khalil was selfish—always had been. I knew what I was doing, but I also knew she deserved better than being treated like a trophy.

"Nah, bro," he said again. "I fucked up bad."

I turned toward him, confused. "Nigga, what you mean?"

Khalil looked me dead in the eyes like he was still tryna convince himself it happened.

"I made Karina my bitch."

I blinked. "Huh?"

He repeated it, slower this time, like he couldn't believe it himself. "I made Karina... my bitch."

I damn near doubled over laughing. Karina?!

She wasn't the worst person in the world, just wild as hell and messy as shit. But honestly... she matched Khalil's chaos.

"Bro," I said between laughs, "y'all are a good match low-key. I ain't even mad at that."

He wasn't hearing it.

"Man, she's a known whore in the P, I can't be doing that."

Shaking my head, I shot him a look. "Half them niggas lied on they dick. The other half just echoing bullshit. You gonna let rumors stop you from fuckin' with somebody you honestly like?"

That hit him.

Khalil nodded slowly, thinking on it. I could tell—he truly liked Karina. He just couldn't admit it out loud 'cause he was scared of how he'd look. The image always mattered more than the truth with him.

"See, bro, that's why I fuck with you," he said finally. "You thorough."

He paused. "But how am I supposed to tell Journee?"

I smirked. "Don't worry about it. I got it."

Truth was, Journee didn't give a fuck about Khalil and Karina. Not anymore. I made sure of that this morning.

"Nigga, you already simpin'," Khalil joked, grinning.

"You don't know," I shot back, both of us cracking up. For a moment, things felt normal again.

His phone buzzed. He checked the screen, and that grin deepened.

It was Karina.

"Aight, bro," he said, standing up, "I gotta get back to my girl. I'ma rap with you later."

We dapped up. "Be safe, nigga."

I watched him hop in the Uber and disappear into the night.

Shaking my head, I jogged up the stairs. When I stepped into my room, Journee was curled up in bed, asleep again, peaceful. Like the storm downstairs never touched her.

And damn if she didn't look like home.

* * *

Karina

The knock on the door was soft.

I didn't answer right away. I just stood there, arms folded, trying to decide if I wanted to let him in or cuss him out.

"Babe, open the door," he said through the wood, his voice calm. "You already know what time it is."

I sighed and walked over, swinging it open. He stood there with that stupid smirk on his face, the one he knew got to me. He stepped inside without waiting for an invitation and closed the door behind him. The second the lock clicked, I turned around, ready to start.

"You saw her," I said frankly, staring at him, searching for guilt in his expression.

He walked toward me slowly, eyes locked on mine.

"I did," he admitted, "but that's not where I wanted to be. I only went to make shit right between me and Omar. So it wouldn't be no weird energy."

His voice was gentle now, low and real. I hated that it calmed me.

"She doesn't want me, Karina. She never really did. But you..."

He closed the space between us.

"You're the one I can't stop thinking about."

I blinked fast, my heart doing too much all at once.

"You always say that," I whispered.

"And I'll keep saying it until you believe it," he replied, brushing his thumb across my cheek. "You be driving me crazy, you know that?"

I tried to keep my wall up, but he leaned down and kissed me, rough and slow, like he wasn't in a rush to prove anything. Just wanted me to feel him. I melted into it without hesitation, my fingers gripping his hoodie as I kissed him back like I hadn't seen him in years instead of hours.

When we finally pulled apart, he rested his forehead against mine.

"I don't want anybody else," he said quietly. "It's you. It's always been you. I was just too blind to see it."

My chest tightened at his words. I didn't know how to trust them, but I wanted to.

He pulled me into him and wrapped his arms around my waist, burying his face in my neck.

"I know I ain't perfect. But I'm not letting you go," he murmured against my skin.

I held him tighter, my breath hitching.

"Do you really mean that?" I asked, needing to hear it one more time.

He pulled back just enough to look me in my eyes. "Yeah, Rina. I mean it."

I reached up and kissed him again, this time deeper—less anger, more feeling. His hands slid under my shirt, his touch gentle, reverent, like he was rediscovering every inch of me.

There was heat, sure, but there was also something else.

He wasn't just trying to fuck me—he was trying to stay.

And for the first time, I let myself believe he might actually mean it.

* * *

Could I Be More to You?

(A Question)

Voluptuous curves, seduction, and smile—
    You compliment me solely on my style.
    But neglect my spirit for a while...
    If I'm not more to you,
    Isn't it time I see the signs?

The missed connections
    when I'm showing you my mind.
    Your interest unguided—
    drawn only to my behind.

Could it be possible
    I'm tagging you in my past?
    Fitting you into failed molds
    and standards that didn't last.
    Holding judgment like a half-full glass—
    But seeing it as nearly empty.

My feelings split—fifty/fifty.
    Being an open book isn't working.
    Too close and I'm hurting.
    Still, I won't say it's not worth it.

Picking apart all the flaws I see, on purpose.
    Could it all be in my head?
    Though I never meant to end up in your bed...

Hair tangled.
    Self-esteem mangled.

Breathing in sharp bits of real pain—
Insecurity hidden behind shiny things.
Bling and bling.

I'm underwritten.
  Hiding scars.
  Dodging commitment.

But which is it?

Is it my smile, or my ass?
  Are you a ghost from my past?
  Am I losing what little sanity I still grasp?

Is this meant to last—
  Or just convenient?
  Settling for shards of easy pickings,
  Risking it all, yet not as your victim.

Willing to bend for this predicament.
  Now, as I fall, you have to choose:
  Pick that, or pick this.
  But do not abuse—

My love,
  My faith,
  My rightful peace.

Choose wisely what you see in me.

You've known the answer far too long.
  Cease from chasing shallow wants.
  Recognize my needs.

I refuse
    to be left in a state of suffering
    when you alone
    could be my recovery.

13

Am I My Sister's Keeper?

I stood beneath the shower head, letting the steaming water cascade through my natural hair and down my back.

My thoughts drifted to everything Omar had done to me—how he touched me, held me, worshiped me—both yesterday morning and again last night. I'd shown up with a full face of makeup, a thirty-inch wig, and lashes that kissed the sky. Now, I stood there completely bare, water dripping from my skin, and I felt no shame.

There was something in the way Omar spoke life into me that made me feel... okay. I know to most people, okay might seem like a dull, unimpressive emotion. But for me? Okay was a gift. It was something I hadn't felt in a long, a real long time. And yes, the sex was amazing—a bonus, if you will—but it was more than that. The emotions I felt in this aftermath were the total opposite of what I felt with Mia. This time, I felt whole.

The intense pleasure of multiple orgasms left me glowing. I felt seen. I felt beautiful.

I closed my eyes, replaying every moment in my mind, when I suddenly felt a presence behind me. Omar stepped into the shower, startling me just slightly.

"Mind if I join you?" he asked, his voice a soft rasp that made my skin tingle.

I looked over my shoulder and stepped forward, making space for him. I didn't mind. He had already kissed every inch of me—there was nothing left to hide. Every time I saw his face, I smiled without thinking. I was falling deep for him, and it was happening so fast, it scared me in the most beautiful way.

My heart fluttered as his hands slid down my belly, fingers trailing lower until they were between my thighs. His touch was commanding and tender all at once, sending shivers up my spine.

"I thought we were going out to eat," I moaned as his fingers found my clit, rubbing gentle, teasing circles that made my knees weak.

"We are," he murmured, lips brushing my neck. "But I need to see you cum one more time. You just look so beautiful right now."

I leaned into him for balance, my body melting into his as pleasure built between my thighs. He quickened his pace, and before I could stop it, another orgasm ripped through me. My juices slid down my legs, and I clung to him, panting, breathless, undone.

He eased his hand away from my center and began to wash me—slowly, attentively—lathering each curve as if I were divine. I watched him through half-lidded eyes, noticing how hard he was, how his thick length twitched at the sight of me. The way his dick stood proudly made my mouth water.

Without thinking, I reached for him, but he gently slapped my hand away.

"Later," he said, his tone firm and demanding. "We already missed our plans yesterday. I've got something special for you today."

Disappointed but intrigued, I pouted slightly. I wanted to return the favor. So instead, I took control.

I dropped to my knees on the slick shower floor, stroking his thick shaft with admiration. My hand could barely wrap around it. Omar never boasted about his size like other men. He didn't have to. He was everything a woman could want.

I licked my lips, then wrapped them around his tip before he could stop me.

"Oh Shit, Journee," he gasped as I took him into my mouth, swirling my tongue around the head before pushing him deeper.
My cheeks hollowed as I sucked him with slow, deliberate hunger, my hands working the rest of his length. I looked up into his eyes, watching him fall apart.

He throbbed in my mouth, and I picked up the pace, gagging slightly as he hit the back of my throat. His taste lingered on my tongue—clean, masculine, addictive. I moaned around him, driven by the need to please him the way he pleased me.

"Baby, I'm about to cum," he warned, his voice tight.

I didn't stop. I took him deeper, ignoring the urge to gag, until the first warm spurt shot down my throat. I kept sucking, moaning softly as I accepted the rest of him on my tongue, curling it to savor the taste. When I finally let him go, he stood there speechless, eyes wide with disbelief.

I smiled, rising to my feet.

"You taste good too," I whispered, turning away to finish lathering my body.

"Damn, Journee..." he said softly, wrapping his arms around me from behind.

"I love you."

We finished our shower together and got dressed. The moment lingered between us like a secret only we could share.

* * *

Outside, the sun beamed in my eyes as I stepped into his truck. Omar shut the door behind me, then slid into the driver's seat.

"Where are we goin'?" I asked, connecting my phone to his Bluetooth, excitement bubbling inside me.

"How many times do I have to tell you—it's a surprise," he smirked, pulling out of the parking space.

"I'm sorry. I just can't help it," I said with a laugh, opening Apple Music and blasting GloRilla. I danced in my seat as Omar joined in, rapping every word like he was in the booth with them.

We pulled up to Ruth's Chris, and I felt relieved I had dressed appropriately. Omar helped me out of the car, his hand warm and steady. We walked in together, and I noticed he had already reserved our table. Everything was perfect, down to the minute.

As we sat down, a small part of me wondered if he could afford this. "You know this place is expensive," I teased, hoping he wouldn't take it the wrong way.

He chuckled, reaching for my hand. "I got it. Don't worry. I just want to show you I'm serious."

I blushed as the waiter arrived and took our order. But even as the night unfolded beautifully, a lingering curiosity tugged at me.

I realized I didn't know what Omar did for a living. He never mentioned work. He never said he had to go anywhere or answer a call.

Trying not to sound nosy, I asked gently, "Omar, what do you do for a living?"

"I'm a driver," he said simply, like that explained everything.

"So... like Uber or Lyft?"

He laughed and sipped his drink. "No, not like Uber or Lyft, Journee."

I still didn't get it. Before I could press further, he leaned in. "I'll tell you more later. Tonight's just about us."

I nodded, sipping my drink as I tucked the unanswered question away. The night carried on in warmth and laughter, but the curiosity about what he truly did stayed quietly in the back of my mind.

* * *

Darren

I sat at the table with my ole lady, and I couldn't believe my fucking eyes. There she was—the same bitch who burned me for over ten grand—sitting pretty at a table across the room, hugged up and grinning with some other nigga like life was sweet.

Journee.

She'd been ignoring my calls for a minute now. I almost thought she blocked me, but nah—my texts were still going through. I watched them kiss, hold hands, all that lovey-dovey shit. My blood boiled. Did she really take my money and break bread with this bum? That bitch had to be playing me the whole fucking time.

She really thought she could finesse me and fuck somebody else like I wouldn't find out? She must've forgot who the fuck I am.

I clenched my jaw, turning my face just enough so they wouldn't spot me. My fists were balled under the table, my heart thudding with rage as a hundred different scenarios ran through my mind—each one ending with me dragging her ass out that God damn chair and making a scene.

My main chick tapped my hand, snapping me out of the spiral.

"You know that bitch over there?" she asked, her voice slick with suspicion.

"Nah. I don't," I lied, keeping my eyes low, praying she hadn't peeped me watching.

"No, I'm saying I know that bitch over there," Jasmine said, her tone shifting quick to an attitude.

I leaned across the table, voice low. "How you know her?"

Jasmine rolled her eyes, cutting into her steak, then chased it with a long sip of red wine before answering. "That bitches mom used to fuck with my uncle. Her sister got my uncle booked, and we all got kicked out after that shit. My siblings and I ended up in the system. Foster care. All 'cause of her fucked-up ass family."

She chewed slowly, getting sloppy now, her words spilling with that drunken slur. "That bitch lucky if she ever hear from me again. I was hella nice to her, and she fucked my life up."

Her voice cracked a little at the end, like the memory hit a nerve she wasn't ready for.

"For real?" I asked, leaning back in my seat as something dark crept into my thoughts. "What else you know about this bitch?"

I stared at Journee like she was a target—plotting, planning, already tasting revenge.

Her and her pussy ass nigga? Yeah, they both had it coming.

* * *

Journee

We finished dinner and made our way to another one of Omar's surprises.

"Seriously, where are we goin' now?" I asked, impatient and curious, unable to hide the smile tugging at my lips.

Omar glanced over at me with that signature smirk of his as we pulled up in front of a hotel. My eyes widened when I saw the glowing Marriott sign overhead.

"You booked us a room?" I asked, excitement bubbling up in my chest.

I had assumed I'd be heading home after dinner—especially since I didn't even pack for longer than three days, the weekend was already approaching, and I was running low on outfits.

"I did," Omar said coolly, stepping out and coming around to open my door. "But that's not the only reason we're here."

Intrigued, I let him help me out of the car. His hand lingered just a little longer than necessary, and something about the way he looked at me made my stomach flutter. We walked into the hotel, and as he checked us in, I stood behind him, admiring the upscale lobby. I'd never been inside a Marriott before. Everything felt... rich. Warm. Classy. Almost like stepping into a dream.

When we got up to the suite, the room was decorated with balloons. A heart-shaped arrangement of roses lay on the bed, surrounded by tons of shopping bags from high-end fashion brands. A beautiful card sat in the middle of it all.
"Wow, you did all this for me," I asked as I walked over, completely in shock.
"Yes, baby, I told you I had no intentions of skipping steps." He replied, his demeanor beaming with pride.

I picked up the card and read it out loud, my heart skipping a beat with each word.
"*Journee,*

I never planned to feel this way about anyone, but here you are—beautiful, fearless, complicated as hell, and still the only peace I've ever known. The way you laugh, the way you hold your pain without letting it define you... It's magnetic.

Being with you is like breathing for the first time. You don't just see me—you understand me. You pull me back when I'm slipping, and without even trying, you remind me of who I want to become.

217

You've touched parts of me no one ever bothered to reach. And when I hold you... damn, it's like the world fades.

So, I'm asking you something I've never asked before. From a place that's real, raw, and yours—

Will you be my girl?

—Omar"

"Yes, yes, yes!" I screeched, rushing over to the man I love. I wrapped my arms around him, kissing him passionately as we stood in front of the windows, admiring the skyline view.

"I wasn't expecting all this," I said, breaking the kiss. "You should've told me. I would have come prepared."

"Me telling you defeats the purpose," Omar said, slipping his fingers into my hair. "It's a surprise, remember?"

His touch was soft, soothing, but I was still pouting. "Well, I wanted to swim with you, but you didn't say anything. I don't even have a damn bathing suit."

"I already bought you one," he replied without hesitation, tilting his head toward the shopping bags, voice low and confident.

That same question crept back into my mind—How? How could he afford this? He was only twenty-two. And yet he moved like he had power. Money. A plan. Something about it didn't sit right. I was just about to ask him again what kind of "driver" he *really* was when a knock came at the door.

"You expecting somebody?" I asked, eyes narrowing as I turned toward him.

He didn't respond. Just walked to the door and opened it.

My whole body stiffened the second I saw who it was.

Karina.

And Khalil.

My shoes flew off as I jumped up, voice sharp as a knife. "What the fuck?!"

Karina immediately let go of Khalil's hand, holding both of hers in the air. "I didn't come to fight, Journee. I just want to talk."

"Bitch, you think I want to talk to your grimy ass?" I barked, my words ripping her to shreds.

Omar stepped in front of me, grabbing both of my hands, grounding me. "Baby, remember where we are right now," he said softly, eyes pleading for me to keep my cool.

I took a deep breath, swallowing the fire in my chest. But my eyes—my eyes were screaming murder. If looks could kill, I'd have been booked on three counts.

How the hell could Omar set me up like this?

Karina must've sensed my fury because she started speaking fast, her words tumbling over each other in desperation.

"I keep texting you. Calling you. I even asked your mom if she could tell you to call me. You got me blocked on everything," she said, voice breaking, tears already sliding down her cheeks.

"I know. I heard," I shot back coldly.

"I saw all the shit you said about me. I read all the text messages," I added, barely holding my composure. "I'm a selfish ass bitch? Bitch, all I ever did was ride for your triflin' ass!"

Karina stood frozen for a second, looking stunned. Then she blinked and asked quietly, "When did you see my text messages?"

Her eyes narrowed as she stared at me, suspicious.

I paused. For a moment, I didn't know what to say. My eyes darted to Omar, heat rising in my chest. I was pissed. He put me in this situation.

But fuck it. They didn't have proof.

"I saw them on Khalil's phone," I said, folding my arms. "His dumb ass didn't clear his recently deleted."

Karina blinked.

"When?"

I shrugged, irritated.

"When, Journee?!" she repeated, stepping forward, voice cracking under the weight of her emotions. She was frantic now. Her whole body was shaking.

"Does it fucking matter?" I snapped, sitting down on the bed, done with the whole damn thing.

Karina stood there looking wrecked. Her face was puzzled. Her lip was trembling.

Then her voice broke again.

"Journee... did you expose my nudes, on my fucking birthday?"

* * *

Karina

I stood there shaking as I watched Journee rise to her feet, brushing herself off like she hadn't just shattered every nerve in my body.

"Oh, *those* were your nudes?" she said, sarcastic as hell, before bursting into uncontrollable laughter.

That laugh—so cold, so loud—cut through the room like a sword. The world went dead silent for a moment.

And then it exploded.

Next thing I knew, we were on the floor, full-blown tussling. Hair, fists, kicks—it was chaos. Journee got in two solid kicks to my stomach while I yanked her hair like my life depended on it.

"Bitch, I fuckin' hate you!" I screamed, my voice cracked with rage.

Omar and Khalil jumped in, each grabbing one of us to pull us apart.

"That ain't news," Journee snapped, pushing her way past Omar to get at me again.

"I saw *everything*, Karina. How ugly, fake, selfish, and weird you think I am."

Before I could catch my breath, she lunged again, knocking me back onto the bed. She was on top of me, swinging, and it took both Omar and Khalil to drag her off a second time.

"Look, Journee—you're fucking my bro, my best friend right now!" Khalil snapped, holding me close as I sobbed into his jean jacket.

"How is what *you're* doing any different?"

Journee's eyes locked on mine, wild and gleaming.

"It was never about you," she hissed. "It's about what *that bitch* said about me. Omar has *never bad-mouthed* you. Ever. I can't say that about my so-called *best friend*."

She threw air quotes around those last two words, and I couldn't even argue. As much as I wanted to deny it, I knew she was right. I had said horrible things about her. I was filled with so much envy, so much bitterness over how the world always seemed to love Journee louder than it loved me. She pulled all the attention, all the love—and it made me hate her. But even through all that hate, I never thought she was a bad person. She was my best friend.

"Journee... I'm sorry," I choked out, still crying.

"Damn. I didn't mean all that shit. I just... I felt like you thought you were better than me. You got Khalil, you pull niggas with money, you're leaving for N.Y.U. Bitch, I felt left behind."

I sat down on the bed, drained. I didn't want to fight anymore. I just wanted her to hear me.

Journee sat beside me, her eyes softer now, but not weak. She looked at me, then slapped the shit out of me. My whole body jumped.

Then she hugged me.

"Are you fucking dumb?" she said, hugging me tighter.

"I wasn't trying to leave you. I don't talk to niggas for money just because I like it. I got no fucking choice. You think I wanted to keep entertaining these weird ass niggas just to get clothes?"

She leaned back and looked me dead in the eyes.

"When's the last time you saw my Momma keep a job? How the hell do you think we've been paying the bills?"

I stared back, stunned. My mouth opened, but nothing came out. Come to think of it, I'd never seen Ms. Semira work. But every time I came over, all of them looked kept up. Clothes were clean. The house was halfway decent. When Miracle or Sincere asked for money, it was handed to them without question. It never crossed my mind how any of it was getting done.

Were Journee and her sisters doing everything this whole time?

"I put that money in her hand, and she don't ask one damn question," Journee said, her voice breaking.

"My mom stopped buyin' me shit when I turned thirteen. Thirteen, Karina. I've been taking care of myself since then."

Tears rolled down her face, and Omar sat beside her, placing a hand on her thigh in quiet support.

I looked up at Khalil. His eyes mirrored mine—wide and stunned, full of questions and guilt.

Journee wasn't just surviving—she was carrying so much I hadn't seen when I was standing right beside her.

And Jealousy clouded my vision, now that cloud was gone.

* * *

Journee

As I finished my sentence, a foul taste crawled up the back of my throat. My stomach flipped and twisted. Gagging, I pushed past Khalil and bolted into the bathroom, my hand clamped tight over my mouth.

My spine arched violently as I hurled, painting the toilet bowl with sour, burning vomit. Memory after memory clawed its way out of me with every heave. I gripped the toilet seat, knuckles pale, as the weight of everything I'd buried came spilling out.

So much had been left unsaid. Too much I'd never dared to speak aloud. The seal on those memories—too raw, too heavy—had thickened into scarred flesh over time. But now, it tore open. Everything I'd hidden behind my smile, behind my sarcasm and silence, broke loose as I vomited until my body trembled.

Omar knelt beside me, his hand gently pulling my hair back. His face was carved with pure worry.

I never wanted to hear myself say the truth out loud. Especially not the kind of truth that came with questions I didn't have the strength—or words—to answer.

I remembered that rented room.

It had a mini fridge, an old TV, and a creaky bed. My mom used to take us there right after the divorce from Mr. Trenton. Maybe it was the financial strain—or maybe something deeper—but whatever it was, the end of her marriage cracked something in her that never healed right.

That room was just the beginning. The first in a string of too many that made it hard to breathe. Bitter peanut butter and jelly sandwiches that stuck to the roof of my mouth until I wanted to lie down and disappear. Warm ginger ale in plastic cups to wash away the taste. But nothing ever went away for long.

I woke up in that darkness too many times. The weight of strange bodies pressing down on me, hands pinching at my thighs. Voices chattering in the background—none of them hers. Sometimes I'd crack my eyes open and see a face. Other times, I flinched at the drop of sweat hitting my skin. Every man smelled different. Some like Musk. Others like stale cologne. But they all felt the same.

Grunts. Groans. Shame.

It was the same sickness I felt with Mr. Trenton.

But I did what my Momma told me: lay still, eyes closed, prayed it'd be over quick.

Afterward, I'd get scrubbed in a bubble bath, but I never felt clean. Not really.

Then came the reward. A smile, a "Pick what you want to eat, baby."

No more PB&J—at least for a while. Until we had to do it again.

Momma used to say her mother, Imani, wasn't shit. Said she made her do it every night. She swore she'd never be like Imani. But now and then, she needed help—"a volunteer," she called it.

"Bills don't pay themselves." At least she was better than Imani, she'd say.

We just had to do what we had to do.

There weren't many people lining up to help a single mother with six kids. No free babysitting, no grandparents stepping in. Daddy was gone—drowned in his addiction. And Momma couldn't hold a job, always forgetting to take her medication.

So we had nothing. Just each other. It wasn't wrong—it was survival.

When I finally lifted my head from the toilet, still shaking, I saw Karina and Khalil standing in the doorway. I ripped off a few sheets of toilet paper and wiped my mouth, leaning my head against the cool wall.

"You okay?" Karina asked, her voice softer than I expected.

I turned away from her eyes, ashamed.

"I'm alright," I mumbled as Omar helped me to my feet. I could feel everyone's gaze—heavy, uncomfortable. Like I was some freak of nature.

I wasn't a fucking weirdo. I didn't deserve to be stared at like I was broken.

"What's wrong?" Omar asked gently.

I closed the door behind me, leaning against it as the weakness pulled at my knees.

"Nothing," I lied, eyes dropping to the white tile floor.

I tried to study the pattern. Anything to avoid his eyes. I didn't want Omar to see through me. Not now. Not like this.

He stepped in closer. "Look at me," he said, lifting my chin.

I resisted, then gave in, letting our eyes meet. Mine, already filled with tears.

"What is it, Journee?" he asked again, firmer this time.

"I can't," I whispered, voice cracking just as someone knocked on the door.

I stepped aside and watched Omar open it.

To my surprise, Karina stood there holding a toothbrush from my overnight bag.

"Here, sis," she said with a crooked smile.

"I know you don't wanna be in here talking to your man with that stank ass breath."

I let out a small laugh. Couldn't help it. What the hell was wrong with this girl?

Karina laughed too, then stepped fully into the bathroom, kneeling in front of me.

"No matter how much you hate me," she said quietly, "you're still my best friend."

She placed a hand on my thigh, and despite all that had taken place between us, I felt the sting of real forgiveness trying to crawl its way through all the pain.

* * *

Karina

I didn't want to ask any questions I wasn't prepared to hear the answers to.

When Journee ran into the bathroom, throwing up like her body was rejecting the very air around her, I couldn't imagine what memory had clawed its way to the surface. Watching her gag and retch from just a conversation—it hit something deep in me. For that moment, all the drama between us didn't matter. Yeah, I was still pissed she exposed me. But now I knew it wasn't Khalil who aired out my nudes—it was Journee, and her reason for doing it wasn't spite. Not really.

Our beef wasn't even about me fucking Khalil. That was just the smoke. The fire was what I had said behind her back. All those ugly, jealous, petty things I spewed. If I'd seen screenshots of her calling me fake, selfish, or weird, I would've beat her ass too. But Journee wasn't built like that. She wasn't the girl who threw hands—she threw truth, and she threw it hard. Exposing me was her way of bleeding out. And even though it stung like hell, I couldn't lie—I was happy it was out. I never really wanted to fight her to begin with.

No one ever taught me how to have a healthy relationship with another woman.

I learned how to love women from women who didn't know how to love themselves. My mother, my aunties—they all came up under claws and tongues sharp enough to gut fish. Everything with them was shade and side-eyes, fake love and loud silence. They were only close when a man did them wrong or when someone died. The rest of the time, it was competition—who looked better, who got the man, who was the favorite.

That's the pattern I followed. I didn't even realize I was repeating it with Journee. Until tonight.

But I wanted to break that shit.

If Khalil and Omar could put their egos aside and talk like men, why couldn't we as women do the same?

It really hit me after the talk I had with Khalil—we were all wrong. Every one of us. But I still loved Journee. Cared for her more than I wanted to admit. She wasn't just my best friend. She was my sister. And no matter what we'd said or done, I wasn't willing to lose her over this mess.

I dug through her overnight bag and grabbed her toothbrush, then stood outside the bathroom door. My heart was racing as I knocked softly, like I was hoping she wouldn't slam it in my face again.

But I knew a part of her still needed me, too.

I didn't pity her. This wasn't about feeling sorry.

It was about letting her know—she wasn't alone.

When I handed her that toothbrush, it wasn't just about hygiene. It was my olive branch. My way of saying, Let's start over. Let's build this the way it should've been from the beginning.

* * *

Secret Recipe

(A Confession)

Sista,
    I'm sorry I ever saw you as competition—
    Maybe even fed the lies whispered by your opposition.
    Truth is, I just longed to be the center of attention,
    Yes, the apple of every eye.
    Craving the same spotlight
    That was snatched the moment you arrived.

People told me I did the same,
    But their eyes twinkled at the mere mention of your name.
    And mine rolled,
    Heavy with shame,
    Laced with a bitterness I struggled to claim—
    Maybe even a flicker of pain,
    Because I, too, wanted that fame.

Why'd you have to be so effortlessly sweet?
    Moving with rhythm, grace,
    Each step a shimmer on the beat—
    Leaving glittering footprints
    Where mine never seemed to reach.
    Oh, the envy that festered quietly in me.

Sista, how I looked at you
    Through a veil of contempt and quiet deceit,
    My jealousy dressed up in silence—

My animosity masked and neat.

Who taught you to move like poetry?
    Because when I try to match your pace, I falter—
    Always glancing back,
    Measuring myself against your perfect stride,
    The one you never altered.

I can't match that walk.
    My body won't align with that tune.

So, Sista, if you'd be so kind—
    Do me just one favor:
    Slip me the secret recipe,
    So I can copy your flavor.

IV

DO FOR LOVE

"To toy with love is to wager one's very soul—
for it is only through the ache of loving sacrifice
that life finds the breath to begin."

— *Dajaha Dior Halliday Blair*

14

Seeing You

I blinked slowly, my eyes heavy with exhaustion, as I watched Omar walk Khalil and Karina out of our hotel room.

I was completely drained, my body limp against the bed as my mind refused to rest. Tossing and turning, I was haunted—ambushed by thoughts that wouldn't let me be. Memories clung to me like shadows, unwilling to release the peace they'd stolen. My mind was the enemy now, cutting me open with every flash of the past.

I felt Omar climb into bed beside me, his arms wrapping around my waist, pulling me in close. He planted a soft kiss on my cheek, and I could hear the breath he exhaled, heavy, as if he was holding something too.

"Talk to me, Journee," he whispered, squeezing me a little tighter.

"Omar..." I started, but then I caught myself.

For a moment, I thought about not saying a thing. Stuffing all the hurt down and pretending that everything was okay. But then Omar sensed it.

"Nothing could ever change how I feel about you. Not this moment, not the past. Nothing," he whispered calmly in my ear.

My eyes watered. Why did God send me this man? I didn't deserve it. I was dirty, I was nasty, I was selfish, but I wanted to change.

"Omar... have you ever felt like you've been broken into a thousand pieces?" I asked, staring blankly into the dim light.

"Like... maybe you didn't just lose your pieces—maybe you destroyed them?"

My voice trembled, not from fear, but from the unbearable weight of knowing.

"Have you ever heard that voice in your head say I told you so, while the voice in your heart just fades... disappears... until you finally accept it? That this—this dream you've been living—isn't a dream at all. It's a lie. A slow-motion crash into the truth: you are alone. Maybe not meant to be. But you are."

I paused, breathing through the lump forming in my throat.

"Think about it. Nobody's meant to be alone. That's why we're born into families. That's the blood connection. And then... there's God's connection—love. The kind that's supposed to find you. Supposed to keep you from ever truly being alone. But what if you lose one of those connections?"

I turned to face the dark ceiling. "Is it impossible to patch it together with the thread of another—even if the thread is fraying?"

My voice cracked as I whispered, "I've lost my dignity. I can't even fake hope anymore—not even to myself. Not even in a daydream."

I took a deep breath, but it came out as a shaky gasp.

"My imagination used to be my safe space. But even that broke. I broke. Into a thousand little pieces of me scattered so far, I can't even find where they landed. I feel like I've forgotten who I am—but my heart still remembers. And that's the worst part. The cruelest part. Because I can't forget that I forgot something."

I turned my head, finally meeting Omar's eyes for just a second before looking away again.

"This... this isn't just pain—it's a closed case, filed under too little, too late. And I know you want to help. God, I know. But don't read me like I'm a story you can flip through. Even if I wrote this pain with my own hands, I didn't do it just to be seen."

I inhaled, trying to find the words, but all I could do was shake my head.

"I searched, Omar. I searched in the dead of night with nothing but the moonlight to guide me. I searched with hope, with fear, with desperation. But when night turned to dawn, I was still standing there—naked in the daylight of my truth. And I hated it. I hated how exposed I was, how much I'd tried to wrap myself in lies just to feel warm."

I leaned into his chest, breathing in his scent like it was the only thing keeping me grounded.

"Even now, even in your arms, even with this moment being the closest thing to peace I've had in years... I feel like I'm drownin' in truth."

My voice softened, barely a breath.

"I don't know who I am. Maybe I never did. But I swear to you... Some part of me used to know. And now I don't. And I don't even know how a person loses something that was supposed to be theirs forever—themselves."

Omar shifted his body, pulling me completely on top of his chest.

"Look at me, Journee," he spoke softly into the dark room that encased us.

His brown eyes held mine, captivated. His arms—solid, tough, rigid—held me in place.

"I don't care if it takes me several lifetimes. I will find every piece. I will replace every moment you hurt with so much happiness it drowns out all the ones where all you did was cry," he spoke, his voice soft yet stern with conviction.

"If time can't heal it, I will. I'll change fate with my own hands. I'd burn this whole world to the ground to save you."

My body relaxed into his. How did he always manage to do it? He said all the right things and showed up exactly when I needed him. God had to create this man just for me.

So did that mean God saw me, too?

* * *

I awoke to sunlight seeping through the hotel curtains, soft layers of golden hues easing my mind, like sorrow hadn't flooded it just hours ago.

Omar was still beneath me, his arms wrapped protectively around my waist, one hand firmly resting on the curve of my lower back. His breathing steady, a rhythm I craved for reassurance that world had not abandoned me to

solitude. I watched him, as I done before. Taking note of the fullness of his lips that spoke light into the even the darkest places of my soul.
The bush of his brows and the scar on his chest, I always wanted to ask him about. I traced it, causing him to stir in his sleep but not awaken. Damn, was he a beautiful man.

Carefully, I untangled myself from his arms and slid out of bed, and the air conditioner pushed out a gust of cold air that instantly made me shiver.
I walked over to the bags of gifts I received last night, but did not open. Beautiful singular pieces and sets were inside. I giggled to myself in approval. My man had good taste.

I walked to the mirror.

My reflection grounded me.
Omar was helping me change the way I saw myself, not just on the outside but within. My puffy eyes looked mesmerizing. My hair, messy from tossing and turning all night, fell beautifully along my shoulder.

I pressed my palms flat against the counter, leaning into the mirror like l was seeing myself for the first time.

"You're perfect, Journee."

A soft knock pulled me out of my trance.

Omar.

"You okay?" His voice was gravelly with sleep, laced with worry but still also gentle, alert.

I cleared my throat. "Yeah... just needed a minute. I just never saw myself as I did just now."

He stepped inside and didn't say anything at first. Just came up behind me, wrapping his arms around my waist again. Our eyes met in the mirror this time. I didn't flinch. Didn't look away.

"And how did you see yourself?" he asked.

"The way that you always see me."

"Oh, so you snuck away just to admire that beautiful goddess in the mirror."

I saw my face turn red as he held me.

He kissed the side of my neck softly. "I hope you admire that woman every single day."

I turned slowly in his arms until I was facing him.

"Will you admire her, no matter what?" I asked, needing to hear him say it.

"I will, now and forever," he whispered, cupping my face. "You are mine."

And I was. His brown eyes told me so. I could see the love that filled them, and I never wanted it to vanish.
Looking at the counter he had notice I grabbed out a blue dress. He smiled in agreement as he used one hand to touch it.
"I see you're wearing this today."
"Yeah, I've just been drawn to blues lately. I couldn't stop staring at it."
Omar chuckled knowingly.
"What?" I giggled, "I wanna know what's funny too."
"Blue is just the color of peace; in psychology, it's associated with calmness and relaxation."

"Oh," I replied, stumped.

I stood back, impressed. This man always managed to surprise me. He was just so different.

"Before we go, there's one more thing I want to do," he announced as he led me back to the bed.
The sheets are still warm from where we'd lain hours before. The morning light filled the room, reflecting off the different hues of our brown skin, mine almond, his dark chocolate.

He pulled me under the covers, not saying anything, just holding me. His thumb traced slow, lazy circles against the back of my hand. My breathing matched his. I was reminded once again that he made me feel safe.

"You fell asleep on me last night and we never finished talking," he pointed out, his hands intertwined with mine.
"I'm gonna tell you something real, and you're gonna do the same," Omar stated sternly.
I love how he said everything with clear intentions. It was a breath of fresh air compared to my norm of people spewing empty words.

"You go first." I insisted still nervous to discuss any question that could arise about last night.
I closed my eyes, bracing myself for whatever he might confess. Silence filled the room.

He didn't hesitate as he broke it.

"When I was fifteen, I used to stay up praying that someone like you existed."

I opened my eyes.

"You are so corny," I said, fighting off my smile.

He fully smiled at me, but his eyes stayed serious.

"Yeah, maybe. But it's my truth. I didn't know your name back then... but I knew what it would feel like. The way I feel right now here with you."

I felt my heart flutter again.

"I guess it's my turn."

"It is," he said. "Remember, don't be afraid, you can't scare me away, Journee."

I closed my eyes again. Afraid that what I was about to admit would change the way he looked at me forever.
"I lost my virginity to my stepfather, Mr. Trenton, when I was nine years old," I spoke, voice trembling, afraid to breathe.

"Look at me, Journee," he demanded gently, "Open your eyes."

My lids slowly parted, and I met his loving gaze.
"You didn't lose anything, your virginity is not something that can be taken. It's given and you didn't give that bitch ass nigga anything'" he said voice wrapped in armor.
"The other day, you gave it to me. I received it, and I claimed it. I meant it when I said I'd change fate, even if I have to rewrite history."

His words hung in the air, thick with meaning. I tilted my head up to look at him.

"Do you genuinely believe that, Omar?" I whispered.

He reached up, brushing my hair from my face.

"Journee... with my whole heart and soul."

He kissed me then. Not with urgency, but with care. Like he had all the time in the world. I needed that. I needed him. My whole life had done a three-sixty in only a matter of days.

I kissed him back, letting myself melt into it. Letting go of the fear. The shame. The weight. The sabotage that screamed for me to run for the hills. Away from him, away from love. And away from the power he was beginning to possess over my heart.
I was madly in love, an emotion I swore I would never feel for any man.

But that vow had been broken inside me, but I didn't feel broken. I felt... found.

Omar saw me exactly for who I was.

I discovered a diary in human form. A person I could share all of my secrets with, knowing they'll keep them locked away forever.

Never using any against me.

* * *

The Soul I See

(A declaration of love)

I find you beautiful—
    Not just in your curves of flesh,
    Nor in the rhythm of the heart beating in your chest.

I find you beautiful,
In the places most never think to look.

If I could explore your soul,
   I'd linger in every cranny—
   Every nook.
   A paradise of pain and grace,
   Of joy braided with sorrow,
   Where hues blend in ways
   My fingers can't help but trace,
   And glance at love, I have no intention to borrow.
   I will claim it as mine.

I am captivated
   By every etched line,
   Every delicate bruise
   You once tried so hard to erase.
   And maybe, just maybe—
   I could reach deeper,
   Run my fingers across the faded scars
   And see them for what they've always been in my eyes:
   Nothing short of art.

You'd see your beauty then—
   Not because I told you,
   But because your soul finally spoke for itself—
   And showed you.

15

The Pot or The Kettle

The weekend came to an end, and it was time to head home. I packed my new clothes, shoes, and accessories into the suitcase Omar had gotten me, my hands moving slower than my heart. I wasn't ready to go.

Omar felt more at home than anywhere I'd ever been.

"You got everything you needed?" Omar asked, reaching for my suitcase before I could lift it.

"Yeah. I have everything," I replied, the sadness in my voice betraying how much I didn't want to leave the comfort of our little bubble.

It was time to get back to life—real life. The one that existed outside of us.

Outside the peace we'd made in a space that had once been chaos.

"You know... You don't ever have to go back," he said, low and hopeful.

But I did.

I had responsibilities. I had brothers who depended on me to make shit

245

happen. Sisters who'd suffered too much to carry my weight on top of their own. I couldn't be selfish.

But God, I wanted to be.

I wanted to be stingy. I wanted Omar all to myself.

"I have to," I whispered.

"I can't just walk away from everyone I've ever loved."

Even though deep down, a part of me wanted to. Not for him—but for me. My soul was tired. But my loyalty... it wouldn't let me rest.

"I would never ask you to," Omar said gently.

"I just wanted you to know you can lean on me."

"I knew that from our first conversation," I said, meeting his eyes.

Because I did. I always knew.

Omar was strong in a way I'd never seen before. Not just physically, but emotionally. He didn't crack under pressure. He stood firm, solid as iron. I'd leaned on him so many times before. He just never noticed.

He packed everything into his truck, and we hit the road. Music blasted through the speakers as the summer breeze kissed my cheeks, the wind catching in my hair as I leaned my head out the window.

One of my favorite songs came on the radio, and I couldn't help it—I sang along, horribly off-key.

"We are lovers through and through
  And though we made it through the storm
  I really want you to realize, I really want to put you on
  I've been searching for someone to satisfy my every need
  Won't you be my inspiration?
  Be the real love that I need
  Real love, I'm searching for a real love
  Someone to set my heart free..."

Omar turned his head, eyes on me like I was something he'd never get tired of watching. He was smiling—really smiling.

"I love hearing you sing," he laughed.

I cringed.

"Boy, you must be tone-deaf."

He shook his head, still grinning.

"Nah, don't get me wrong, baby. You can't sing. But watching you sing? I could watch that performance every day."

I laughed even harder, cheeks burning.

"I know I can't sing. I don't need you telling me that!" I teased, nudging him playfully.

When we pulled up in front of my house, my heart sank. The weight of reality came crashing back down.

Did I have to go?

Did I have to leave him?

I dragged my feet getting out of the truck. Omar came around and walked me to the door, hand on the small of my back, grounding me one last time.

"When can I see you again?" he asked, rubbing his thumb along my cheek.

"Whenever you want," I said truthfully, aching for him to say now, to take me back with him, to make time stop.

"Tomorrow?" he asked, searching my face.

"Yes," I breathed.

He kissed me on my forehead—soft, lingering—and I floated through the front door still glowing, smiling.

Until I saw her.

"J... Ja... Jasmine?" I stuttered, my throat closing around the name.

"Hey, Journee. I've missed you, girl," she said, rising from the couch with a warm smile.

I blinked.

Serenity sat across from her, grinning like she hadn't just cracked my world open.

"I told you she'd be happy to see you," Serenity beamed, clearly proud of herself for this reunion.

It wasn't that Jasmine wasn't important to me. She was. But she was also part of a lie, a lie that was the catalyst of my self-destruction.

"Are you happy to see me?" Jasmine asked, her tone holding something I couldn't quite place.

"Of course," I answered, trying to center myself. "I'm just shocked to see you. It's been... years."

I turned to Serenity.

"Where's Momma?"

Serenity chuckled like nothing about this moment was surreal.

"Her and Daddy went on a date."

I needed air.

What the fuck was going on?

Had I stepped into the Twilight Zone?

I turned around, opened the door, and stepped outside. My heart raced, palms slick with anxiety. Why the hell did Serenity bring her here? I wanted to call Omar. I wanted to run. Escape.

But I remembered what I told him—I wanted to change. I wanted to be better.

So I stepped back inside. Sat down next to Jasmine. Serenity quietly exited the room.

And before my brain could catch up with my mouth, I started apologizing.

"I'm so sorry for what I did to you."

Jasmine's smile was plastic.

"Girl, I'm over that. We grown now. Leave that shit in the past. What were you, like ten?"

"Twelve," I replied flatly. "You don't know how many times I tried to find you. It's like you vanished into thin air."

Jasmine's jaw tightened.

"Oh, I didn't vanish," she said bitterly. "I just ended up in foster care."

"Foster care?" I repeated, the guilt crawling up my throat like bile.

"Yeah. Nettie overdosed that summer. That selfish bitch could never leave those pills alone."

She said it like it was a line from a movie, like she hadn't just dropped a bomb on my chest.

"Ms. Nettie... died?" I gasped.

My brain spun. No one told me. But then again... I never asked. I didn't want to face what I'd done. Didn't want to look into the aftermath I left behind.

And now... here it was. Right in front of me. Waiting to be reckoned with.

"I'm sorry that happened to you." My voice was low, thick with remorse.

Was I the cost of all this?

"Girl, that bitch had it coming'," Jasmine replied, her voice cold, distant.

"And with me? Shit, it was bound to happen sooner or later. I told you how fucked up my life was."

I could vaguely remember. Back then, her stories sounded like adventure—sneaking drinks, partying, sex she didn't truthfully want but said she did. At twelve, that didn't sound so bad to me. Not through the lens of my childhood turmoil.

But now, as a woman?

That shit sounded like hell.

"Yeah... I remember," I said quietly, trying to hold space for her pain.

And Jasmine fell into conversation like no time had passed at all. We talked about everything. Laughed until I was clutching my stomach, tears rolling down my cheeks. We swapped wild stories, ones we probably should've never lived through—but did anyway. Some of them were funny. Some were tragic. All of them were ours.

Eventually, it was time for her to leave.

She stood up slowly, hesitation displaying in her body language, like she wasn't sure she wanted to go.

"Listen," she started, smoothing her shirt.

"I'm only in Philly for a little bit—just visiting Kiki and Kevin. I'm leaving soon, but I got an Airbnb for the weekend, and I'm throwing a little get-together..."

She paused. Something flickered in her expression—something deeper than casual.

"And I want you to come," she finished, almost shyly.

I smiled. Not just because of the invite, but because she was willing to let bygones be bygones. She wasn't holding it over my head. And if she could let it go, maybe I could too.

"I'll be there," I told her, meaning it.

For the first time in what felt like forever, life was falling into place.

* * *

Still, the situation with Jasmine had thrown me off completely. I was supposed to drop off my luggage and meet Karina for brunch—clear my head, reconnect, remind myself that healing wasn't just an idea, it was a choice.

We'd promised to work on rebuilding our sisterhood. I had every intention of honoring that. But my heart still felt tangled in the mess of the morning. Seeing Jasmine forced me to confront my past. That wasn't a part of the plan. Not something I wanted to do. And now it followed me around like a dark cloud.

When I arrived at the restaurant, Karina was already there, waving like a little kid who'd just seen her favorite cousin. Her energy was bright, unfiltered, and light. I needed that right now more than ever.

"Girl, what took you so long? I almost started drinking your mimosa," she teased, her grin stretching wide.

I hadn't seen Karina smile like that in a long time. It looked good on her. Like something had finally settled inside of her. Maybe confessions truly were good for the soul.

I slid into the seat across from her, my heart still heavy.

"I don't even know how to tell you this shit, 'cause it sounds crazy even coming out my mouth. When I got home, guess who was sitting on my couch?"

Karina squinted like she was trying to read between the lines.

"Hmm... was it Darren?"

"Hell no, girl. I cut that nigga off," I said with a laugh that barely masked my nerves.

"Bitch, then who?" she asked, her curiosity growing with every passing second.

"Sis—it was Jasmine."

Karina's whole face changed. Her jaw dropped like I'd slapped her across the mouth.

"I know the fuck you lying. Jasmine? Your stepdad's niece Jasmine?" Her voice was sharp with disbelief.

I missed this. Brunch with Karina always turned into the messiest conversations. Only now, the drama wasn't gossip—it was my real life unraveling.

"Yes, bitch. I damn near ran for my life," I admitted, half-laughing, half-shaking.

"What the fuck did she want?" Karina asked, her eyes narrowing with suspicion so thick I could feel it pressing against my chest.

"To invite me to a get-together."

Karina froze, blinking like she couldn't process the words. Then she leaned in.

"Oh hell nah. Bitch, you ain't going. That's that scary movie shit. After what you did, and she just popped up, all peace and good vibes? This bitch tryna kill you, Journee."

I laughed harder than I meant to—maybe out of shock, maybe out of disbelief. Karina was dramatic, but not always wrong. Still, part of me wanted to believe Jasmine had come to make peace. I needed to believe that. Because if she could forgive me, maybe I could finally forgive myself.

"Rina, that shit happened when I was twelve. Do you hear me? Twelve. She probably let that stuff go," I said, trying to convince her, trying to convince me.

Karina wasn't letting it go.

"Do you really think she just forgave you out of the blue after all these years?"

Her words hit like a slow blade. Shame crept up my throat like smoke, bitter and choking.

"Didn't I forgive you?" I snapped, the words escaping before I could catch them.

Karina flinched, her eyes darkening with pain. I hated the silence that followed, heavy and loud all at once.

THE POT OR THE KETTLE

"I didn't mean that," I said quickly, heart sinking.

"I'm sorry. That had more to do with my personal shit than it had to do with us. I forgive you, Karina. Honestly. You're my day one."

She sat up straighter, composed herself.

"Nah, you right. It's just the pot calling the kettle black," she muttered, voice low.

"You might not see it for what it is, but I don't trust that bitch. But if you insist on going, I'm coming with you."

I nodded, grateful for her protectiveness even when it came dressed as paranoia. She was right—I couldn't walk into this alone.

Not again.

* * *

Karina

I sat there at brunch, mad as hell that Journee wouldn't listen to me.

Yeah, I had betrayed her trust recently—but all the other times I didn't came flooding back. I'd been her rider. When bitches came around ready to mix, I always swung with my bitch with no hesitation.

But look at us now.

My mind flipped back and forth as I sipped my drink, watching Journee try to hold it all together like she wasn't breaking apart inside.

"What day is the get-together?" I asked, sarcasm dripping from my tongue.

Journee shook her head, her voice tight. "It's this Friday."

I could see the war in her eyes—loyalty clashing with fear. Journee had never been confrontational, but I guess our fallout had changed her. Hardened her.

"I'm not saying you're right, Rina. I hope to God you're wrong," she said, locking eyes with me. "But if you aren't, and this bitch is on some weird shit..." she paused, her voice steady, "...I'm not running."

We held each other's gaze. So much unspoken pain sat between us—some caused by our own hands, some by all the shit life threw at us that we never talked about.

"I got you," I said, and I meant every damn word.

Her face softened, her eyes shining with something I hadn't seen in a long time—relief. Trust. Love. It filled something hollow in me I didn't even know was empty.

The rest of the brunch was easier. We laughed, swapped updates, and avoided the heavy. I missed this. I missed her. Before the world crept in and poisoned everything, this was how it used to be.

When we finished, we hugged tightly and went our separate ways. I headed back to North Philly, where my family and I had moved last year.

My phone buzzed.

Khalil.

My heart skipped.

"Hey, Daddy," I answered, sweetness coating my voice.

"Wassup, sexy. Where you at right now?" he asked, his voice smooth but stern.

I smiled, but something about his tone made me pause.

"Just leaving brunch with Journee," I said, unsure now.

We'd moved past that weird tension after the hotel fight. I didn't think it would be that easy, but with Khalil, it was. We locked in quick. Real quick.

"Where at?" he asked again, firmer this time.

"The Pink Olive. Why?"

Now I was catching an attitude. What the hell was with the third degree? He'd never been on this type time before. If he was turning into the jealous boyfriend type, I wasn't with it. I had way too much going for me to be caught up in that.

"Aight, bet. Stay there. I'm less than ten minutes away."

He hung up before I could respond.

My stomach flipped. Did he just flip the switch on me? Was this who he really was? I didn't know, but a part of me needed to see it through.

Ten minutes later, a car pulled up close as hell, making me jump. The window rolled down—

"Damn ma, you bad as shit," Khalil grinned from the driver's seat.

Fear melted into excitement. I ran to the passenger side as he jumped out to greet me.

"Oh my God, is this yours?" I asked, eyeing the fresh wheels.

"Yeah, baby. This all me," he said, arms wrapping around my waist.

I melted into him. He smelled so damn good, and he was fine—finer than anyone I'd ever dealt with. I wanted to be alone with him, feel that energy again.

"I been missing your pretty ass all day," he murmured against my neck.

I felt him stiffen against me. Yeah, we were on the same type time. I loved that about us.

"I missed you, too." I sang back, happy to be wrapped in his embrace.

"Come on, let's go," he said, opening the door for me like a gentleman.

I blushed. He was spoiling me, and I was loving every second of it.

"Where you headed?" Khalil asked as I buckled in.

"Back home," I muttered, trying to keep my voice light.

The truth was—I didn't wanna go home. My Momma had been tripping. Ever since I turned eighteen, she stayed on my ass about everything. Any small situation could trigger a conversation about when I was moving out.

Like I asked to be born into her mess. The woman was a weirdo, straight up.

"Aight, bet," he said, pulling off.

When we got to my house, Khalil insisted on coming in. I should've said no. I should've warned him. But I couldn't. I didn't want to. Not yet.

Before I even stepped on the porch, I heard it. Screaming. Shit breaking.

I froze.

I wanted to run, head back to Journee's like I used to. But Khalil was there, and he stepped in front of me.

"What the fuck going on in there?" he asked, walking up the steps like he was ready for war.

The door flung open.

My mom's drunk-ass boyfriend stumbled out, reeking of liquor.

"Nigga, who the fuck is you?" he slurred, glaring at Khalil.

Khalil didn't flinch. "Better keep that shit pushing, old head," he said coldly.

I was mortified. This was not how I wanted him to see my life. My chaos.

The man stumbled past us and down the block.

"I'm sorry about that," I whispered, my face burning.

"Man, don't even worry 'bout it. Old head was on some weird shit," he said, brushing it off.

I stepped inside first. The place was a mess. Trash everywhere. Momma was slumped on the couch, leg twitching as she faced a blunt like it was her last breath.

"Oh shit, who this fine motherfucka?" she slurred, eyes barely focusing on Khalil.

I walked straight past her, straight to my room. I didn't want to see the look on his face. I didn't want to see his pity.

"Bitch, I know the fuck you hear me!" she screamed, and something shattered behind me.

I didn't even flinch.

I just shut the door.

Inside my room—the only neat part of the house—I locked the door behind us and let out a heavy breath as I sank onto my bed.

Khalil stood there, quiet.

Too quiet.

His face was unreadable. No smirk, no raised brow, no slick comment—just silence. My heart pounded. Was he mad? Disappointed? Turned off by all the chaos he'd just walked into?

The worry settled deep in my stomach, coiling like a knot I couldn't untangle.

I wanted to ask him what he was thinking, but I was too scared of the answer.

Too scared to break whatever this was before it even got started.

* * *

Khalil

I sat there in Karina's room for the first time, gathering my thoughts.

It looked exactly how I thought it would—pink everywhere, soft, delicate. She was definitely the girly type. The shit was cute, though. Made sense for her.

Walking into Karina's crib, seeing the chaos, hearing her mom wild out like that—it didn't bother me. Not one bit. I was used to that kind of dysfunction. It ran through my own family like blood in our veins.

My mom was a crackhead. Dropped me off at my grandparents' house when I was a baby and never looked back. I was raised by my grandmother, my mother's mother. I'd see my mom now and then, but never sober. She was always floating in and out like a ghost in real life.

That look on Karina's face? I knew it too well.

Shame. Embarrassment. Fear.

And a big part of me wanted to make it all disappear the way I knew how— get her naked, pull my dick out, eat her pussy until she moaned so loud she forgot her own name. That's what I usually did. That was how I made girls feel better.

But I chilled.

Damn. Omar really was rubbing off on me.

Instead, I sat beside her, hand resting gently on her thigh.

"What's on your mind?" I asked.

She looked so fucking edible. Those full lips pouting, her sharp, pretty eyes glistening under the soft light. My dick got hard instantly, just being close to her—but I fought it. I wasn't gonna make the same mistake. Not with her. Karina was different. She was my peace.

"I'm just sorry you had to see all that shit," she muttered. "My Momma always acts like that."

"Baby, I'm off that. I don't give a fuck about none of that," I said, brushing a thumb across her leg.

"I done seen worse. That ain't phasing me."

She smiled at me, eyes softening as they roamed over me. She knew what she was doing.

I couldn't help myself. I leaned in and kissed her, deep and rough, my hand gripping her throat, gently but firm, pushing her back on the bed. She loved that kinky shit. But just when it started to heat up, I stopped myself.

I had to stay grounded. I had something more important on my mind.

"What's wrong?" Karina asked, sitting up with concern in her voice.

"Nothing," I said, catching my breath. "I just wanna talk."

"About what?" she shot back, her defenses rising quickly.

I could see her walls going up, and I softened my tone.

"Rina, it's not like that. I just wanna understand. How long has it been like this with you and your moms?"

She sighed, that deep, tired kind of sigh.

"She has always been like that. The only time she switches up is when my aunties come around."

"And your dad?" I asked, my voice gentle but steady.

Her eyes hesitated before she answered.

"I don't even know who that nigga is."

I nodded slowly. "Me either."

She turned toward me, shocked.

"I was raised by my grandparents," I admitted. "Don't know where my mom is, don't know shit about my dad. Just got through life with the people who decided not to leave."

Karina stared at me, eyes locked like she was searching for something deeper than my words. It made me nervous, how quiet she got.

"I'm just keeping it real with you," I told her. "So you know—none of this shit changes how I feel about you. You're my girl."

"Khalil," she whispered, voice full of emotion, "you one of the realest niggas I ever met."

She leaned in, lips finding mine again. Her hands moved to my jeans, reaching for my dick, but I gently swatted her hand away.

"Not yet," I murmured, pushing her back onto the bed.

I had something on my mind from the moment I picked her up from brunch, and now was the time.

I lifted her dress, slid her panties down slowly, savoring every second. Then I dropped to my knees and went to work with my tongue.

I wanted her to feel how much I cared. I needed her to know—without saying another word—just how much she meant to me.

So I showed her the best way I knew how.

Karina lay breathless beneath me, her chest rising and falling, a dazed smile tugging at the corners of her lips. Her fingers tangled in my curls, gently pulling me up toward her. I kissed her slow, deep—our breaths syncing like we'd done this dance a hundred times before.

"That felt like love," she whispered against my lips, her voice barely audible, trembling with something raw.

I looked her dead in her eyes.

"That was love, Rina."

She closed her eyes for a second, like she didn't know whether to believe it or protect herself from it. I recognized that hesitation. That fear of something good not lasting.

I pulled her into my arms, letting her rest her head on my chest. For a while, we just laid there. No words. No drama. Just silence, wrapped in the warmth of something real.

Then her phone buzzed.

She didn't move. I felt her tense up.

"Who is it?" I asked softly.

"Journee," she murmured.

"Probably checking on me."

"You wanna answer it?"

She shook her head against my chest. "Not right now. I just wanna stay here."

I held her tighter. "Then that's what we gon' do."

A knock echoed on the door.

Both of us flinched.

"Karina! Open this damn door!" her mother's voice slurred, angry and ragged.

Karina sat up quickly, fear flashing across her face. I could see her going into survival mode—her body stiff, her breathing shallow.

"Nah, she's not about to do this again," I said, getting out of bed and pulling on my shirt.

I unlocked the door and cracked it open.

Her mom swayed in the hallway, eyes bloodshot, leaning against the wall for balance.

"Who the fuck said you could come in here disrespecting my house?"

"With all due respect, you were disrespecting your daughter," I said calmly, my voice low but firm.

She stepped forward like she was about to say something slick, but I shut the door in her face before she could. Locked it tight.

Karina looked at me, mouth open. "Khalil..."

"Nah. You don't deserve that," I said. "She doesn't get to treat you like that. Not while I'm here."

Tears welled in her eyes, but she blinked them back.

"I'm getting out of here," she whispered. "I don't know how or when. But I can't stay here much longer."

I stepped closer, cupping her chin in my hand. "You won't have to. Whatever we gotta do, we'll do it. I got you."

She nodded slowly. "You sure?"

"I'm sure."

And I meant that. I felt it, I wanted more than just a fuck. I wanted a future with her in it.

* * *

Her Beauty and His Beast

(A dangerous love story)

For once,
   She felt as if she belonged.
   From place to place—
   Always houses, never homes.

Her mother?
   Who? She barely knew.
   Her father?
   Long and gone.
   No true connection,
   But Grandma's blessing.
   From her, she learned the difference
   between right and wrong.

From place to place,
   He bounced.
   His pain?
   He never announced.
   Outside, he held his ground.
   If only his grandmother could see him now.

Gun in hand,
   Zero plan,
   He walked without a beat.
   Fatal attraction

From a simple transaction—
The two had come to meet.

His home lay in the streets,
   Hers within the sheets.
   Together,
   They became a duo:
   Her Beauty and His Beast.

16

I Won't Run

The Next Day...

I waited anxiously for Omar to pull up. I was ready to sink back into our little bubble and savor it for as long as possible.

When he arrived, his truck looked freshly detailed, gleaming under the afternoon sun. He hopped out and opened my door like a gentleman, and my heart flipped—like I hadn't seen him in ages.

"I missed you so much," I blurted the moment I walked up to him.

Instead of getting in right away, I wrapped my arms around him and held him tight. I needed that. Needed him. Especially after everything that had unfolded—everything I still hadn't said out loud.

"I missed you, too," he said, his voice low, filled with something deep and sincere.

I pulled back and slid into the passenger seat, but I could already tell—he knew something was up. He didn't say a word. Just placed his hand on my thigh as we drove, his eyes locked on the road, the silence stretching between us like a slow-building storm.

Then, without warning, he pulled over and parked. No words. No warning. Just silence and tension.

"What's going on?" he asked finally, turning to me. His eyes were sharp with concern, their seriousness making my throat tighten.

"Nothing," I lied, trying to keep my voice even.

"We're not going anywhere until you talk to me," he said, pulling the key from the ignition and slipping it into his pocket.

I wasn't ready. Not to talk about Jasmine. Not to explain another layer of my past that might shift how he saw me. But the look on his face told me I couldn't run from this—not from him. He saw right through me, past my smile, past the front I was putting up.

* * *

Omar

I sat there, waiting for Journee to explain why she was putting up this front with me.

She knew me—knew she could trust me, lean on me. So why lie?

Something was wrong. I saw it in her eyes, felt it in the way she clung to me earlier, like she was afraid to let go. My gut told me—she wasn't okay.

"Look, Omar, I'm sorry I lied," she finally said, her voice cracking. "It's just… yesterday, some crazy shit happened."

My heart tightened. I softened my tone, not wanting to push her but needing to understand.

"What happened?"

She hesitated, and the silence between us grew thick. I didn't want her to feel forced—whatever it was, I wanted her to share it because she trusted me. Because she knew I'd carry it with her.

"My ex-stepfather's niece… she was at my house yesterday. After you dropped me off. I walked in and—she was just sitting there."

I studied her face, her posture, her energy. There had to be more. Way more than just some uninvited relative showing up.

"Did she hurt you?" I asked, my eyes scanning her body, searching for any sign of pain she hadn't spoken out loud.

"No," she whispered, barely audible.

I leaned in, gently taking her chin between my fingers so she had to look at me. Her eyes were glossy, full of the weight she hadn't let drop yet.

"Journee," I said, my voice tender but steady, "please don't shut me out."

"I wanna tell you," Journee whispered, her voice trembling. "But I'm so fucking afraid."

Then the tears came—deep, uncontrollable sobs I hadn't seen from her since that night at the hotel. I leaned in closer, my chest tightening even more.

"You can tell me anything," I said gently. "Nothing will change how I feel about you, I promise."

I wiped her tears, my thumb brushing her cheek as softly as I could.

She inhaled sharply, trying to steady herself.

"When I was twelve... I did something bad. So bad, it messed up my life, her life... everybody's life."

She rocked slightly, staring at the floor, hands clenched in her lap. I didn't say a word.

"I didn't know what my stepfather was doing was wrong. I thought rape meant screaming and bruises. I didn't know it could be quiet. Subtle. I didn't know it could hide in plain sight. I told Jasmine some of what happened. I ain't even mean to, before I could even understand what I was saying, it came out. Not everything—not that he raped me. Just... the touching."

Her voice cracked again, and another wave of sobs hit.

"It's okay," I said softly, rubbing her back. "I'm here. I got you."

She pushed forward, like she needed the words out of her before they destroyed her.

"She taught me what he did was wrong. She explained to me what rape looked like, what molestation was. She helped me understand things no one else ever took the time to ever explain. And you know how I repaid her?"

She looked at me with eyes full of shame.

"I fucking lied. I lied on her. Got her sent to foster care. And all she was just trying to do was fucking help me."

I pulled her into my chest.
"I ain't never told nobody what he did to me but you. I ain't never said it out loud," she cried into my chest.

My arms wrapped tighter around her, steadying the storm inside her.

"None of this... not any of it is your fault," I whispered, my voice steady even though my heart broke for her.

I felt the tension in her shoulders ease, her sobs slowing like the calm after a hurricane. Her breathing leveled out as her weight sank into me, safe at last.

"Thank you," she said softly—just that.
   But it held the weight of everything she'd been carrying.

As we left the parking lot behind, the silence between us wasn't uncomfortable, but it was heavy with unspoken words. I could feel the weight of everything she'd shared, and I wanted nothing more than to help her forget the pain, even if just for tonight.

I kept my hand on hers as we drove, the road ahead lit by streetlights that flickered like distant stars.
Journee leaned back in her seat, but her body was still tense, but somehow softer, like she was on the fence of releasing and bracing herself for something at the same time.
I knew better than to think that her opening up about it was enough— She knew better than to think I didn't notice the pain that still clung to her below the surface. But I wasn't pushing. Not tonight, she had been through

enough.

"How are you feeling now?" I asked, my voice low, just enough for her to hear.

She glanced over at me, her eyes soft, red, tired.

"Better," she whispered, the faintest smile tugging at her lips.

"It's just nice to be here. To not think about anything else for a while."

"You don't have to think about anything else tonight. Just focus on you. Just focus on me," I said, my voice firm but gentle, the promise in it clear. I would protect her. No matter what it took.

The silence between us softened as we crossed the bridge into Camden, the Philadelphia skyline dimming in the distance. We were close now. The Adventure Aquarium was just up ahead, and I could already feel the shift in the air. It was the perfect surprise.
The moment she stepped out of that car, I wanted her to feel something other than the crushing weight she carried on her shoulders. I wanted her to feel safe. I wanted her to feel free.

When I parked the car in front of the aquarium, I could already see her eyes light up. There was something about water that always seemed to calm her, to give her the peace I knew she deserved but had never really known.

I got out of the car first, walked around to her side, and opened the door for her. She took my hand quickly, allowing me to help her out. I could feel the unspoken trust between us.

"Let's take our time, okay?" I said softly, my eyes meeting hers to provide reassurance. "We'll leave everything else behind here. This is for us."

She nodded, a quiet "Okay" leaving her lips.

We walked together through the entrance, and I kept my hand securely around her waist. She didn't pull away. She didn't flinch. She was allowing me to see her willingness to remain open, and that was something I would never take for granted.

The air inside was cool, salty, a refreshing reminder that we weren't alone in this world—we were together.

As we moved through the exhibits, I watched her eyes change. The tension in her shoulders started to release. The wonder in her gaze as she watched the sea turtles glide gracefully through the water reminded me of everything I loved about her: her quiet strength, her beauty, the way she could look at something simple and see it for what it truly was. I wanted to hold onto this moment forever.

I moved closer to her, our shoulders brushing lightly, letting her feel the constant presence of me by her side. I wasn't going to let her go. I wasn't going to let anyone else hurt her.

"Look at that," she whispered, pointing to a school of fish darting through the water. "They move together. Like they know where they're going."

"They're strong together," I replied, my hand sliding around her waist, pulling her in a little closer. "And so are we. We'll figure this out, piece by piece. But right now, you don't need to carry anything but this moment."

She looked up at me, eyes filled with a softness that almost shattered my heart. "I don't know what I'd do without you," she said, her voice low but full of emotion.

"You'll never have to find out," I said, my voice firm. "I'm right here. And

I'm not going anywhere."

We continued to walk through the aquarium, the quiet hum of the water, the gentle swish of fish, creating a peaceful rhythm that made everything feel just a little bit better. We moved from exhibit to exhibit, but I was always aware of her, always keeping her close, always making sure that I was the one who was holding her together. I didn't care about anything else right in that moment.

When we reached the massive tank filled with jellyfish, the light in the room dimmed just enough for them to glow, their translucent bodies drifting lazily through the water. It was beautiful, almost magical, and I could see the calm settle into her face.

"This is my favorite," she whispered, her hand resting in mine, the touch gentle but sure.

I nodded, watching the jellyfish as they floated effortlessly, their bodies glowing in the soft light.

"They're peaceful," I said, squeezing her hand. "Like you. You deserve to feel this peace. No more fear. No more worry."

She leaned into me, her head resting on my shoulder, and I wrapped my arm around her, pulling her in even closer.

"I'll make sure you always feel safe," I promised. "I'll protect you, Journee. Always."

And for the first time that day, she let out a deep breath, a sigh of relief. Her body softened against mine, and in that instant, I knew that she believed me.

We didn't need to say anything else. The quiet was enough. As we stood there, watching the jellyfish glide effortlessly through the water, I knew one thing for sure: no matter what she had been through, no matter the darkness that tried to pull her down, I would always be there.

All intentions were pure, Journee will always be safe. She will be protected. With me. For as long as I had breath left in my body.

* * *

Journee

It felt so good to see Omar again. Every time we were together, he peeled back another layer of dead weight I didn't even know I needed to shed. Just being in his presence grounded me, reminded me of the softness I still had left.

As we stepped out of the aquarium, my heart felt lighter. I had told him another one of my darkest secrets—and even though the forgiveness hadn't come from Jasmine's lips herself, his understanding and care made that pain vanish from a place deep inside me. He didn't look at me differently. If anything, he held me closer.

"Shit, there's something I forgot to tell you," I blurted out as we reached the car.

"What is it?" he asked calmly, slipping into the driver's seat. Omar never lost his cool.

"We're supposed to be meeting Karina and Khalil for dinner," I explained, buckling myself in.

"It's still early. We're only twenty minutes away," he said, his tone smooth as ever. "Play some music, relax, turn your brain off. I told you—tonight is about you."

The double date with Karina and Khalil was something I was actually looking forward to. I had to admit, Omar was right—Karina and Khalil were way more compatible than Khalil and I had ever been. Honestly, I don't even think we were compatible at all. People just assumed we were because we looked good together. That was never enough.

I smiled to myself, silently grateful I had taken the risk and ended up sitting here, next to Omar instead. I bet Karina felt the same way about Khalil.

I must've been grinning a little too hard because Omar interrupted my thoughts with a smirk.

"I better be the reason you over there blushing," he teased, eyes locked on the road but hand sliding over to grip my thigh.

I shivered at his touch and, without even thinking, I spread my legs slightly in invitation. His hand wandered further, fingers pressing firmly against my hot spot.

"This is all mine," he growled, voice low and possessive.

"All yours," I breathed, my brain too clouded to form a full thought.

He smirked and moved his hand away just as quickly, leaving me aching.

Why did he do this to me? He knew exactly how to push every single button... then he'd just stop. Like he enjoyed watching me squirm.

"I got you later," he said with that same smug grin as we pulled up in front of the bar.

And I believed him. Every word.
We walked into the spot, a little hole-in-the-wall bar and grill off South Street, where the wings were always fire and the drinks hit harder than they should for happy hour.

Karina and Khalil were already there, posted up in a booth in the back. Khalil had his arm around her shoulder, but they were in deep conversation— well, more like a silent roast battle by the way Karina was cheesing and side-eyeing him at the same time.

As soon as she saw me, Karina's whole face lit up.

"Ayyye bitch, y'all finally made it! We was 'bout to order without y'all slow asses."

"Girl, relax," I laughed, sliding in beside her. "We had to take a little detour. You know... romantic shit."

Omar just nodded, cool as ever.

"Had to show my girl a good time first."

Khalil squinted at him.

"Oh yeah? Looks like she's walking just fine to me, bro. You sure you did your job?"

"Boy, shut up," Karina smacked his chest. "You always tryna start something."

"I mean…" Khalil shrugged. "I'm just saying—if it was me, my bitch would need help sittin' down."

"Wow." I rolled my eyes, sipping the drink I hadn't even ordered yet. "Y'all still on that demon time, huh?"

Karina smirked. "That's his love language. Ignorance."

"And yours is violence," Khalil said, rubbing his arm dramatically. "You my mans bro, She be fightin' me in her sleep, I swear."

Omar chuckled low, wrapping his arm around me. "Y'all toxic for real."

"Nah, we just spicy," Karina corrected, snapping her fingers. "There's a difference."

The waiter came over and we ordered way too much food. Khalil had to be extra and asked for "every flavor of wings y'all got—on one plate."

"Sir, that's not on the menu."

"It is now."

Karina was already on her second drink, telling stories about how Khalil almost burnt his grandmother's kitchen down trying to fry fish with no flour.

"This nigga put the fish in the grease frozen. Had the pot sounding like it was fighting for its life."

"You tryna embarrass me or tell the story right?" Khalil laughed, "I was making some official shit. Y'all ain't ready for the new methods."

"Nigga, ain't nobody tryna eat your experiments," I said, choking on my laughter.

Omar leaned in, whispering in my ear, "You needed this."

And he was right. This was the last test to past that showed that out toxic situation fizzled out and no bonds were broken. I was surrounded by people who were loving out loud, laughed hard, and weren't afraid to be soft in the right moments. Sitting between Karina's wild jokes and Omar's steady warmth, I finally felt safe.

And in Philly? That's a rare kind of luxury. For people to lock back in after, shit had hit the fan. I was glad I didn't run from it.

After dinner, we all stood outside the restaurant, full as hell and laughing like we hadn't just smashed wings, sliders, and two orders of crab fries.

"I ain't gonna hold y'all," Khalil said, rubbing his stomach. "I need a nap or a new stomach, no bullshit."

"You need a job in a kitchen," Karina clowned. "That way, you can finally learn the difference between sauté and set it on fire."

He rolled his eyes, pulling her into a side hug. "You lucky I fuck with you."

"Nigga you know what it is," she smirked.

I watched them bicker and banter while Omar stood behind me, arms around my waist, chin resting on my shoulder. The smell of his cologne meshed in with mine, and I swear the city noise around us faded when he was close like this.

"You ready to head out?" he whispered, lips brushing my ear.

I nodded. "I'm ready."

We said our goodbyes, exchanged hugs, and promised a brunch that we all knew might take a month to plan.

Once we got in Omar's truck and pulled off, the city lights danced against the windshield. He reached over, lacing his fingers through mine on the center console.

"I meant what I said earlier," he said, eyes still on the road.

"About what?"

"Tonight is about you. I just wanted you to smile. Laugh a little. Feel all the shit disappear."

"I did." I glanced at him. "You made that happen."

He looked over briefly, then smirked. "Good. 'Cause I'm not done with you yet."

My brows lifted. "Oh?"

He didn't say anything, just turned the volume up on the playlist he made just for me—slow, sexy vibe, and full of songs that made you feel like love wasn't scary.

By the time we hit the bridge back to Omar's spot, I found myself resting my head against the window, his hand still in mine. I didn't say it out loud, but I didn't have to.

This was what I always wanted.

* * *

We arrived back at Omar's spot, and I could barely hide my excitement. There was something about being there—about being his—that made my skin hum with anticipation.

Walking upstairs to his room, I eased onto his bed, the same bed where he had once taken me to places I didn't even know existed. My mind wandered there now, temptation dancing in my head, licking at my thoughts like flames on dry wood.

He stood across from me, rolling up a blunt, and every motion he made only turned me on more. The way his fingers moved. The flick of his tongue when he sealed the wood. That smirk he shot me when he caught me staring too long.

My body reacted before I could even speak. My thighs pressed together, trying to quiet the throbbing need between them.

"You said you weren't done with me yet," I said, voice low, laced with desire.

He paused, placing the blunt to the side.

"You're so impatient," he said, that deep voice of his sending chills down my spine.

Then he walked over, slow and intentional, standing over me like a king who knew exactly what he was about to do to his queen. His eyes, dark and full of hunger, locked onto mine.

He unbuckled his pants, never breaking that gaze. My heart beat so loud I could hear it in my ears. I had seen what was underneath before, but something about this moment made it feel brand new.

"You want it?" he asked, voice heavy with power and promise.

I swallowed, heat surging through me.

"Yes."

He kicked off his pants, watching my every move with that same crooked grin that drove me crazy. He knew I was captivated.

He knew I was his.

He leaned down, his breath brushing my cheek, warm and teasing. His fingers hooked under my chin, tilting my head up so I had no choice but to look at him.

"Nah, say it like you mean it," he whispered, voice thick with desire.

"Tell me how bad you want it."

My lips parted, but the words caught in my throat. My body was already speaking for me—arching up, reaching for him, aching in places only he could soothe.

"I want you, Omar," I finally breathed. "So bad it hurts."

That was all it took.

His mouth crashed into mine, devouring my words. His hands roamed my body like he was retracing a map he'd already memorized, pulling my shirt up and tossing it to the floor like it offended him.

"Lay back," he commanded softly, his tone sending shivers down my spine.

I obeyed, trembling under his gaze.

He slid my pants down slowly, taking in every inch of skin like it was his first time seeing me. Then his lips followed—kisses down my stomach, the inside of my thighs—until I was squirming, whispering his name like a prayer.

He took his time.

Licked me slow.

Savored me like I was the sweetest thing he'd ever tasted.

And when I came undone, he didn't stop. He held me still, tongue and fingers working in perfect rhythm until I was gasping, grabbing the sheets, and trying to remember how to breathe.

Only then did he rise, hovering above me, eyes wild but tender. "I told you I got you."

He slid into me slow, deep, filling every part of me like he belonged there. Like my body was designed to accept his. Only his.

Our bodies moved together like they'd been created just for each other. Every thrust was deliberate, every kiss grounding. He didn't rush, didn't hold back either. He let me feel all of him—his love, his hunger, his protection.

Then there it was again his finger circling my clit, making me climb the wall as he stuffed me to completion.

"Don't run from me." He commanded.

My body continued to shudder.

"Oh Fuck, Omar I can't take it," I screamed involuntarily.

My thighs soaked with my own cum.

"You can do it, I know you can."

My body tensed, another orgasm.

"That's my girl."

I tensed again, flooding his stomach and manhood. I felt it twitch and swell inside of me.

"I'm so proud of you." He growled.

His body stiffened as I continued to fuck him back trying my hardest to match his intensity.

Then it happened, I felt the warm gush I've learned to crave fill my tummy.

We collapsed into each other, breathless and tangled in the sheets, satisfied.

Not just in his arms—but in the truth we shared, the secrets he held without judgment, and the love that was starting to feel more real than anything I'd ever known.

17

My Hell or Yo Hell Nigga?

I sat down in my room, doing my makeup as I stared at my reflection in the mirror. My heart thudded louder with each stroke of my brush. Was I truly ready to do this? To see Jasmine, Kiki, and Kevin in one space—after I caused their separation? No telling how they would react to me, especially since they were so young when it happened. What if they had no positive memories because of me?

That thought made my chest tighten. My stomach hadn't stopped turning since I got the confirmation text from Jasmine. Tonight was the night. No more running. No more hiding behind the mess I made.

Despite the nervousness digging at my insides, despite the intense, sinking feeling in the pit of my gut, it was time to look my past dead in the face, confront it, and close that door behind me forever.

My mind drifted as I brushed some powder across my cheeks, and that's when Faith walked into the room.

"I must've missed something, 'cause why Karina down there chillin' on our couch?" she asked, hand firmly planted on her hip like she was ready to interrogate somebody.

Faith was home again for one of her quick visits and couldn't wrap her head around the fact that Karina and I were still friends. Not after everything that went down between us. I wanted to explain, really, but there wasn't time—and truth be told, I didn't have the emotional energy to unpack all of that.

My mind was already spinning from everything else.

"Girl, we got over that shit," I replied flatly, eyes still glued to the mirror.

"I'll tell you all about it when I get back home tonight."

"Aight, you better tell me," she teased, her voice light, but I could feel her curiosity heavy as she walked out, music already blasting in her headphones again.

I stood up and gave myself one last look in the mirror.

I kept it simple tonight—cute lounge set, sneakers, my hair pulled back in a claw clip. I wasn't trying to impress anybody. This wasn't a fashion show—it was a confrontation.

I headed downstairs, my nerves crawling beneath my skin, but I moved with purpose. At least I had Karina by my side.

"How far is the Uber?" I asked, trying to keep my voice steady as she sat on the couch scrolling through her phone.

"Girl, is you crazy? I ain't riding in no Uber to some random ass BNB," she muttered without even looking up.

"Khalil takin' us."

I froze. My stomach dropped even lower.

"If I ain't want Omar there, why the fuck would I want Khalil?" I asked, my face scrunching with irritation.

"Because I ain't you. I ain't walkin' into nobody crib I crossed without some kind of protection."

I sighed and shrugged. As much as I didn't like it, she had a point.

We walked outside, the night air hitting my skin like a warning. We got into Khalil's new car and drove off toward the address Jasmine had sent me.

The closer we got, the more off everything felt. When we pulled up, my breath caught in my throat.

Men were posted up all over the steps, staring hard like they were guarding something—or—someone.

This did not look like a small get-together.

Khalil peeped it instantly. I saw his whole demeanor shift. He reached for his strap, his voice dropping low.

"I don't know about this shit," he said, eyes locked on the scene ahead.

He didn't even pull up all the way, just sat there scoping the spot from a distance.

"This shit don't even look right."

"Maybe it's the wrong address," I said, clinging to optimism like it could protect me.

"Ain't no fuckin' wrong address. I'm tellin' you, Journee—that bitch is on some weird shit," Karina snapped, her voice laced with suspicion and heat.

That was it for me. I needed answers.

I opened the door and stepped out of the car, nerves on fire. I dialed Jasmine's number as I walked up the street, my hand trembling slightly. Karina followed close behind, her eyes scanning everything around us like she was expecting something to jump off.

I glanced back just as Khalil pulled up to the corner and parked, watching us, his eyes sharp, body tense.

Something about this night felt wrong. And yet, I kept walking.

Jasmine picked up after the third ring.

"Hey, girl, where you at?" she asked, music blaring so loud I could barely hear her voice.

"I'm outside," I replied, trying to hide the nerves twisting my stomach into knots.

"Aight, here I come," she said quickly—and hung up before I could say another word.

Karina caught up and stood beside me, her body tense, eyes cutting sideways at the men still standing on the steps like they were security at a club nobody asked for.

"What that bitch say?" she asked, inching closer.

Before I could answer, Jasmine walked out—drink in hand, smiling like this was just another chill night. A few of the men moved aside and went inside, but the rest stayed posted like they were watching for something.

"Bitch, you ain't tell me this was a house party," I said, my voice edged with irritation, though I tried to keep it playful.

"Girl, I said a get-together," she replied, a smirk playing on her lips.

"It ain't hardly nobody in there—just family."

That was the problem.
   It was her family.
   Not mine.
   And that meant one thing—Mr. Trenton's family was in there, too.

"Yeah... I don't know if I can do this," I muttered, already taking a step back.

"Girl, stop. Don't nobody even remember who you is," Jasmine said with a laugh as she grabbed my hand and pulled me inside like I was just being dramatic.

Karina followed behind, still trying to keep it cute, but the look on her face said everything. She was just as uneasy as I was, or maybe worse.

The house was packed. Loud-ass music thumped through the walls, making the floor vibrate under my feet. Weed smoke hung thick in the air, mixing with sweat and cheap cologne. Bodies moved to the beat, too many eyes lingering too long.

"You said you wanted to talk, right?" Jasmine yelled over the music, tugging my hand tighter.

I tried to look back—make sure Karina was still with me—but she was gone.

Swallowed by the crowd.

Before I could panic, Jasmine dragged me into a side room. The door closed behind us, muting the chaos outside to a dull bass that thudded through the walls like a heartbeat.

I looked forward.

My heart sank straight to the floor.

In front of me stood someone I thought I'd never see again.

Darren.

"What the fuck!" I screamed, panic slamming into me like a freight train.

I spun around, desperate to get back through the door, but Darren was faster.

He grabbed me by the back of my neck, tight, so tight it felt like he was trying to crush it like a soda can.

"Where you think you going, lil' bitch?" he spat before throwing me to the ground.

I hit it hard. My body slammed against the concrete of the garage floor, the breath was knocked out of me in an instant. I looked up through blurry vision, my eyes locking with Jasmine's.

She just stood there.

Smiling.

I scrambled for my phone, my hands shaking as I tried to unlock it, but

Darren snatched it before I could even get past the screen.

"Did you think you could burn me for my bread like shit was sweet?" he growled, then he began kicking me—over and over again in the stomach, each blow sharper than the last.

I screamed in agony.

"Stop—please, stop!"

But no one could hear me. Not over the pounding bass of the music outside. Not through the walls, smoke, and drunken bliss.

No one knew.
  No one cared.

Darren didn't stop.

Fueled by rage, his kicks turned into slaps, then punches. A full-blown assault. Fists crashing into my face, my ribs, anywhere he could land them.

"I'll give you back the money! I have it—I swear—it's in my account. If you let me go, I'll cash app it to you right now!" I pleaded, tears and blood pouring from my face.

"Please, just let me get my phone back!"

Jasmine strolled over like it was nothing.

"Don't worry, I got you, boo," she said, lifting my swollen, battered face to unlock my phone.

She opened the app, casual as ever, then turned to Darren.

293

"How much was it again?" she asked smugly, like this was some kind of joke.

He paced back and forth like a lion in a cage, eyes never leaving me.

"Ten grand," he said coldly.

Jasmine typed in his Cash App tag, found his name, used my face again to verify, and sent it.

A moment passed.

"You got what you want," I said through gritted teeth, blood dripping from my forehead. "Please, just let me leave."

Darren shook his head, dark fire still burning in his eyes.

"Nah," he muttered. "That ain't all you owe me."

He stepped toward me.

I shook my head frantically, body trembling, heart about to explode. I didn't want to die, not like this. Not in a dark room. Not now that I had finally just discovered the joy of being alive.

"Please... I promise—I swear—you'll never hear from me again. I won't tell a soul," I cried, my voice breaking into sobs.

Darren didn't speak.

He just started unbuttoning his pants.

My stomach turned. My body froze.

I looked up at Jasmine. Her smile was gone now—vanished completely, replaced by something close to fear.

"What the fuck are you doing?" she asked, voice low and shaking.

Still, he said nothing. Just kept moving toward me.

My eyes locked with hers, wide, pleading.

Begging.

Then she turned and ran.

She dashed out of the room and disappeared back into the party, leaving me behind.

* * *

Karina:

I searched through the crowd, heart thudding in my chest.

Where the fuck did she go?

Panic crawled up my throat, thick and choking. Journee was just gone. Like she vanished into thin air. I knew this was a bad idea.

"Where the fuck did this bitch go?" I mumbled to myself, pushing past dancing bodies.

I pulled out my phone, thumbs flying as I texted Khalil. I wanted to call, but the music was too loud for that shit.

'I can't find Journee.'

That's all I wrote. No time for anything else. I pushed deeper through the crowd, heading toward the kitchen.

Nothing.

No sign of her.

I doubled back toward the front, still panicking, brain running in circles. Where could she have gone?

Eyes followed me as I moved, some curious, some calculating.

"Yo, let me talk to you," a voice said as a hand slid around my waist from behind.

I whipped around, ready to curse someone the fuck out—until I saw Jasmine.

Her face was pale. Frantic. She looked like she'd just seen death itself and couldn't look away.

"Where the fuck is she?" I demanded, grabbing Jasmine's arm with a grip that made her flinch.

"I'm sorry," was all she whispered before pushing past me.

My stomach dropped.

I sprinted toward the back, heading to where I first saw her. A door. I tried to open it, but it didn't budge.

Locked.

I pressed my ear to the wood, heart pounding, and then someone yanked me back.

I spun around, fists up—ready to fight—only to freeze.

Two masked men stood in front of me.

Ski masks.

Before I could bolt, I heard Khalil's voice through the muffling fabric. Omar stood beside him, silent but deadly.

"She's in there?" Khalil asked, eyes burning behind the mask.

Before I could answer, Omar kicked the door clean off the hinges.

We stormed inside.

Panicked screams exploded from the corner.

"Nooo! Get the fuck off of me! Please!"

My jaw dropped.

Journee was curled into the corner, trying to fight Darren off with everything she had. He was tugging at her clothes, hands wild and shaking.

She grabbed a fistful of his dreadlocks, yanking them hard, a war cry erupting from her throat.

"Oh my God!" I gasped, surging forward, but Omar and Khalil were already on him.

They didn't waste a second.

They ripped Darren off her and began unleashing a deadly ass whopping.

Punch after punch, each one heavier, deadlier than the last. Bones could be heard cracking under the weight of each hit. A storm of fists rained down on him, blood splattering from split skin painted the floor beneath them.

I dropped to my knees beside Journee. Her top was shredded, her face swollen, eyes nearly shut. A painful rage consumed me.

"Shit," I whispered, tears spilling as I unzipped my hoodie and wrapped it around her shoulders.

She flinched when I touched her.

"It's okay, I got you, girl," I whispered, choking back sobs.

"Thank you," she cried through busted lips.

I gently helped her up as Khalil and Omar kept swinging. The floor was stained with Darren's blood, and still, they didn't stop.

"Did this pussy do what I think he did?" Omar snapped, finally pausing long enough to take in her torn clothes, bruises, and the way she could barely stand.

It was rhetorical.

The calm look Omar usually wore was replaced by a wrathful darkness.

He pulled out his strap and grabbed Darren by his dreads, yanking his head back before smashing the butt of the gun into his mouth.

Blood and teeth flew.

Darren hit the floor, groaning in pain as Omar stomped him—his head, ribs, and chest. No mercy.

"You know you fucked up, right?" Omar growled, voice low and seething.

"That bitch burned me," Darren gargled, spitting blood between broken teeth.

His whole front grill was gone.

Omar didn't flinch.

He just stomped on Darren's chest again. No words. No emotion. Just vengeance.

The music outside still blared, loud and dumb. Nobody inside had a clue what was happening. The hell hole that Darren initially planned out for Journee. It was now his.

Khalil pulled out his own strap, eyes fixed on Darren's bloody, broken body.

They looked like grim reapers—black-clad, merciless, calm in chaos—as they debated his fate.

"Let me smoke this pussy," Khalil said, gun ready.

"Yeah, babe, kill that bitch!" I shouted, rage flooding my veins.

"No! Please..." Journee begged, voice shaking. "Don't..."

Omar didn't say a word.

He just lifted his strap.

And emptied the whole clip.

Screams erupted all around as people heard the gunfire. Feet scrambled. Bodies shoved past each other, trying to escape.

Journee and I both screamed—instinct, shock, pain—but our eyes stayed locked on Omar.

Omar, who stood there, calm, with an empty gun in his hand.

He walked over to Journee like nothing happened, scooped her up in his arms, and without a word—

We all walked out the back door.

V

Today's Product

"Murderer! Blood is on your shoulders
Kill I today you cannot kill I tomorrow
Murder!"

— Buju Banton

18

A Safe Space

Journee

The night air hit my skin like ice, stinging every wound, every bruise, every part of me that had been torn open.

Omar carried me like I was weightless, but I felt everything: the sting in my ribs, the burn in my face, the shame buried deep in my soul. This was all my fault. I played Darren and brought Karina, Khalil, and Omar into this situation.

Behind us, Karina's voice cracked through the dark.

"Oh my God, oh my God, oh my fucking God—"

Her panic felt louder than the gunshots that still rang in my ears.

"Is she okay? Journee, are you okay? I swear to God, this is too much—"

"I'm fine," I whispered, but I wasn't. Not even close.

Omar didn't flinch. Didn't speak. His jaw was tight, hands steady, breath even. He looked down at me once—just once—and I saw something dangerous in his eyes. I don't know if it calmed me or frightened me.

It wasn't fear.

It was control.

Khalil walked beside us, calm like he had just left a corner store. Gun tucked, hoodie up, mouth set like stone.

"Car's around the corner," he said low.

"Did anybody see y'all?" Karina asked, still frantic, eyes darting, breath ragged.

"No," Omar said flatly.

"Fuck, Omar! You just killed somebody!"

"That pussy had it coming," Omar replied calmly.

We reached the car. Khalil opened the back door, and Omar gently slid me inside. I winced, trying not to cry. Karina climbed in next to me, shaking. Looking at me with eyes that wished they could heal.

"You're bleeding," she whispered, pulling me close, her hands hovering, not sure what to touch or what to do.

"I'm okay."

"You're not fucking okay, can you stop saying that shit!"

Her voice cracked, tears spilling as she gripped my hand like it would anchor her.

She was right, pain shot through me from all directions. Physically, mentally, emotionally. I wasn't broken. I was shattered. I had just witnessed the man I love kill for me.

Khalil got in the passenger seat. Omar started the car and pulled off smoothly, like we hadn't just left a murder behind us.

The silence inside the car was loud. Too loud.

"I—I didn't know she would set you up like that, I thought she'd just get you jumped or something, not this," Karina whispered. "That bitch is evil."

"I trusted her," I said, voice flat, hollow. "I walked right into it."

Karina broke again. "This shit ain't right, J. This shit ain't normal!"

Khalil turned slightly in his seat. "That's why I told y'all not to go."

Karina wiped her face. "I didn't know it was gonna go down like that."

"It always does," Omar said, his eyes locked on the road. "You just never know when."

We rode in silence for a while. The adrenaline started to fade, and the pain crept in.

My face throbbed. My ribs screamed. My dignity was buried under blood and betrayal.

"Where are we going?" I asked weakly.

"Somewhere safe," Omar said. "Just for the night."

Karina looked like she was about to argue, but bit her tongue. Her whole body was trembling, and for the first time, I saw fear in her eyes—not just for me, but for what they were capable of.

"You've done this before," I said, barely able to get the words out.

Omar didn't answer. But the silence spoke for him.

I watched in silence as Omar drove us away from the city. Long-winded roads and trees flew past our ride. I closed my eyes and drifted into sleep from exhaustion.
When I opened them, we were there. The safe house was quiet. Too quiet.

No music. No voices. Just the low hum of the refrigerator and the sound of my shallow breathing.

Omar carried me inside like he had done it before. Like I was something fragile, broken, but still worth holding. The lights were dim. The space was clean—too clean—like no one actually lived here. Just came when they had to disappear.

Karina hovered behind us like a ghost, eyes wide, still shaken. Khalil soothed her into the house until she was fully inside. He locked the door behind her, checked the blinds, then disappeared down the hall like he'd done this routine a thousand times.

Omar laid me on the bed, adjusting the pillows under my head.

"I'll get some ice," he said quietly.

Karina stepped forward. "I'll help," she said, but her voice cracked.

They both left the room, and for the first time since the attack, I was alone. My body felt like it didn't belong to me—bruised, sore, violated. But my mind? My mind was still screaming. Still trapped in that garage.

I stared up at the ceiling, blinking back tears until Omar returned with a cold cloth, a glass of water, and something else I didn't expect—softness.

He sat beside me, gently pressing the cold cloth to my face. His hands were warm. Steady. Careful.

"I'm sorry," he said low. "I should've been there sooner."

I didn't know how to respond. So I just looked at him. Peering deep into his eye. His jaw clenched, eyes dark, haunted. This wasn't just rage. This was history. Pain hid behind it all.

"Thank you," I whispered.

He didn't say anything, just leaned in and kissed my forehead. It was soft. Unexpected. It made the pain bearable. God, did I need his comfort. I was so happy he had come to save me. No one had done so before.

Karina came back in with Khalil, both of them carrying supplies—gauze, pain medication, clothes. But the energy had shifted. Why did they have all of this here?

Khalil glanced at Omar, something unspoken passing between them. That same eerie calm. That same practiced silence that I witnessed back at the garage.

Karina paced with some supplies still in her hand.

"This place... this isn't a regular crib. There's nothing in here. Not even family pictures."

Khalil sighed, finally breaking the quiet. "Because it ain't for family. It's for business. We don't come here to relax."

Karina froze. "Business?"

Omar rubbed his temples. "Look, I wasn't tryna drag y'all into this shit, alright?"

"Into what?" I asked, heart starting to race again.

Khalil looked right at me. "We move weight, Journee. Big weight. Out of town, in town, ports, stash spots. All of it."

Karina's mouth dropped.

"What the fuck you mean?"

Omar didn't flinch. "Exactly what he said. We built an empire off survival. Ain't proud of it. But we ain't ashamed either."

I stared at him, my heart thudding.

"So that's why you have all that money. Why did you lie to me and tell me you were a driver?"
I paused, waiting for an answer.
Khalil just chuckled.

"Nigga, you told her you were a driver?"
Omar shot him a glare that said 'not now'.
"How many times have you done the kind of shit that you just did tonight,"
I asked, grateful but concerned.

"Enough so that I survived," he said, locking eyes with me. "Enough times that I just saved you."

Karina sat down on the edge of the bed, stunned and silent.

Khalil placed a hand on her shoulder. "I didn't bring you here for this. I brought you to protect you."

"And now what?" she asked, trembling. "We just pretend like none of this happened?"

"No," Omar said, eyes back on me. "But we don't let it break us either."

I couldn't stop staring at him. The layers I had barely started to peel back. The softness beneath all that hardness. It was so much about him that I wanted to know. He wasn't just violent—he was dangerous with reason. Protective. Strategic. And somehow, right now, that made me feel safe.

He leaned down again, brushing a strand of hair from my face.

"You don't have to worry," he whispered. "I told you I would burn down the world for you."

And in that moment, with the room dim and my body aching, I let my head fall gently against his chest.

Karina and Khalil talked quietly in the corner, their voices low, tension still buzzing in the air.

But for the first time all night, I closed my eyes with a sense of peace.

And let myself feel protected again. I knew Omar would do exactly what he said he would: burn it all down if I asked him to.

* * *

Omar

The whole night been running back in my head like a fucked up movie on repeat, while Journee laid knocked out on my chest.

My jaw locked just thinking about it.

She didn't even tell me she was linking with Jasmine. If she did, I would of shut that goofy shit down before it even started. If Karina ain't hit Khalil up to drop them off, ain't no telling how far that weird-ass nigga Darren would of took it.

As soon as bro hit my line and told me what was going on, I told him, "Say less," and grabbed my shit. Couldn't even take my truck. Too hot. Too flashy. If shit got active, I needed to move low.

Slid in the wheel with my ski rolled like a beanie, hoodie tight. Ready for war. Khalil was, too. That's just how we moved.

He got the drop from Karina as soon as we pulled up.
Journee was missing, and that's all I needed to know.
The crib was packed, music dumb loud, air thick with smoke and bullshit energy. We dipped right in, heads on a swivel.

Khalil peeped Karina off rip. Scooped her fast. She was crashing out, trying her hardest to get the door open. I could tell she knew something was off. So I didn't hesitate, I kicked it in.

I wasn't tryna talk. I wasn't tryna negotiate. I saw red. Darren touched her, and I knew what he was about to do. I don't give a fuck what line I crossed—he had to go. That pussy had to die.

But still... I never wanted Journee to see me like that. Not as a killer. Not as a monster.

I felt her shift. Looked down—she was up. Staring at me with them big brown eyes, locked on mine, soft and serious. She always did that when she fell asleep on my chest—woke up watching me. I always wondered what was on her mind.

"You good?" I asked, voice low, hand rubbing the small of her back.

"I'm good," she whispered. "I hope you know... what happened tonight doesn't change the way I look at you."

Damn. That shit hit different like a bullet piercing straight through my soul.

"I'm sorry I kept this shit from you," I said, voice thick with guilt.

"Omar," she said, palm to my cheek. "You don't gotta say sorry for tryna survive. We all got shit we ain't ready to say out loud yet. I'm just now telling you mine."

I looked away, tryna hold that lump in my throat.

"I wish I were as brave as you," I muttered.

"You are," she said, smiling through her bruises like they ain't even there. "You're the bravest man I know."

"I'm just tryna be that for you."

I looked at her face—black and blue, swollen, eyes puffy but still soft. Still her. I could feel the guilt eating at me, begging for somewhere to go.

She saw it all over me.

"Don't do that."

"Do what?"

"Put the weight on yourself when I walked into that shit. You saved me."

That word hit different, too.

Saved.

She was fucked up all over and still looked at me like I was her hero, not her mistake. I wanted to tell her everything, but it was like my emotions were in separate plastic bags, suffocating. I didn't even know how to put my feelings into words.

She leaned in, forehead pressed to mine, her breath warm and sweet like she hadn't just been through hell.

"You are my calm in the storm," she whispered. "My only safe space."

I closed my eyes.

No Sirens, No noise.

Just her heartbeat.

And for once in my life...

I ain't feel like just a villain.

I felt like hers. As we both drifted back to sleep.

* * *

Journee

The next morning, I woke up late, not remembering falling asleep. All I know is, when I opened my eyes, I was warm—safe even.

His chest rose and fell under my cheek. Calm. Steady. His warm embrace that cradled me all night was the first thing that didn't feel violent in hours.

Omar.

The name echoed in my head like a whisper and a prayer. His arm was wrapped tight around me, fingers laced against my hip like he was scared to let go. I didn't wanna move. I didn't wanna break whatever this was.

But the bruises reminded me I was still in my body. Every breath I took came with a sting.

My ribs. My face. My pride.

I stirred.

His hand shifted instantly, like he could feel the pain radiating through me.

"You up?" he asked, voice rough, like gravel and honey.

"Yeah," I whispered, my voice dry.

"You need water?"

I nodded, and before I could blink, he was already up, moving quietly. I watched the way he moved, like he'd been trained for shit like this. Like he wasn't new to seeing someone broken.

He came back, kneeling in front of me, one hand on my leg, the other holding the glass. I took it slow. My lip split again, and I winced.

"I got you, ma. Take your time."

That "ma" hit different. Soft. Intentional.

I leaned back, letting the water settle in me. I could feel him watching me, but not like he had before. This was... distinct. He watched me like I was art that got torn up, and that he didn't know how to piece back together, but was ready to try.

"You ain't have to get up, I felt you checking on me all night," I said, voice low.

He tilted his head. "You think I could have slept knowing you're hurting like this?"

I blinked hard, trying not to cry. My face hurt too much for that.

"You seeing me like this, I don't like it," I said, my voice cracking.

He moved closer, thumb grazing under my chin.

"I still see you no different than I always have."

I broke. Tears rolled slowly down the sides of my face, and he wiped them away one by one.

"I should've told you about Jasmine inviting me there," I whispered. "I should have— I should have protected you, like you protected me. What if you get arrested? I can't lose you, Omar."

"She set you up," he said, anger flickering in his tone. "What I did is done, this ain't my first body. Won't be my last. I'm not going anywhere."

I looked at him. His face was stone, but his eyes burned.

He leaned in close, forehead pressing against mine, gently.

"I been in this shit too long. Seen too much. Did too much," he said. "But you? You still got light in you. I'll kill any nigga before I let them snuff it out."

"Now that I'm here, you fear no man. Let me hear you say it."

"I fear no man," I repeated.

He kissed my forehead.

"Never forget it," his voice laced with something I had never heard before.

I let that sit. Let it wrap around me like a blanket in December.

He lay back down, arms open. I curled into him slowly, wincing with each shift, but it still felt better than any hospital bed could. Better than anything else.

I was still a little scared. Still hurt. But right there—in his arms, feeling his heartbeat under my cheek again—I knew I had nothing to fear.

Omar had me.

* * *

I spent the next few days with him and I just in the room together alone.

The soft hum of the TV played in the background, but I wasn't watching. Just staring. Still processing. My body ached less than it did days ago, but the bruises lingered, faded to red and blues like paint on my skin.

Omar stood in front of me, throwing on sweats and grabbing his keys.

"I'm heading to the store," he said, pausing in the doorway. "Need anything?"

I shook my head. "No, I'm good."

He watched me a second longer, like he wasn't sure if he should leave. His jaw clenched, then relaxed. Finally, he nodded once and stepped out.

The silence that followed settled like a cloak over me. I didn't mind it. Not anymore.

A knock pulled me out of my thoughts. Not loud. Just enough to be felt.

Then I heard Karina's voice. "Hey Journee, it's me."

I called out, "It's open."

She and Khalil stepped in, moving slowly like they didn't want to startle me. Karina's eyes scanned me immediately, then softened with relief. Khalil stood behind her, unusually quiet, hands in his hoodie pocket.

Karina crossed the room in two seconds flat and wrapped her arms around me. Carefully.

"I been losing sleep thinking about you," she whispered, her voice trembling.

I hugged her back, feeling the familiar comfort I didn't know I needed.

"I'm okay," I said, though I wasn't sure if I believed it yet.

She pulled back, looking at me like she was scared to hurt me. "You look better," she said. "Stronger."

"I'm trying."

Khalil gave a small nod. "You on the other side of this shit. That's all that matters."

They sat with me for a while—the room filled with quiet conversation and long pauses. No one pushed me to talk. Karina just held my hand like she always had.

"I don't think you should be alone right now," she said finally. Her eyes took me in I could see the worry inside them.
"We were thinking—maybe we all chill here for a while. Make sure we all good before heading back to the city." Khalil said

I knew they were talking about me being okay specifically. Even though I had no broken bones, thankfully, I was still a long way from being good. I knew they had my back.

Still, I looked at them, surprised.

"Y'all don't have to do this."

"We want to," Khalil added. "This place is quiet. Out of the way. Safe. I'll dip here and then to handle business, but you and Karina staying in this jawn gives me peace of mind."

That word. Safe. I hadn't felt since Omar walked out the door. It echoed in me, soft and necessary.

Karina smiled. "I can cook. Talk. Not talk. Whatever you need, sis."

I nodded slowly. "Just don't let Lil step anywhere in the kitchen." I joked.

"Y'all stay tryna bid." Kahlil laughed.

I felt the tension in the room melt away.

* * *

The next two weeks passed in a haze of slow healing. There were no sudden movements, no loud noises, just the rhythm of recovery.

Karina kept me laughing when my face allowed it. She did my hair on the days I didn't feel human. Khalil cooked—surprisingly well with Karina guiding him—and helped Omar keep busy so he wasn't always glued to my bedside watching over me like a watchdog.

I checked in with family to keep them updated, told them I was visiting my boyfriend's family down south. A lie I knew was necessary to keep everyone safe. The only one who truly knew what was up was Serenity, to keep an eye out for anything odd.

Through it all, Omar never pressed me to talk. He was just there. Patient. Kind. And when I'd cry in my sleep, he'd pull me closer, whispering soft things I couldn't always make out, but always believed.

The bruises faded. My body loosened. The house started to feel less like a hiding place and more like a home.

I wasn't all the way okay, but I was headed there.
"You're up again," Omar said with a soft smile as I stepped out onto the back porch.

"Yeah... I just needed some fresh air."

His eyes lingered on the bruises that remained. My lips had healed, and the swelling around my eye was gone. But my ribs were still tender—still a painful reminder of everything.

"You hear any stories going around yet? About what happened?" I asked, sitting beside him.

"Some shit. But don't worry about it."

He said it like it didn't matter. Like he couldn't tell me.

But I saw the shift in him. Whenever he stepped out to handle "business," the man I loved became someone else entirely—distant, hard. I missed the way we used to be. I missed him.

"Omar, please stop lying to me. I ain't afraid."

"It ain't even like that."

"Then what is it?" I snapped, my voice dry. "'Cause you ain't talkin' to me like you used to."

That hit him. I saw it all over his face.

He pulled one of his hands out of his hoodie pocket and wrapped his arms around me. Strong. Tight.

"I ain't tryna overwhelm you. You haven't even told me everything that happened yet. I need to know you good before anything else. All that other shit can wait," he said, his head resting gently against mine, worry thick in his voice.

I hadn't realized how much he was holding back for me. He was being patient, being kind, I knew that part. I loved that he was waiting for me. But in my silence, I'd unknowingly created a space between us.

"Babe," I whispered, "I'll tell you everything. If you do the same."

He didn't say a word—just nodded, eyes locked on mine, steady and patient.

I looked down at my hands, twisting my fingers to keep them from shaking.

"You already know Jasmine set me up. I know that. But I never told you why they actually came after me."

His jaw clenched, but he kept listening.

"They thought I had money on me, and I did. More than ten bands. I'd been stacking for months. Most of it came from Darren."

Omar blinked, then sat forward a little, brows furrowed.

"I made him think we were gonna sleep together," I admitted, my voice low.

"Flirted. Sent pictures. Played mind games. But I never touched him. I couldn't. I just needed the money... for bills, groceries, Momma. My brothers needed clothes. I was tryna save for school, too."

I looked up at him, my breath shaky.

"It wasn't right. I know that. But it was either finesse or watch everything fall apart again. So did it, not just to him but a couple niggas."

He didn't look away.

"I would block them after, and I did the same thing to him once I got the last deposit." I paused.
"But this time I was done, I had met you and I wanted to change. But word must've got around. Jasmine must've known. Probably told them what I did to her and used our past to trap me." My voice cracked.

"That's why they had me in that garage and why I ended up like this."

Omar reached for my hand, firm but gentle, the kind of touch that said *you're safe now.*

"Journee," he said, his voice thick with emotion, "you did what you had to. Don't let anybody make you feel dirty for surviving. You hear me?"

I nodded, but the guilt still sat in my throat like a stone.

"And on some real shit," he added, "There's been a lotta dumb shit goin' around—none of them even close to what really went down. Niggas always talk, but I ain't feed into none of that shit. As long as they ain't talkin bout me or mines."

Tears welled in my eyes, but I didn't cry. I felt seen, yet again. Time after time, he kept seeing me exactly for who I was and not for what I had done.

He pulled me into his chest again, holding me like he wasn't ever gonna let go.

"We good?" he asked softly.

I nodded against him. "Yeah. We good."

* * *

One week later...

"Yo, I can't wait to breathe air that ain't got the smell of cow shit in it," Khalil said, dragging a trash bag of clothes down the porch steps like it owed him money.

"Boy, you act like we was in jail, I kinda liked being up here with all these farms and shit" Karina shot back, rolling her eyes but smiling.

"Shit you trippin! I ain't slept right since we got here. Beds hard as fuck, we ain't buy shit in this bitch for comfort."
I laughed, arms full of folded clothes and a plastic tote. "You too fucking dramatic."

Omar came up behind me, tossing another bag in the trunk. "Nah, he's right. This air stinky as shit. And I'm low-key starting to think this bitch haunted."

"I told y'all I heard whispering the first night!" Khalil said, shaking his fingers like he was finally validated.

Karina gave him a sideways look. "That was the TV, dumb ass. You fell asleep watching horror movies."

Everyone cracked up.

I leaned against the car for a moment, looking at Omar. "You sure you're ready for this?"

He looked at me like I was the only thing worth staring at. "Been ready. I want to wake up next to you. In our own crib, not a place like this."

My cheeks flushed, but I nodded, heart full. "Then let's do it."

Khalil watched us like a proud cousin at a cookout. "Awe, look at y'all—black love and all that shit. I fuck with it."

Karina elbowed him. "What about us, huh?"

He smirked. "What about us? I already know I'm bout to start looking at two-bedroom. I ain't tryna keep drivin' up North when I could be laid up with you."

Karina squinted. "Is that your way of asking me to move in?"

"I mean... yeah, fuck you think I'm asking you.," Khalil grinned. "I ain't gon' get on one knee and beg."

"Boy, shut up and grab the rest of my bags."

"You see how she treats me?" he called to Omar, lifting Karina's pink suitcase like it was full of bricks. "See how the good niggas get talked to!"

Omar shook his head, laughing as he opened the car door for me. "Y'all niggas trippin'."

I slid in and looked back at the house one last time. "It's over, right?"

Omar nodded. "Yeah. Now it's just us."

And with that, we pulled off—windows down, music low, the hope we felt riding shotgun.

19

Home Is Where The Heart Is

I'd been here more times than I could count just to chill, vibe, relieve my mind. Spent many afternoons and nights posted on his couch. Been in his shower plenty of times, in his bed the same. Sometimes we'd fall asleep talking, other times not talking at all, our mouths too busy doing other things.

But today felt different.
   This time, I wasn't just here to chill.
   This time, *I was moving in.*

Omar held the door open like he always did, but his eyes stayed on me longer. Like he could tell I felt the shift too. This was becoming real, not just a distant fantasy we whispered to each other while laying in bed. It was happening.

"You know where everything at," he teased casually, grabbing my duffle bag. "I ain't doing the whole welcome home tour."

"You already gave it— plenty of times."

He smirked. "Aight, then act like you know."

I stepped inside and kicked off my slides. Same cozy scent—lavender and sandalwood. Same clean floors, same gray couch with the permanent dip where I always curled up. But now, there was an empty row of hangers in his closet and a toothbrush waiting beside his in the bathroom.

This was different, everything was moving so fast.

I trailed behind him into the bedroom, heart thudding even though I'd lain in that bed a bunch of times before. Laughing. Healing. Moaning his name. I didn't want what was already happening between us to change because of that night.

"You really sure about this?" I asked, watching him unzip my bag and start folding my clothes like he already considered them part of the drawer.

"Journee, if I wasn't, you wouldn't be here. I wanted this since the moment I slid inside you. The moment I made you mine."

I nodded, flashbacks of the heat that took place between these very walls came tumbling into my mind.

Still, I needed to know. "I mean, it's not like we've been dating for years. I just don't want us moving too fast."

He came over, real close, and rested his forehead against mine. "How can love move too fast when it's real?"

That made me smile. I wanted to stay in that moment with him.

He kissed me once, slow, then pulled away like he wasn't trying to make it a whole thing—even though it kinda was.

"You hungry?" he asked, already headed toward the kitchen. "I got wings, or we can go grab something from a spot nearby."

"Wings and a drawer? You really tryna lock it down," I teased, following him.

"We already locked in, baby."

And just like that, we fell into it easily, like we always did.

Only this time, I didn't have to go home after.

I was home.

* * *

Later that day, I invited Karina over.
I heard her voice hit the door before she even knocked.

"Girl, bring yo loud ass in here." I shushed her.

"Yo! Don't be acting brand new now that you shacked up bitch!" She laughed.

Omar shook his head, grinning as he opened the door. Karina breezed in like she owned the place, Khalil trailing behind her with a cheese steak platter in his hand and an Arizona mango in the other.

I plopped back on the couch, hoodie on, socks mismatched, and my bonnet still halfway off from earlier.

Karina took in everything I was wearing and immediately let out a dramatic gasp.

"Oh, you real comfortable now, huh? That's what movin' in look like?"

"Don't start," I warned, laughing as I adjusted myself.

She flopped beside me and looked around. "Nah, this is cute though. Grown-folk livin'. Look at y'all. Cohabitating and whatnot, it's cute."

Khalil plopped down next to Omar at the kitchen island. "So when we signing the lease, Karina?"

Karina twisted her neck to look at him. "I'm waiting on you to pick a place so I can be in that bitch looking like Journee." She teased, pointing at my socks.

"Waitin' on me? Shit we ain't never gon find shit."

She rolled her eyes, but her smile gave her away. "Boy, I promise we'll start lookin' tomorrow."

Omar laughed from the kitchen. "Maybe Journee could help y'all, she loves looking at houses on Zillow."

"I'm preparing for the future!" I said, clutching my chest like he just shared my darkest secret.

"Bitch Zillow, hoe is you forty," Karina joked playfully reaching for my feet.

I leaned into the couch, laughing so hard I nearly spilled my juice. It felt good, normal. No tension, no weight. Just friends bidin' and talking shit in a house that finally felt like home.

Karina nudged me. "So, how does it feel? Living with your man, waking up to morning breath and all?"

I grinned. "Like I should've been here the whole time."

She smirked. "You said that with your whole chest. I love that for you."

And I did. Because right now, life wasn't spinning. It wasn't perfect, but it was mine. And I had people who loved me enough to laugh with me through it all.

* * *

The nighttime quickly approached. The house had finally quieted down. Karina and Khalil left with the wings we didn't finish, two cans of ginger ale for their stomachs, and more jokes than necessary about "how they can't wait to be fucking all over their own house."
The TV was still on, Martin reruns playing in the background, casting soft blue light across the room.

I was in bed, curled under the blanket, bonnet fixed this time. Omar came out of the bathroom in a fresh T-shirt and gray sweat pants, his chain catching the light as he climbed in beside me. He looked so damn good.

We laid there in the quiet for a minute. Him on his back. I curled toward him, head resting on his chest, hand splayed out over his heart like it was mine to guard.

"You good?" he asked, voice barely above a whisper.

I nodded, but then paused. "Yeah... just thinking"

"'Bout what?"

I exhaled. "How just a few months ago, I had no clue we'd end up together.

Now I'm here. With you. Laughing. Living. Like... it doesn't even feel real sometimes."

He ran his fingers along my arm, slow and grounding.

"It's real. All of it."

"I know. It's just... the peace feels unfamiliar sometimes."

"I get that."

"I ain't used to soft."

"You deserve it, though. The only thing hard you need is this." He stated rubbing my hand across his hard dick.

It had been a minute since we made love, and just that touch made me shiver. But was I ready?

"I miss him," I admitted, softly watching his manhood grow larger by the second.

"I miss her." He replied, kissing me softly on the forehead.

We sat in the stillness a little longer, just the two of us and the steady rhythm of his heartbeat beneath my ear.

I looked up at him. "Thanks for not rushing me."

"I'm never gon force nothing. I want you ready. For this...." he said taking my had and wrapping around his dick. "And for us."

"I think I am now."

He smiled, one of those deep, quiet ones he only gave me when he really couldn't help it. "Then I got you."

I leaned up, kissed his jaw, kissed his neck, and continued down his chest. I could hear him grunt.

I didn't stop, I sat up slightly and went further down his stomach. Until I made my way to what was mine. Pulling it out, I slid him right inside my mouth.

"Shit, baby you got it," he said voice laced with lust.
I worked my way up and down, relaxing my throat so I could take him even deeper. I wanted him to feel just how amazing he made me feel.

"Fuck," he wrapped his finger in my hair, stroking my face slowly and I slurped him like I was on a mission.
I couldn't help but moan and slurp harder as I looked up at him. He was just so damn fine, biting his lip as I worked my magic.
I watched as his eyes rolled back, his body tensed, and warm liquid poured into the back of my throat.
I gulped, grateful to receive it.
"Damn."

That was all he could manage to say as he planted a firm kiss on my lips.
I curled up beside him. That's all I wanted for the night. Now I could sleep peacefully.

We had each other.

Every day after that deepened that feeling.

* * *

We began another morning as we had become accustomed to. The pancakes were fluffy, eggs perfect, and turkey bacon crisp just how I liked it.

We sat across from each other at the little table by the window, legs brushing under the surface. Omar kept stealing my bacon, like I wouldn't notice. Me picking through the eggs, debating if I was going to finish them.

"I saw that," I said mid-chew.

He grinned around a bite. "Saw what?"

"You real bold now that I moved in." I giggled, scraping my eggs onto his plate.

"You said what's mine is yours, right? No harm, no foul."

"Yeah, but that ain't mean *my food*, greedy."

He reached over, wiped syrup off the corner of my mouth with his thumb like it was second nature. "You talk tough, but you ain't built."

I didn't even argue. Just smirked and sipped my juice.

We were mid-bite when a knock tapped against the kitchen window.

I jumped.

Omar didn't flinch. He already knew.

He stood up, pulled the curtain back just a little, and sighed. "Miss Bernice."

I peeked, too. There she was— Robe, slippers, rollers in her hair, arms crossed.

He cracked the window.

"Boy, I thought I seen another head up in there this morning," She said with zero shame. "I told my daughter, 'Omar got company. You know that boy has always been quiet, but it's a woman in there today. I feel it."

I blinked, completely caught off guard. Omar just chuckled.

"Good morning to you, too, Miss Bernice," he said.

She squinted past him. "Mmhm. Yeah, she's real pretty. You be good to her, you hear me?"

I waved awkwardly. "Good morning..."

"Hi, baby! You eat? He can cook when he wants to, but don't let him act lazy. He be faking tired."

"Got it," I nodded, grinning.

Bernice nodded back with full approval. "Alright now. I'll be watchin' y'all."

She walked off like it was nothing, adjusting her robe as she shuffled back across the porch to her own door.

Omar shut the window and looked at me.

"Welcome to the neighborhood," he said.

I shook my head, laughing. "Oh, this is gonna be fun."

We sat back down, still smiling. The kind of moment you don't plan for, but end up remembering.

Home wasn't just a roof.

It was laughter over pancakes, syrup-sticky fingers, and a nosy neighbor knocking on the window like it was her business.

And I was finally a part of it.

20

I Can Feel It In The Air

Six months later...

I awoke to find Omar gone again.

The clock read five in the morning. Early. But this had become our pattern—me falling asleep curled in his arms, only to wake to an empty bed. Just me, alone in the quiet stillness.

I slipped out from under the sheets and wrapped my robe around my waist. I already knew where he'd be. This was our new normal.

The faint hum of movement echoed down the hall, drawing me toward the gym. I didn't need to guess—it was him. The intensity of his stride on the treadmill grew louder with each step I took.

I reached the door and quietly peeked inside.

There he was.

Shirtless. His chest glistened with sweat, muscles flexing in rhythm as he ran. His arms moved like they were designed for it—synchronized, precise— his entire body a well-oiled machine in motion.

I stood there, just watching, silently caught in the raw beauty of him.

His pace began to slow, then stopped altogether. He hadn't even looked at me.

"You can come in, if you want," he said, voice calm, steady—like he hadn't just been running full speed for God knows how long.

"I know," I murmured, stepping into the room fully.

"How'd you sleep?" I asked, already knowing the answer.

At first, I thought it was me—that my presence made him restless, kept him on edge. That maybe he was adjusting, trying to learn how to share space with someone else. But I'd been here long enough to know better. Omar didn't sleep. He rested. Lightly. Briefly. As if too much stillness left him vulnerable.

"Good," he said simply.

He grabbed a towel from the arm of the machine and dabbed the sweat from his face, his chest rising and falling with quiet control.

"I'll get breakfast started soon."

He leaned in, kissed me on the cheek, and headed toward the shower.

This was his ritual.

And somehow, over time, it had become mine too.

As I returned to the room, I could already hear the soft patter of water and the low simmer of Omar's presence behind the curtain of steam. He was in the shower.

I let my robe slip from my shoulders, peeled off my clothes, and quietly stepped in behind him.

The steam wrapped around our bodies like a blanket of silence, warm and heavy.

"Come to the front," Omar said with a smirk, his voice smooth, almost teasing.

He didn't turn around, but I could see the map of scars etched across his back, mirroring those on his chest. My fingers traced them gently, just as they had countless times before. And, like always, my mind wandered to the memories he'd entrusted to me—the stories buried in each line and ridge.

Pain.
  Torture.
  Conditioning.

Omar hadn't been raised on love and blinding ignorance the way I had—if you could even call my childhood that. No, he'd been forged in fire. Taught to steal. To lie. To cheat. And worst of all, to kill.

I moved to stand in front of him. The water rained down between us, cascading over our skin. His arms slipped around my waist—firm, leveling, but laced with something impossibly tender. I looked up into his eyes— those haunted, beautiful eyes that held more truths than his lips ever would admit.

They spoke volumes without a single word.

I pressed my forehead against his, letting the water wash over us both. It wasn't just about getting clean—it was about release. About shedding pieces of pain, we didn't have the language for.

Reaching for the sponge, I began to wash him. Slowly. Reverently.

I bathed his chest, his arms, his back—every scar, every muscle, every inch of him—just as he had done for me so many times before.

He had made me feel clean once. Not just my body, but my soul. And now, I needed him to feel it too. To know that he wasn't alone.

I wasn't his savior. I didn't want to be. But I was here. Willingly. A passenger beside him on his long, fractured road to redemption.

"I'll find your pieces, Omar," I whispered, the words barely louder than the steam around us.

His eyes met mine.

And in them, I saw it.

He knew exactly what I meant.

* * *

By the time we stepped out of the shower, the sky had shifted from deep indigo to the soft gray of early morning. Light crept through the edges of the curtains, but the warmth between us lingered longer than the heat from the water.

Omar moved through the room with quiet purpose—methodical, focused. His ritual. Dark jeans. Plain T-shirt. Diamond-studded watch. Strap holstered at his side like it belonged to him as naturally as his breath.

He was going to work.

And work, for Omar, meant stepping into a world soaked in blood, silence, and the sting of betrayal. Everyone was clawing for the top.

I sat on the edge of the bed, the towel around me beginning to cool. My fingers tightened against the fabric as I watched him zip up his jacket, tuck a second clip into the inside pocket, and press a kiss to the gold chain that hung around his neck. The same one his older brother died wearing. The same one I had once tried to take from him during a night of rage. Begging him not to fall to the same fate. He never let it go. Not even in sleep.

Countless mornings had looked like this.
  The same motions.
  The same deadly silence.
  The same fear was rising like bile in the back of my throat, ready to be expelled.

But today felt different.

Not because the danger wasn't there—it was always there. But because for the first time, I wasn't bracing for the worst.

I was grieving the possibility that this life would always be his.

That I would always be left behind, pretending not to count the minutes, the hours, the calls that didn't come. I was scared, yes. But it wasn't just fear—it was something deeper. Sadder. Like standing at the edge of a cliff and realizing the person you love is about to jump off without a parachute.

"You gon be okay?" he asked, standing in the doorway, looking at me with that unreadable expression he wore like armor.

I nodded. A lie I'd told a hundred times. But my eyes must've said something else because he lingered.

"Journee," he said softly. "Don't carry me while I'm gone. Read, write, watch TV. Don't worry. You hear me?"

I swallowed hard. "Don't tell me to do something you can't even do."

He exhaled through his nose, jaw tightening. Then he stepped back, disappearing down the hallway, boots hitting the floor like a countdown.

The door closed behind him.

And the silence that followed wasn't peaceful. It was hollow.

But this time, I didn't cry.

I just sat there, towel damp against my skin, heart beating like it knew something I didn't.

The door clicked shut.

And still, I didn't move.

I sat there, towel wrapped tight around me like a shield, staring at the space he'd just left, as if his absence had drained all the hope from the room. A weight fell over me, the kind that settles in your chest and refuses to leave. Just stayed there claiming it's mark. I couldn't breathe.

Something wasn't right.

I couldn't explain it—not with words, not even to myself—but I felt it. A slow, creeping dread consumed the air around me as it shifted. I rubbed my tummy softly, looking down at what I hadn't disclosed. Not yet able to tell the man I love what now grew inside me.

I'd felt fear before. Every time he left. Every time he kissed me goodbye and disappeared into streets that didn't love him the way I did. Didn't cherish him for who he was. But this was different.

This wasn't fear.
  This was foreboding.
  Heavy. Cold. Final.

My skin prickled, goosebumps rising despite the warmth of the room. My heart beat a little faster, out of rhythm with no obvious cause. Maybe this is what pregnancy felt like, I told myself as I sat there growing cold from the air that kissed my skin.

I closed my eyes and tried to breathe through it. Tried to convince myself I was just being paranoid. That this life-this new edition of it—had trained me to expect the worst. But even then, I couldn't shake it. I reached for my phone to check his location.

Not far, still close enough for me to say *'Come home'*. For me to tell him the feeling that slammed against my heart.

I wanted to call him. Just to hear his voice. Just to release this wave of emotion that stirred inside of me.

But I didn't.

Because I knew him. And I knew what he would say.

"Don't carry me while I'm gone."

But I was. I always was. And now, something in me knew—I might not be able to hear him say it, again.

Something was coming.

And this time, I wasn't sure if love alone could save either of us.

My mind darted in every direction as I fought to push back the thoughts that were crashing into me like waves.

I wanted to tell him.

We were having a baby.

The missed contraception pills had been forgotten during the haze of recovery after Darren's attack.

The comfort of being with Omar eased all worry. It wasn't planned. Nothing about it was deliberate. And now, eight weeks in, I was sitting in our home, wondering if bringing a child into this world of chaos and fear was fair.

This panic that lived in my chest—it wouldn't just be mine anymore.
    It would be ours.
    Ours and the baby's.
    A baby who never asked to be here.

I scrolled to Omar's number. My thumb hovered for a beat. Then I swiped the screen away and tapped on Faith instead.

"Hey, sis," I said, forcing a brightness into my voice that felt fake even to me.

"What's wrong?" Her voice snapped to alert, mirroring the storm I'd been trying to hide.

"Nothing," I lied. "Just checking on y'all. How's everybody?"

"We good," she said. "Momma's up cooking, me and Daddy helping. Everybody here but Mir." She paused to giggle. "He finally got a girlfriend."

"Eww," I said dramatically, managing a soft laugh. "Who would ever date him?"

"Apparently, there's somebody for everybody."

In the background, I heard my mother shout.

"Girl, if you don't get off that phone and cut them onions!"

I smiled at the sound of her voice. I was just there a few days ago, but I missed her already—missed the noise, the smell of food, the ease of being in a place where love was louder than the pain.

"Aight, Journee, I gotta go."

"Okay," I replied quietly.

The phone call grounded me for a minute. It gave me something real to hold onto. A break in the storm. But as soon as the call ended, the silence returned—and my thoughts circled back to Omar like a bad habit.

I needed a real distraction.

I got dressed, grabbed my bag, and drove to Karina's apartment. It wasn't far, and maybe being around someone who didn't handle me like glass would shake me out of my head.

A few minutes later, I was standing at her door, texting I'm here.

She yanked it open fast, wide-eyed, like she'd seen a ghost.

"Did anybody see you come up here?" she asked, scanning the hallway behind me.

"No..." I answered slowly, confused. "Why?"

"Good!"

A fresh wave of panic rose in my chest.

"What's going on?"

"Nothing," she muttered, peeking through the crack in the door before pulling me inside.

"I'm tryna catch this bitch who keeps stealing my damn packages."

My shoulders dropped. Relief washed over me like cool water.

"Girl, you almost gave me a fucking heart attack."

Everything about today had me on edge. My nerves were shot and I didn't even know why. But Karina saw it. She always did.

"What the fuck is going on with you?" she asked, eyebrow raised, arms crossed.

I didn't answer right away. Just took a deep breath, reached into my bag, and pulled out the folded paperwork from my doctor's office.

I handed it to her without saying a word.

She opened it. Read. Looked at me.

"Bitch!" she screamed, throwing her arms around me.

"Oh my god! You're pregnant!"

"Yes," I exhaled. "I don't even know how this happened…"

Karina pulled back, eyes wide. "Girl, now you know exactly how this shit happened," she said, smirking and doing an exaggerated grinding motion.

I burst into laughter, shaking my head. God, I loved her. But I could've slapped her, too.

"This is not the time to joke," I said, half laughing, half crying. "I'm serious."

* * *

Omar

As I eased out of the parking spot, I pulled off slowly, my gut twisting in a way I couldn't explain. Something was off—I could feel it in the air, in the way my chest tightened with every block I passed.

I hated leaving Journee behind, hated the quiet way she looked at me this morning, like her soul was screaming without her mouth moving. But I knew being home was the safest place she could be. That's what I kept telling myself.

Still, I wanted to turn around. I wanted to hold her and promise her things would change. That she wouldn't always have to worry every time I walked out the door.

But I had places to be.

And I'm a man of my word.

I pulled up to the spot right on time. Smooth, clean. Just like it was supposed to be. I didn't want to linger. My whole spirit was screaming to handle this shit and go home.

Khalil was already waiting inside. I walked up to him, dapped him up, and grabbed the bag out his hand.

"This is it?" I asked, scanning the weight of the package with my eyes before I even bothered to look inside.

He nodded.

"You get in touch with that nigga Crazy Mike yet?"

"Yeah," Khalil said, licking his bottom lip. "He said pull up at two."

I checked my watch, jaw tightening.

"How the fuck we supposed to do that and still drop this jawn off ya-mean?" I asked, heat rising in my voice.

"I tried to tell that nigga that, bro. His ass drawlin'—talking 'bout it gotta be at two. You know I can't do it, I gotta stay to meet Big Tee here." Khalil shook his head, just as irritated as I was.

"Man, I ain't dropping this jawn off by myself. Wouldn't be a smart move."

Khalil gave me that slick smirk he always wore when he was about to suggest something reckless.

"Bro, take that nigga Tyree. If shit get weird... You already know."

I nodded once. "Aight. Bet."

As I walked off, the weight of the day pressed harder on my back. The streets felt louder. The wind felt colder.

That unease?
    It didn't just follow me.
    It crawled up my spine and settled at the base of my neck.

I pulled out my phone, fingers quick, and texted Tyree:

'Pulling up now. Be ready.'

I pulled up to the curb slowly. Tyree was already outside, bouncing on his toes, grinning like he just got called up for the league. I shook my head.

This young bull better not be on no nut shit.
    Not today.
    Not when I got somebody waiting on me to make it back.

He hopped in the passenger seat, dapped me up.

"Wassup, bro?"

"Wassup."

I pulled off without another word. Traffic lights slid over the windshield, flashing like warnings. Neither of us spoke. Silence sat between us—thick, sharp, like a blade resting on my thigh.

I cut through it.

"When we get in there, let me talk. You don't say a word. Just hold the bag, hand it off when I say so. That's it. After we dip, cool, you can run your mouth. But until then?" I glanced over, jaw tight. "Don't say a fucking word."

Tyree nodded quickly, his face serious now. The grin was gone. He knew I wasn't playing.

He was solid, but he wasn't Khalil. He and I had years in. Didn't have to speak—we moved like one body in two frames. I needed that today. I needed his backup, but Tyree was all I had instead.

The drive stayed quiet. Just the hum of the engine and the city crawling past. I had too much in my head—Journee's face haunting my rear view. The way she looked this morning, like she felt something coming.

And now I did too.

Tyree sensed it. He sat stiff, like even breathing too hard would set something off. He kept glancing at me, probably wondering what was running through my mind. But I wasn't about to spill shit.

Not until this was done. Not until I got home.

The sun was out, sky clear, but the heat didn't do anything to ease the chill crawling up my back. Broad daylight always made these moves riskier. Cameras, eyes, too many people pretending not to see what they damn sure saw.

I hated making drops when the city was wide awake.

We pulled up to the spot—neutral ground, tucked between an abandoned Papi store and some boarded-up row homes . I clocked the area before the wheels even stopped spinning. No kids. No old heads. Just concrete, graffiti, and tension in the air like gunpowder.

Tyree shifted in his seat.

"That him right there?" he asked, nodding toward the dude standing by a dark Charger, arms folded, head on a swivel.

"Yeah," I said. "That's that nigga Mike."

Crazy Mike was posted up like he owned the block. Hoodie on pulled low, diamond grill gleaming even in the shade. I could see that twitch in his jaw. Dude always looked like he was five seconds from blacking out. That's what made this tricky. Mike was a ticking time bomb but he was necessary for business.

I threw the car in park and looked at Tyree one more time.

"You remember what I said?"

He nodded. "Don't say nothing. Hold the bag. Pass it when you say so."

"Aight. Let's go."

We stepped out. Sunlight hit me in the face like a spotlight. I didn't flinch. Just kept walking, my body calm, but my mind running a mile a minute. So many alarms were going off when nothing was happening in front of me.

Crazy Mike met me halfway, grinned widely like we were best friends.

"My nigga Omar," he said, dragging out the vowels like he was trying too hard to sound friendly. "Heard you had something for me."

I gave a slow nod, hands empty, eyes on his.

"It's all there. But we keeping it light today."

"Always, my nigga." He looked over at Tyree, then back at me. "Who this nigga?"

I didn't answer. Just lifted my chin toward Tyree.

"Pass it."

Tyree stepped forward, quietly like I told him, and handed off the bag. Mike took it, popped it open for a quick peek, and gave a satisfied nod.

"Aight then. We good."

I didn't say shit. Just turned around and started walking back toward the car. Tyree was on my heels.

I didn't like the way Mike was still standing there, like he was waiting for something. But I wasn't sticking around to find out what.

As I slid back into the driver's seat, I caught a glimpse of a black truck parked two cars down, engine running, windows tinted darker than legal.

My jaw clenched.

Something ain't right.

Skrrrt!

I pulled off hard, tires screaming as I dipped through lanes. The truck behind me hugged every turn like it was glued to my bumper.

I reached for the strap under the seat—cold steel in my hand. Ready to return fire, but right now, I needed to escape. I bent corner after corner, no brakes, no signals. Just red lights turned suggestions as I flew through them.

I glanced in the rear view—yeah, they're still on me.

A trash truck rolled into the lane in front of me, movin' slow as hell.

"Yo, get the fuck out the way, dick head!" I barked, punching the horn. My heart was beating out of my chest.

Tyree cracked a smile, dumb as fuck actually relieved. "Yo bro, I think we cooked them niggas."

Before I could even respond, a truck pulled up on our side.

POP! POP!

Glass shattered. The window blew out, and Tyree took one straight to the chest. His body jerked, eyes wide, mouth gasping for air that wasn't coming.

The trash truck peeled off, and the sanitation workers on the back scattered like roaches. One of 'em damn near dropped off mid-run.

I ducked low, popped up with my strap, and let that shit rip.

BOOM! BOOM! BOOM!

I lit the passenger seat up—caught that nigga slippin'. His body jerked back as blood sprayed the inside of their windshield. I didn't stop. My foot hit the gas, wheels screeching as I dipped.

Eyes on every mirror, head on a swivel. My body was running off adrenaline now.

"Fuck!" I yelled, the word ripping from my throat.

My shirt was wet—hot. Blood. I'd been hit. Multiple times. I could feel it now. The sting, the weight. My hands were slick on the wheel.

Tyree was wheezing beside me, blood bubbling out of his mouth. Gasping. Still trying to breathe.

I looked over—regret cutting deep. I brought him out here. He wasn't built for this, not yet. Not really. He only jumped off the porch 'cause I opened the gate.

I turned my eyes back to the road just in time to see brake lights.

I slammed the pedal—
    Too late.

BAM!

We crashed into the back of a stopped car at the red light. My head snapped forward. Metal crunched. Horns blared. The world spun.

Everything went quiet.

* * *

Journee

I doubled over like I'd been kicked in the gut—sharp, raw pain ripping through my stomach out of nowhere.

"What's wrong?" Karina asked, voice rising with panic. Her eyes darted to me, full of confusion and fear.

But mine were locked on the screen in my hand.

Car Crash Detected.

The words hit harder than anything I'd ever read.

Karina leaned over, reading it too. Her eyes widened, her lips parting without a sound.

I couldn't breathe.

Omar.

I took off, rushing out the door like my legs had a mind of their own. Karina was right behind me.

"I'm coming with you," she said without hesitation.

I drove fast, recklessly. Red lights didn't exist; stop signs were just sticks on the corner. My heart thundered in my chest, louder than the sirens I was racing toward. My mind screamed no, no, no, over and over, but my mouth couldn't make a single sound.

When I reached the scene, the flashing red and blue lights greeted me like a nightmare come to life.

Omar's truck—
    Smashed. Crushed like a tin foil.

My chest tightened. My knees buckled.

"No... no, no, no!"

A body lay on the ground, covered in a white sheet stained with blood.

"Oh God... oh God!" I screamed, voice cracking as my legs gave out beneath me.

My body folded. Karina caught me, held me tight as I struggled forward, desperate for answers.

A firefighter stepped toward us, helmet in hand, face lined with sympathy.

"Are you a family member of the victim?"

I opened my mouth, but nothing came. Not a damn word.

"Yes," Karina said, stepping up without missing a beat. "This is his wife. I'm her sister."

His wife. She said it with her whole chest, like it was gospel. And in that moment, it was.

Sirens still wailed in the distance, but everything else faded. I was drowning in the stillness. My hands were shaking, my heart shattering piece by piece.

Then I saw it—

Omar's watch.

His arm was dangling as his body was being wheeled onto a stretcher. Unconscious. Bloodied. But alive.

My knees hit the pavement as I cried out, this time from pure gratitude. My hands reached toward the sky.

Thank you, God. Please don't take him. Not him. Not now.

I pressed a hand to my belly. We need him. I need him. Our baby needs him.

As they loaded him into the ambulance, I ran after them, breath ragged.

"I'm his wife," I told the EMT, voice trembling but fierce.

They looked me over once, then nodded.

"Alright. Get in."

I climbed inside, never taking my eyes off the man I loved. I gripped his hand, blood and all, as the doors shut behind me and we sped toward the hospital.

* * *

At the hospital, they rushed Omar into surgery.

I sat helplessly in the waiting area, the cold chair beneath me barely registering against the storm inside my chest. Karina showed up first, out of breath and worried. Khalil came soon after, face grim, hoodie pulled low.

There was no family to call.
   No mom. No dad. No bloodline to lean on.
   Omar was an orphan.
   The only people he had in this world... were us.

When I saw Khalil, something in me snapped.
   I stood up, stormed toward him, rage and fear making my voice shake.

"What the fuck happened?" I barked, my chest rising fast.

Khalil didn't say a word.
   But he didn't have to.
   His face was riddled with guilt.

"Not here," Karina said quickly, stepping between us. Her tone was calm, but I could see the fear in her eyes, too.

I backed up, wiped my face with the sleeve of my hoodie.

My thoughts were everywhere. My chest was tight. My world was crumbling in real time.
   The love of my life was back there—bleeding, broken, fighting.

My voice cracked as I looked at them both.
   "Please... somebody tell me something. Anything."

Khalil stepped forward and grabbed my hands. His grip was firm, steady.

The first thing that felt real all night.

"Trust me, Journee," he said.

And I knew what that meant.
   He'd tell me what happened...
   And he was gonna handle it.
   One way or another.

We waited for what felt like forever.

Khalil came back with paper cups full of hot, bitter coffee. We sipped in silence, too heavy with pain to speak.

The room buzzed with fluorescent lights and the low hum of machines, but I didn't hear any of it.

All I could hear was my heartbeat pounding.

Then, finally, a doctor walked up.

"The surgery was a success," he said. "He sustained serious injuries due to the crash, but with proper physical therapy, he should make a full recovery. As for the gunshot wounds, he's lucky to be alive. All the areas of impact were nonfatal."

My knees nearly buckled.

I let out a long, shaking breath. A prayer in itself. Tears pooled in my eyes, but didn't fall.

"When can I see him?" I asked.

"As soon as he's settled in his room. We'll let you know right away."

The doctor turned and walked off.

I stood there, heart still racing, eyes closed tight.

Thank you, God.
    Thank you for not taking him from me.

21

All or Nothing

I sat by his hospital bed, waiting.

Minutes blurred into hours—long, aching stretches of silence broken only by the soft, mechanical beeping of the machines, a subtle reminder that he was tethered to life.

Then, finally, he stirred.

My heart leapt.

He grunted, his face twitching, lips dry and cracked as he tried to speak.

"I'm right here," I whispered, my voice cracking as the tears already began falling. "I'm here, baby."

His eyes fluttered open—glassy, dazed.

"Journee..." he rasped, heavy with anesthesia.

"I love you," I breathed, leaning in closer. "So much. I can't even put it into words. I'm just... I'm so damn grateful I didn't lose you."

He coughed, jaw tightening from the pain.

I grabbed the cup of water and held it to his lips.

He sipped, wincing. "How long was I out? Them niggas hit Tyree..."

He tried to sit up, panic flashing in his voice.

"Not long," I said, pressing my hand gently to his chest. "But please—just breathe. I almost lost you, Omar."

"But you didn't," he murmured, voice dry, frayed. "I told you... I ain't going nowhere."

I shook my head, eyes fixed on the bruises, the bandages, the dried blood crusted along his skin.

"No," I whispered. "You were close. Too close."

"Come here," he said, lifting his uninjured arm, reaching for me. "Look at me. I'm good."

I leaned in, letting myself be pulled into the lie, the comfort of it—even though the truth clung to me like sweat.

Nothing was the same.
    Nothing could be.

"Look at yourself," I said, voice trembling. "You're lucky it was just your leg, arm, and hand. What if it had been your head, Omar? What then? You can't keep living like this."

"I *am* thinking," he snapped. "Them niggas still out there, Journee. And when they find out I'm alive, who do you think they're coming for next? You. Khalil. Karina. I can't let that happen."

My heart broke all over again.

"I can't do this anymore," I said quietly. "Things have changed."

"What's changed?" he scoffed, wincing. "This ain't my first time getting shot. It won't be the last."

"Don't say that!" I cried, the words ripping out of me. "Don't you ever fucking say that!"
   He stared, stunned.

I stepped closer, voice soft but shaking. "We can't lose you..."

"We?"

He blinked, confused.

I took his uninjured hand and placed it gently on my stomach.

"Yes. *We*, Omar," I said, tears falling again. "We."

His hand stilled against my belly, unsure.

His eyes searched mine, disbelieving.

"What do you mean, 'we'?"

I didn't answer right away. I let the truth settle in his chest, slow and heavy.

"I'm pregnant," I whispered. "I didn't want to tell you like this—not here.

But I couldn't wait. You need to know what's at stake."

He turned his head, swallowing hard. His eyes glossed, but no tears fell. He wouldn't let them.

"Damn…" he murmured. "You serious?"

I nodded, biting my lip. "I found out a few days ago. I was gonna wait. I thought maybe you'd be ready… that maybe I'd feel safe."

He looked back at me, softer now.

"That's why you kept looking at me like that," he said quietly. "Like you were saying goodbye."

I nodded again. "I've been terrified, Omar. Not just of losing you, but of raising this baby without you. Waking up one day and you're not coming home. Because of *this* life."

Silence fell again. But this time, it was thick with truth. He brushed his thumb gently over my belly, closed his eyes, and exhaled a long, shaky breath.

"Aight," he said finally. "After this… I'm done."

My breath caught. "Done with what?"

"This shit," he said, looking at me—really looking. "The game. The streets. All of it. I ain't lettin' my son—or daughter—grow up without a father."

My heart cracked wide open.

"You serious?" I asked, afraid to hope.

He nodded slowly. "Real shit. I can't keep doing this to you. To us."

And in that moment, I let myself believe him.

Because a life without Omar wasn't a life I was ready to live.

* * *

Omar

I lay there stunned.

That was the best news I got all day. Journee was having my baby.

I smiled faintly at her. She smiled back through tears, soft and scared, but full of love. That shit hit different. It was time for me to lock in. I ain't got time to be playing out here no more. I had even more to live for now—them.

The door swung open, and Khalil walked in wearing a fresh black Nike tech, different from what he had on earlier. As soon as I saw it, I knew what time it was.

"Yo, bro... welcome back to the world of the living," he said, half-laughing as he dropped a bag on my lap.

I didn't waste any time.

I yanked the IV out of my arm and swung my legs over the side of the bed, ignoring the throbbing pain. Journee panicked instantly.

"Whoa, what the fuck are you doing?" she asked, rushing over.

I was already unzipping the bag. My own Nike tech. Fresh sneakers. Black ski mask. My second skin.

"I'm getting the fuck out this bitch while we got the chance," I told her, my voice low but sure.

Journee shook her head, eyes wide, damn near on the verge of tears again. "You just had surgery! You ain't even get discharged—what about your leg?"

I stepped toward her and kissed her slowly. My palm pressed gently against her belly.

"My leg was grazed. Ain't nothing. The last place I need to be is here. Trust me."

She stared at me for a moment, her jaw tight, then finally nodded. "I trust you."

I got dressed fast. Khalil checked the hallway, then nodded.

"Let's move."

We slid out of that hospital like I didn't just dodge death. Moved casually. Calm. Walked straight to Khalil's other whip and hopped in. As soon as the doors shut, I reached over, popped the glove box, and grabbed my strap.

"We gotta drop her off," I said, tone flat.

"Drop me off?" Journee turned to me. "Omar, what are you about to do?"

I didn't answer. I looked her dead in her eyes.

"Omar..."

That was all it took. Her whole body softened.

She exhaled, barely audible. "Okay."

We dropped her off at Khalil's crib. Karina came out and pulled her inside.

That was the last soft moment of the night.

Now it was time for war.

Khalil slid through North like a shadow, weaving through traffic, windows tinted, bass silent. I sat in the passenger seat, gripping the steel in my lap like it was an extension of me. Every part of me was locked in.

"Where we hitting him?" I asked, eyes forward.

"Spot off Ridge. He posted up in the projects across from the Barbershop. Crazy Mike got two old heads with him. We pull up quick and fast, we got it easy."

I nodded once. "Say less."

We rolled up two blocks away, parked, and moved out on foot. Night was falling, but the streetlights gave just enough glow to make out movement.

Khalil pointed toward the alley. "Back there. I seen that dick head's chain he always wear. The minute he comes this way, it's over."

I gripped my strap tighter.

As we crept closer, I heard laughter. Crazy Mike's voice—loud, ignorant, like always. Talking like he ain't just tried to kill a nigga.

I turned the corner and stepped out before he even saw me.

"Nah, fuck all that. We ain't waitin'," I said loudly, voice cutting through the laughter in the air.

Mike looked up, confused at first, then his face dropped.

"Omar?" he stammered, stepping back.

"Thought I was dead, huh nigga?" I cocked my head, taking slow steps forward. I wanted to walk this nigga down personally.

He reached for his strap quickly, but he wasn't quick enough.

POP!

One of his niggas dropped first, Khalil's shot slicing through the air clean.

Mike tried to run, but I was on him. I grabbed him by the back of his shirt, slammed him against the brick wall. His gun fell.

"You tried to line me, pussy." My voice was low, my breath calm, but my heart was a storm.

He started begging, bleeding from the mouth, nose was broken from the impact.

"I ain't know—ain't mean it like that—"

"Shut the fuck up. You knew what it was nigga, stop cappin' motherfucka."

I pressed the barrel against his forehead.

"I should end you right here... but that would be too fucking easy."

He cried out, squirming, but I wasn't done. I cocked the gun, but at the last second—I changed direction.

POP!

His leg.

He howled.

"Yeah nigga," I whispered.

Aiming at the other leg, letting another one go.

POP!
He screamed.
I laughed, "Next ones yo fucking head."

"Who ordered the hit?" I gritted through clinching teeth, barrel pressed against his dome.
"I can't, that nigga gon kill me."

"Pussy I'm gone kill you." I spat.
"It was that nigga Trenton." Crazy Mike cried, blood gushing from both legs.
Trenton? I thought to myself, I heard that name before. Then it hit me.

Journee.
"Who the fuck is Trenton?" I questioned my finger itching to pull the trigger

"That nigga Big Tee."
I looked at Khalil—we locked eyes. No words, just that unspoken stare that

said everything.

"Now come on let me go nigga, you know me I ain't gon say shit."

"Yeah, I know you won't," I replied, letting the last shot ring.

POP!

Putting a bullet right through his left temple.

I shook the blood from my hand as Khalil and I ran off.

"That nigga Big Tee never showed earlier," Khalil muttered angry at himself for not peeping scene.

"It's cool cause we gon show up just for him." I smiled.

Khalil and I backed off, disappearing into the shadows.

This shit wasn't over, I still had murder on my mind. Now it was time to put a bullet in that nigga Trenton.
To be continued...

www.ingramcontent.com/pod-product-compliance
Lightning Source LLC
Chambersburg PA
CBHW031144050726
47495CB00018B/514